MW00458914

Published by Scrivenings Press LLC
15 Lucky Lane
Morrilton, Arkansas 72110
https://ScriveningsPress.com

Printed in the United States of America

Paperback ISBN 978-1-64917-212-9

eBook ISBN 978-1-64917-213-6

Editor: Susan Page Davis

Cover by www.bookmarketinggraphics.com.

All scriptures are taken from the KING JAMES VERSION (KJV): KING JAMES VERSION, public domain.

The Death
COLLECTOR

A SACKETS HARBOR MYSTERY

Sandra Kay Vosburgh

SANDRA KAY VOSBURGH

Scrivenings
PRESS
Quench your thirst for story.
www.ScriveningsPress.com

And they lay wait for their own blood; they lurk privily for their own lives. So are the ways of every one that is greedy for gain ...

Proverbs 1:18, 19

1

Sheriff Leo Meriday leaned over the body pulled from Lake Ontario. He'd worn the badge for nearly three decades, yet a queasiness invaded his gut the same way it did when he faced down his first corpse.

A breeze toyed with the gray hair that lay matted against the ashen face. Blue lips, open mouth, she stared coldly at the gulls gliding above the water. In spandex jogging pants and an Adidas tee, the woman looked fit except for the fact that she was dead.

He straightened and drew in a calming breath.

Midmorning rays shot through the sprawling maples and weeping willows that dotted the bank, while blue lights flashed from the cruisers parked along the blacktopped lane of the retirement village.

At his feet lay a cocker spaniel, whining.

Meriday's jaw tightened. He called to his deputy scouting the shoreline. "Bidwell, take the mutt to Kroft. Tell him to find it a home."

"Sir." The rookie tugged the leash and coaxed the dog away from his deceased owner.

Duncan Kroft sat on a bench at the top of the knoll, his shirt and jeans soaked from his plunge to retrieve the old woman's body. Behind him hovered a woman with a black bouffant, towel drying his hair.

The deputy posted the dog at Kroft's bare feet, then hustled back and began a search of the hedgerow near the edge of the lake.

Meriday turned at the smack of a car door. *Finally.* The coroner.

Dr. Fred Albright dipped his head in greeting then knelt beside the body, shoved his horn-rimmed glasses up the sharp slope of his nose, and opened his kit. "Any ID yet, Leo?"

"Nita Beavers. A resident here."

The coroner studied the dead woman. "Wasn't in the water long."

An ambulance arrived without pulsing lights and sirens. Warning beeps sounded while the driver backed the vehicle across the grass.

Meriday chafed at the sound of mounting babble. A small crowd of Willowdell residents had gathered around Duncan Kroft. "Bidwell."

"Chief?" Bidwell rose and brushed the grass from the knees of his tan uniform.

"Did you get a statement from Kroft yet?"

"Yes, sir, when I first arrived."

"Then send him on his way along with the nosey parkers."

The rookie dipped his blond crewcut and hiked once more up the knoll toward the village square. The dog darted at his approach.

The snap of latex gloves grabbed Meriday's attention.

"Received a blow to the side of her skull," Fred said, standing. "Could have happened before she went into the water, or she could have hit her head on the rocks when she fell in. I'll let you know what I find in the autopsy." The coroner cued the paramedics waiting at the open back doors of the ambulance.

Meriday moved to the spot where Mrs. Beavers likely went into the lake and examined the two-foot drop from the grassy bank to the rock-strewn water. What caused her to lunge into the lake?

He scanned the ground for evidence of a struggle.

The roots of an old maple jutted above the soil. Nita could have tripped while jogging. Or lost her balance when she reached the edge of the lake. Perhaps while looking down, she rammed her head into one of the low-hanging branches.

Slow and silent, the ambulance moved toward the front gate, followed by the coroner. With his hands on his hips, Meriday turned back to the water poppling golden in the late-morning sun. Seagulls cried and circled overhead.

To his left, the hedgerow bordered a wooded area marked with walking trails. To the right, the lake's shoreline stretched uninterrupted except for the occasional willow dipping its tendrils into the water for a drink.

Willowdell looked peaceful. Just outside the village of Sackets Harbor, the senior living community seemed a perfect place to live out the retirement years.

"Sheriff?"

He spun around.

"May I have a word?" Ada Whittaker's blue eyes narrowed beneath the pink straw hat that housed her ivory bird's nest hairdo.

Meriday crossed his arms. His linebacker build towered above her petite frame. The retired schoolteacher never lost the tendency to correct everyone's paper. He bristled. "Something on your mind, Miss Whittaker?"

"Yes, indeed."

Of course. There would be.

She pointed toward the bungalows that lined the north and south sides of the Willowdell square. "My sister lives in number eight. The yellow one closest to the lake." She looked at him. "Frances—"

"Frances Ferrell? She called it in. She's your sister?" *Don't tell me there are two of you.*

"Yes, she saw Nita Beavers this morning and has a theory as to what happened to the poor woman."

He clipped his thumbs in his belt and splayed his fingers over his weapon. "I prefer the coroner's theory."

The old woman raised an eyebrow and spoke firmly. "There's no denying that, but if you are interested in the truth, and I assume you are, I would urge you to speak to my sister." She stared him down, and he somehow knew she had maintained control of her classroom.

With an inward groan, he yielded. "Give me a minute."

Meriday rubbed the nape of his neck while Ada Whittaker marched toward the yellow bungalow. He detected an ill wind. Ever since that scandal at Stonecroft, it seemed whenever Ada Whittaker stuck her nose in something, she'd pick up the scent of murder.

Maxwell Bailey tucked a book under his arm, grabbed a mug of coffee and a bag of yogurt-covered pretzels, and headed toward the back patio of his bungalow. At the kitchen door, he paused at his reflection in the smudged glass.

His hair poked from his head like gray spikes, while dull, dove-gray eyes looked back at him. His fleshy cheeks and jawline attested to weeks of comfort feeding.

He mumbled, "Whatever," and opened the door.

In a cushioned chair at the patio table, Maxwell opened the sci-fi novel he had picked up in the Willowdell library. He munched pretzels and slipped deep into the storyline.

Minutes later a lake breeze swooped in and tossed the pretzel bag. Maxwell reached to retrieve it and became aware of the increasing volume of sirens. Their screams chilled the retirement village. Residents trickled from their bungalows, all astir and chatty, and toddled toward the lake and the flashing blue lights.

The coroner's car arrived, and he wondered who bit the dust.

The impulse to run to the scene and offer spiritual aid and comfort had left him the moment the elders plopped him on the curb outside Westlake Community Church. His pastoring days were over. He no longer concerned himself with the matters of others.

Maxwell returned to his beige walls, barren except for the WCC calendar hanging on a nail in the kitchen. Unwashed pans and baking dishes filled the stainless-steel sink. Amid the clutter on the granite countertop sat a new stack of paper plates and a ream of Styrofoam cups he'd ordered online.

Maxwell pulled a brownie mix—also ordered online—out of the pantry and within minutes placed the batter-filled baking pan in the oven and withdrew to his bed.

Stretched out on his bedspread with pillows propping his head, Maxwell stared at the five-tiered bookcase holding his choicest volumes. The remainder of his vast library lay boxed in climate-controlled storage two miles away, at SafeSpace Storage in the village of Sackets Harbor.

For thirty-five years he collected Bibles, commentaries, study guides, and biographies of great men and brave women. For thirty-five years, he prepared sermons and stood behind the pulpit of Westlake Community Church. Faithful to his call, preaching the gospel, he gave himself unceasingly to the work of the ministry.

What had it all come to? Five tiers of shelved theology.

The scent of warm chocolate lured him to the kitchen. The timer sounded the same moment he put a K-cup in the Keurig. Blowing on a plate of double-chewy brownies, he stepped out onto his porch, sat in one of the wicker chairs, and placed his mug on the table in front of him.

Oh, blissful moment ...

The irritating voice of his next-door neighbor reached him. "Yoo-hoo. Max." Gladys Blumm stood on her porch flapping an arm. "Do you like them?"

He frowned. How could Gladys see the plate in his lap from thirty feet away?

The tall, stout woman with hair the color of pale butter pointed a finger. "The geraniums I put by your pillars."

Two large flowerpots holding a mix of red geraniums and silver fox had been placed near the two front pillars of his porch. "Wow," he mumbled. The woman had crept onto his property and left him with something that required work to maintain.

He called out, "That's very kind of you, Mrs. Blumm."

"Call me Gladys. We're friends."

He groaned.

"Look in the front." Gladys Blumm's wrinkled face glowed.

Reluctantly, Maxwell set the plate on the table and moved off the porch. Next to an azalea bush, a garden flag waved in the breeze. A frog sat on a lily pad beneath an umbrella. It read, *Welcome to My Pad.*

Oh, Lord ...

"Remember, Max. F-R-O-G. Fully rely on God." She smiled and waved, then went back into her gray bungalow.

He wiped his forehead with the napkin in his hand.

A dog whimpered. *Oh, no. She didn't* ...

Maxwell turned to see Stanley sulking about the square, his leash dragging in the grass. That was odd. Why would he be out wandering by himself? Maxwell looked up and down the sidewalk, then crossed to the square with a crinkled brow.

He knelt by the dog and stroked its mahogany coat. "Where's your lady, Stanley? Huh, boy? Where's Miss Nita?"

2

Leo Meriday left the lake area and walked toward the square. Late spring blossoms colored the scattered flower beds, and a dozen or so cast-iron benches had been placed strategically near shade trees. In the center of the square, water glistened while it spilled over the rims of a three-tiered fountain surrounded by a patterned brick walkway.

Just beyond the square lay what resembled an elongated lodge, yellow sided, white trimmed. An open porch lined with Shaker style rockers ran the length of the building. On the many glass doors, black lettering read, *Gym, Pool, Clinic, Lobby, Café, Lounge,* and *Library.* A tall planter of mixed blossoms and trailing vines guarded each side of each door.

Meriday paused near a maple, debating whether to rest a moment on the bench. He'd been on his feet for hours. A few small branches lay in the dirt and grass under the tree. Could that be what happened? A rotted branch fell on Nita Beavers when she jogged by? Tragedy so often happened like that. Being in the wrong place at the wrong time.

He ran a hand through his hair and moved on.

At number eight, the bungalow of Frances Ferrell, Meriday again resisted the impulse to sit. Like a picture from his wife's *Home and Garden* magazine, the porch invited him to rest on one of the padded swivel rockers set amid pots of flowers and ferns.

He stepped to the blue door and reached to prove to himself the white tulips in the swag were fake when the door opened. A woman of about seventy with smooth, chin-length white hair stood with one hand on her hip. Her eyes were dark with mascara and shadow, her cheeks forced to flush with rouge, and her thin lips stroked with deep rose lipstick.

Meriday straightened his shoulders and deepened his voice to counter his embarrassment. "Mrs. Ferrell?"

"Come in, Sheriff."

He found it hard to believe this woman and Ada Whittaker were sisters. Frances Ferrell wore glitz. A red silk blouse, white slacks, and fine gold jewelry around her neck and on her wrists. Ada Whittaker—from what he had ever seen—always wore a denim skirt, a plain, buttoned-up blouse, and what were called sensible shoes.

Mrs. Ferrell waved him to a crème-colored chair, then perched her tall, thin frame on the edge of the matching sofa and planted her feet squarely on the blue marbled rug.

He sank down in the soft leather. Relief flooded his aching feet.

"Someone pushed Nita Beavers into the lake." Mrs. Ferrell clamped her hands together. "I'm sure of it."

Ada came in carrying a frosted glass of lemonade and set it on the coaster beside him. "I made a pitcher this morning. With fresh lemons. I thought it best to have some refreshment on hand in case anyone stopped in to talk about the tragedy." She joined her sister on the sofa. "I do find people like to talk about tragedy, don't you?"

"Living at Willowdell now, Miss Whittaker?" She wore no makeup or jewelry, except a simple wristwatch.

"Mercy, no. I'm still on Fairfield Lane. But Gwen—you remember my secretary-slash-companion? I'm afraid she's taken it upon herself to oversee the remodeling of the bathrooms. I couldn't object too loudly to her proposal. The old Victorian is well over one hundred. Of course, the bathrooms aren't that old." She blushed. "I'm staying with Frances until the contractor is finished. Would you care for a chocolate?"

Ada lifted the lid off a small brown box with gold lettering that read *Hegler Chocolates* and held the box out to him.

The frown on Frances Ferrell's face told him they were expensive. But what the heck, if she lived at Willowdell, she could afford it. He reached for one.

Mrs. Ferrell pinched her lips. "Sheriff, may I continue?"

"Please." His mouth watered while he removed the gold foil wrapper. He chewed the chocolate cloud and fought to keep drool from leaking out the sides of his mouth. With his little black book in hand, he jotted down a note while she spoke.

"About eight thirty this morning, I heard Nita calling for Stanley to come back. Stanley is Nita's dog." She leaned forward. "That's when I looked up from watering the ferns on my porch and saw Stanley racing toward the lake, barking. It struck me as odd."

Meriday studied her firm jawline and sculpted neck and wondered if Frances Ferrell had undergone plastic surgery.

"In the eighteen months I've been living at Willowdell," she went on, "I'd never heard Nita yell or seen Stanley run away from her. Probably chasing after a squirrel or a rabbit. Anyway, at the maple tree near the bank he stopped and barked at something in the tree. Or maybe at someone behind the tree."

Meriday grabbed the glass and eyed the little brown box on the table near Ada.

"Are you listening?" Frances Ferrell squinted at him.

"Yes, ma'am." Meriday shifted and forced himself to focus on her story. After all, the woman might say something important.

"Nita caught up, but she'd gone behind the tree. I couldn't see her. The next thing, I heard a splash. Ever so faint, but nonetheless a splash. I waited. But Nita never came back into view. That's when I called the office. I wanted someone to check on her."

Meriday returned the empty glass to the coaster. "Did you see anyone besides Mrs. Beavers down by the lake?"

Ada picked up the open candy box and held it out to him.

Why not? He took a white chocolate this time and twirled the rich cream on his tongue while he waved for Mrs. Ferrell to continue.

"I saw no one. But someone must have been there. Crouching behind the tree."

"Isn't it possible"—he wiped his mouth—"Mrs. Beavers slipped on the grass, or perhaps tripped on a tree root?"

She shook her head. "You don't understand. Nita Beavers was a fit woman."

"Oh my, yes," Ada agreed. "Very active. Swimming aerobics. Hiking. Bicycling. Even tennis—and that's so demanding."

He had noted the toned muscles of the seventy-four-year-old victim.

"You see," Frances said, "if Nita had tripped into the water, she could have easily gotten herself out. She had to have been incapacitated in some way, unable to assist herself. Do you see what I mean?"

More clearly than Frances Ferrell knew. But without an

eyewitness to foul play or, better yet, medical evidence, he chose to consider the woman's death an accident.

"Yes, ma'am. I appreciate the information. If you think of anything else or hear or see anything out of the norm, please contact the station." He rose from the chair, and before tucking his notebook into his shirt pocket he glanced at his only entry, *Hegler Chocolates.*

Ada walked with him to the door and spoke in a hushed tone. "You didn't take many notes."

"Yes, ma'am. That's true."

"Then let's pray a pop quiz doesn't land on your desk."

He tilted his head. "A pop quiz?"

"Yes, Sheriff. On murder."

3

Gwen Dunbar sat on the floor of the downstairs bathroom, glaring at the shredded strips of daisy patterned wallpaper and chunks of smashed drywall lying about her. Gray dust coated the vanity, the mirror, the cupboards, and her clothes, and irritated her eyes.

In an attempt to save Miss Ada money in the remodeling of her bathrooms, Gwen had undertaken to do the preliminary work herself. In her zeal, she had dismissed the fact that she had entered her forties a few years back. Every muscle ached.

She scowled at the maze of copper pipes that, she assumed, connected to the pipes of the second-story bathroom of the three-story Victorian.

Janet, Ada's cook and housekeeper and Gwen's nemesis, paused outside the door with a dust rag and a can of furniture polish. Her large brown eyes scanned the walls and the floor. "Mm-mm-mm. Miss Ada will not be happy." She shook her head and moved on.

Gwen crawled to her feet with a groan and brushed the

drywall dust out of her frizzy red hair. She acknowledged her defeat and mumbled, "Okay, not my most brilliant idea." She needed a contractor. Now.

Dread gnawed at her stomach while she dragged herself to the telephone. The crew that could start immediately, she remembered, had submitted the highest bid.

The day after the tragedy, Leo Meriday sat on the edge of a chair in the living room of Duncan and Miriam Kroft. Deputy Bidwell took up his position near the door. The overstuffed room felt suffocating.

They had entered a rainforest. Chairs upholstered with garish, exotic flower and bird patterns sat amid a forest of artificial bamboo and palm trees. Bamboo side tables presented a glut of glass lovebirds and budgies. A large porcelain peacock posed on each side of the fireplace, while an exhibit of colorful parrots lined the mantle. Framed paintings of macaws and cockatoos overwhelmed the green walls.

Meriday pulled his notepad from his shirt pocket. "I understand, Mr. Kroft, you reached Mrs. Beavers first and pulled her out of the lake."

The coroner's report that morning revealed Nita Beavers hit the water alive, but Fred could not determine conclusively if the blow to her skull occurred just prior to or after she entered the lake. Either way, something caused the victim to plunge into Lake Ontario, where she drowned.

Meriday had no choice but to look deeper.

"Yes, that's right." Duncan Kroft looked mid-seventies. A full, eggshell-colored mustache skirted his large nose.

"How long have you and your wife been residents at Willowdell?"

Kroft leaned back on the sofa and pressed his lips in thought. "Well ... I guess about—"

"Two years and six months," Mrs. Kroft said. She sat beside him with her red-rimmed smile, a black bouffant hairdo, and a loud, gaudy blouse over orange slacks. There was nothing vanilla about Miriam Kroft.

Mr. Kroft cocked an eye at his wife and scowled, then looked back at the sheriff.

"Yeah, around that." He straightened and shifted his position.

"What can you tell me about Nita Beavers?" Meriday looked to both of them for an answer.

Miriam waved her hands while she talked. "The woman meant well, always trying to encourage the residents to make healthier choices at the café. Telling everyone they should be more active, and how they could improve the quality and length of their lives."

Duncan Kroft mumbled, "Lot of good it did her," and leaned back and crossed his long legs.

Meriday found the man's constant fidgeting distracting. "Something bothering you, Mr. Kroft?"

"I think my sugar's dropping."

"Well, Dunc, why didn't you say so?" Miriam edged off the sofa and trekked through the jungle toward the kitchen.

The clock cuckooed, and a blue budgie peeked out a tiny open window ten times then retreated.

Meriday glanced at his deputy. Bidwell maintained his wooden stance.

"Miriam had to have that stupid clock," Duncan Kroft griped. "Spends money like it grows on the stupid forestry around here." He lowered his head. "Sorry. I get a little irritable when the sugar's low."

Meriday sniffed and tapped his fingers on his notebook.

Miriam Kroft returned with a glass of orange juice, and after drinking the juice, Mr. Kroft seemed to relax.

His wife rejoined him, and Meriday continued the interview. "How is it, Mr. Kroft, you happened to be the first to arrive at the lake? Did you see Mrs. Beavers fall in?"

"No. Miriam and I were sitting at the kitchen table having our morning coffee when we heard Samantha—"

"Samantha Milsap, the property manager," his wife said.

Kroft briefly closed his eyes and took a deep breath. "As I was saying, we heard Samantha yelling for help. I ran outside and saw her plodding toward the lake, screaming something about someone falling in."

Meriday frowned. "You reached the lake before Miss Milsap?"

"Of course," Kroft said matter-of-factly. "Sam's so portly, a one-legged dog could outrun her."

Miriam playfully swatted her husband's knee and chuckled. "Dunc thinks anyone with a BMI over twenty-four is portly. But he is correct about Samantha."

"When you arrived at the lake, what did you see?"

"Stanley, at first, which told me if someone fell in the lake, it'd be Nita. Sure enough, that's when I saw her body in the water."

"Was the victim struggling in any way? Trapped in an undercurrent, perhaps?"

Duncan Kroft scoffed. "No. Not a kick. Not a scream. Just floating. Facedown."

Meriday placed a fist on his hip. "Did you see anyone else near the lake at that time?"

"No one. Except Sam. She came up behind me, puffing like a bellows. Once I dragged the old girl to the shore, Samantha helped me pull her out."

"Did you move anything? A fallen branch. A rock. Something that may have been in the way of you reaching Mrs. Beavers? Did you touch anything?"

The old man paled. "You sound like the guys on *NCIS*. You asking if I tampered with a crime scene?"

"Oh, Dunc, don't be dramatic." Miriam Kroft rolled her eyes and shook her head. "The sheriff wants to know if Nita could have tripped over something."

Blood flow returned to the old man's face. "You stopped my heart, Sheriff. There's enough of us dropping dead around here without having a murderer in our midst."

Later that afternoon, Meriday entered the Willowdell lobby to interview Samantha Milsap. In the small office of the absent owner, she sat in a hard-backed chair positioned against a wall, rubbing her palms over her ankle-length print skirt. Duncan Kroft had accurately described the property manager.

"Tell me about the call that came in." Meriday took out his notebook.

Samantha shifted in the chair and made a noise with her throat. "The phone at the front desk rang, and when I answered—"

"At what time?"

"Before nine. Possibly closer to eight thirty."

"Were you here alone?"

"Yes. Simon had been in earlier but left before the phone call."

"Simon Hilton is the owner of Willowdell?"

"Yes."

Meriday gave the little room a once-over. File cabinets. A

small desk. A bookshelf. One framed snapshot of Hilton—he recognized him from the political posters—his parents, and a sister, perhaps. "Is Simon Hilton married?"

"I don't think he has ever been married."

Meriday settled into the desk chair. "Tell me about that call."

"Mrs. Ferrell rang the front desk. She told me Nita Beavers may have fallen into the lake, and she wanted someone to check immediately."

"May have fallen? Those were her words?"

"I don't know. Maybe she said 'pushed into the lake.' I don't—"

"You called 911?"

"No. Not until Mr. Kroft and I pulled Nita out of the water."

"Why not? Why didn't you call 911 on your cell phone while you rushed to the lake?"

Samantha Milsap blew out of the side of her mouth. "Because if anyone could get themselves out of the lake, Nita Beavers could."

"Yet, you ran to the lake and yelled for someone to help you."

"Of course. We couldn't risk liability."

"When you arrived at the lake, what did you see?"

"Mr. Kroft taking off his shoes."

Meriday glanced at the clock.

"He jumped in and grabbed her." Samantha Milsap gave a slight groan and held her hand to her stomach. "It makes me kind of sick to think about."

He understood. "Did Mrs. Beavers respond in any way?"

Samantha dipped her head and shook it side to side.

"Tell me your opinion of Nita Beavers."

Her jaw stiffened. "She was rude." Samantha swiped her palms on her skirt and lifted her shoulders in a quick shrug. "I don't know, maybe she did care about my health, but she didn't care about me. So, I didn't care about her. I mean, I didn't want her to drown, but …"

"But it's okay that she did?"

The young woman jutted her chin and looked away.

4

Ada stood in the lobby of Willowdell the next morning, her ivory strands nestled under an orange straw hat, a white envelope in her hand. Frances leaned on the counter and waited for Samantha Milsap to check with Simon Hilton regarding Frances's request.

Hilton stepped out of his office. Thirty-something, trim build, dark hair, tight beard, charming smile, midnight-blue eyes. Exactly as he appeared on the political posters that marred the landscape of Sackets Harbor.

Samantha scuffed behind him toward the counter.

"I'm sorry, Mrs. Ferrell," Simon Hilton said. "We can't give out the addresses of family members. It would be a violation of their privacy. I'm sure you understand our position. Miss Milsap will be glad to assist you in any way she can." He rapped his knuckles on the counter, dismissing the matter, and returned to his office.

"Thank you, Simon." Samantha's eyes lingered on the retreating man. When he disappeared, she turned back to Frances. "I'm sorry."

Frances spoke firmly. "Just how is my sister to forward a sympathy card to Nita's family?"

The property manager gave Ada a sympathetic smile. She reached no more than five-feet-two and likely would torment the clinic scale if she were to step on it. Samantha's fingers shook slightly while she ran them over the long strands of hair descending over her buxom chest. Her attempt to dye her red hair blond resulted in a Halloweenish gold-rose. "I can address the card and place it in our outgoing mail, if you like."

Ada stepped closer and spoke in a hushed tone. "I understand Mr. Hilton is running for the New York State Senate."

Samantha's pale green eyes lit up. "Isn't it exciting? We've placed yard signs all over Sackets Harbor." Her voice sank. "We don't allow any signs here at Willowdell. Residents say they trash the landscape and lend to disagreement."

"Oh my, I'm sure they would. It sounds like you're helping with the campaign."

"Volunteering."

"I noticed a moving van in front of number eleven. Do you have a new resident moving into Nita's bungalow so soon after her death?"

The woman flinched but recovered. "There's a waiting list for admittance to Willowdell. We try to accommodate the next applicant quickly." She reached out a chubby hand. "Would you like for me to put that in the outgoing?"

Ada clutched the card. "Don't bother with this, dear." She tucked it into her tote bag. "Frances can help me offer my condolences online. That's the way so many do now. Seems rather impersonal to me, but what can one old woman do but downgrade with the times?" Ada sighed and headed toward the lobby door.

Outside, Frances put on her sunglasses. "Now what?"

Ada started toward number eleven at a determined clip. "Come along. I want to speak to the movers."

"Seriously? You are going to bother those men? They probably know nothing about Nita Beavers's family."

"They must know where they are taking her possessions."

"Really, Ada. You can simply offer your sympathies on the funeral home's website. Or even attend the funeral and speak to her family in person. And must you speed walk everywhere you go?"

"I doubt there will be a funeral." Ada paused and waited for Frances to catch up. "Nita Beavers had no family."

Frances lifted her sunglasses and squinted. "Then why ask about mailing a sympathy card to the family?"

"The envelope is empty. I merely hoped to obtain the name and address of whoever is handling Nita's estate."

"Why? Did she owe you money?"

"Mercy, no." They continued toward number eleven, where two men tried to finagle a couch out the front door. "But I believe her estate to be fairly large. Her son, a medical doctor, passed away over five years ago and left his estate to Nita. That's how she could afford to live at Willowdell."

"If she had no family, what happens to her estate?"

"That's what has me curious." Ada stopped beside the van, which read, *King Tut Movers. We Reign & Shine.* She grunted. Of all the words in the English language at their disposal ....

She waited while the men positioned the couch in the back of the truck then said, "Good morning, Tut." Ada read the name embroidered on the older man's sweat-soaked shirt. She smiled an intended-to-disarm smile. "You must have cleared your court to get here so promptly."

King Tut brushed past her.

With a silly grin, the younger man said, "Don't mind him.

He gets grumpy when the queen messes with his schedule." He laughed and started toward the bungalow.

"Oh, young man," Ada said.

He stopped and looked back at her. "Ma'am?"

"Where are you taking the load?"

"To the warehouse."

"Warehouse?"

"At the old shipyard."

"Kid," Tut barked, "ignore the biddies and get to work."

Kid slipped Ada another silly grin, then grabbed the chair the king had set outside the door.

Ada turned and stared at the lake, tapping an index finger on her lips.

Frances moved up beside her. "What's going on in that head of yours?"

"I need to borrow some of your clothes."

Just before dusk, Gwen parked Ada's gray Volvo sedan in front of Frances's bungalow. Frances and Ada, dressed in black, sprinted to the car and leaped in.

Gwen scanned them with sharp green eyes. "Why are you dressed like that? And why am I taking you to the shipyard?"

"We need to case the warehouse." Ada tied a dark scarf over her head.

Frances spoke from the back seat. "We learned the movers who cleared out Nita's home took all her possessions to the warehouse at the old shipyard."

"And that concerns you both, why?" Gwen drove onto the main highway leading to the marina.

"The young man said they were taking the load to the

warehouse," Ada said. "I have the distinct impression that's the standard practice."

Political signs lined the main thoroughfare into the village of Sackets Harbor. Simon Hilton's charismatic smile greeted Ada every few hundred feet.

"So?" Gwen said. "Until the family arrives and decides what to do with everything, the stuff has to go somewhere."

"There is no family. That's the issue."

Gwen gave a sigh and focused on the road.

Ada had seen that resignation many times over the past four years. Times when Gwen did not understand the reasoning behind her whims but had learned to comply. When Ada turned sixty-five, Frances suddenly objected to her living alone. Janet lived in, but still Frances fussed.

Gwen was a sister to Frances's daughter-in-law. When Frances learned of Gwen's broken engagement, she believed Ada's home in the quaint lakeside village of Sackets Harbor would be the perfect place for Gwen's fractured heart to mend.

Contented, Gwen stayed on, and Ada grew to depend on her as her secretary and driver.

Frances leaned forward. "I wonder what happens to the furniture after it goes to the warehouse. Maybe it gets donated to charity."

If that were the case, Ada believed the truck would have simply taken the load to the door of the charity. "My concern lies with the deceased's major assets. I hope to find some clue that could reassure me no one is misappropriating the funds from Nita's estate."

Beyond the marina, Lake Ontario shimmered with the deep gold rays of a setting sun. Darkness descended quickly after sunset. They had to hurry.

Gwen turned the Volvo into the yard of the once-thriving boat manufacturing business everyone called the shipyard.

The windows of the fabrication building were boarded with sheets of plywood. Cranes, with their booms lowered, crouched in a hedgerow.

"Pull up there, Gwen." Ada pointed to a large steel building that covered much of the back lot. "No one will see us."

Gwen parked close to the back of the building, near an area overrun with weeds.

Large tires had made a path to an overhead door of the warehouse. Farther down, a chain and padlock blocked entrance through a green steel door. A footpath led to a large dumpster in the brush near the tree line.

Ada and Frances got out, and Frances drew a navy ball cap from her pocket and tucked it on her head. They weaved through the overgrowth. At the warehouse, Frances peered through a dusty window. "Looks like a furniture storeroom. Couches. Beds. Dressers."

Ada looked around and spotted a pile of bricks and cement blocks. She called to Gwen. When Gwen got out of the car and walked toward her, Ada pointed to the pile. "Do you think you could bring a block for me to stand on?" So often, her five-four height left her dependent on others.

Gwen gave her a look, but went at Ada's bidding.

Seconds later, Ada stepped up and gripped the windowsill. "Oh, mercy. I see what you mean."

"There's a staircase. Must be a second floor."

Ada focused on the office door near the staircase. "Wish I could search that office."

Frances turned her deep-gray eyes on her. "How is any of this going to help us find out who inherits Nita's estate?"

"Let's check the dumpster." Ada turned from the window. She had no answer to her sister's question but would keep hunting. Not knowing would gnaw at her. Someone would benefit from Nita's death, and she wanted to know, were they friend or foe?

Ada blamed Agatha Christie for this engrained bent toward suspicion. Her mystery novels, read over the decades, had sown seeds of distrust in Ada's subconscious mind like tares sown among wheat.

Nonetheless, she had to know the answer.

Gwen and Frances helped her stack a few cinderblocks by the dumpster, then Ada and Frances stepped up. A rancid smell swirled in the lake breeze.

Frances crinkled her nose. "I bet the movers throw everything from the refrigerators in here."

"I need to poke around in there," Ada said. "Can you hoist me in?"

Her sister cocked her head. "I'm not sure that's wise."

"No, it's not." Gwen peered at her.

Ada pressed her lips tight in a grimace.

Gwen sighed. "All right. Move over."

Ada scooted over while Gwen heaved herself over the edge. She landed on a pile of discarded clothes and blankets, plates, pans, and cleaning supplies. "What am I looking for?"

"Papers, forms, journals," Ada said. "Letters. Business cards. Notes on a scratchpad. Anything that clues us in to the name of Nita's attorney."

"What is that red cloth by your knee?" Frances pointed.

Gwen unfolded the swimsuit.

"That's Nita's." Frances looked at Ada. "She wore it to water aerobics class."

Gwen searched the bin for several minutes but found nothing of significance.

Purple swathed the evening sky. Ada said, "You better come out now, Gwen. It will soon be dark."

"Ouch." Gwen pulled her hand out and checked it.

"Do be careful."

"I'm okay. Just a little cut from this light." Gwen held up a chipped lamp of Southwestern design.

"That belonged to Charlie Snell," Frances said. "I admired it when I took soup to him a couple weeks ago. His death shocked everyone. We all thought he'd recover."

A chill swept in off the lake and trickled down Ada's spine. Her mind raced with questions. Could there be a pattern? She quickly chastened herself and refocused on the mystery at hand. Who is profiting from the death of Nita Beavers?

5

Under duress, Maxwell went to the barber and made himself presentable. So many residents had dropped in on him over the past week to check on Nita's dog that his embarrassment shamed him into action.

For weeks he had avoided driving into the village of Sackets Harbor, not wanting to risk being seen by one of the progressively minded elders from his former church. He believed in grace, but at this point he didn't know if he had enough of it to get him through such an encounter.

Gladys Blumm and her middle-aged daughter even now sat in his living room, eating his brownies.

"It's kind of you, Mr. Bailey, to take pity on poor Stanley." Selma Potter shook the front of her lime-green muumuu, sending the cheap gold chain necklace she'd been wearing to the carpet along with brownie crumbs from her lap. She sighed and picked up the necklace. "The clasp is always coming undone."

Her light brown hair held an array of waves and curls without any definitive plan. The strands in front of her tiny ears had been rolled and held against her temples with a cross of bobby pins.

Gladys scowled at the dog lying at Maxwell's feet. "The fella still looks kind of lost."

"He's a bit—"

"My Addison put a tiny piece in the *Ontario Times* a couple months back when the new pastor took your place at Westlake Community Church." Selma attempted to hook the chain around her thick neck while she spoke.

Her grin did not lessen the sting of her words, or the reminder of that full-page article lauding the young man fresh out of seminary. His vision for growth. His plans to reach into the community with giveaway programs. There had been no indication in the article that the young pastor intended to preach the gospel or had a burden to reach those lost in sin.

"He's too young." Gladys took another brownie. "He ain't turned enough corners or climbed enough hills. Know what I mean?"

"Traveled enough roads?" Maxwell added.

Gladys snorted. "You got it."

Selma licked a finger and picked up a crumb off the coffee table and put it in her mouth. "Did I mention my Addison is the editor of the paper?"

"I surmis—"

"You should join us for bingo in the rec center." Gladys wiped her mouth with a napkin. "The prizes aren't too shabby. In fact, every July we play a tournament, and this year I hear the prize is a cruise."

Selma checked her watch, its silver links stretched around her wrist. "Ooh, I'd better go, Mother. Addison expects his supper to be on the table when he gets home from the paper."

"He always has." Gladys lifted her solid frame and moved toward the door. "Thanks for the tea and sympathy, Max. If you don't mind my saying so, I think you need something to interest you. There's life after retirement, you know."

Selma asked coyly, "Mind if I take one for Addison?" The woman took the remaining two brownies.

At last, he closed the door behind them and rested his head on the windowpane.

Ada pillaged through sports equipment in the recreation building. "There has to be a croquet set somewhere." To get Frances's mind off Nita Beavers's death, Ada had suggested a game.

The incessant interviews conducted by the sheriff and his deputies since that day had generated rumors. Lots of them. The residents began to conclude Nita's demise in Lake Ontario may not have been an accident and began to look at one another with suspicion.

"Ah, here." Ada pulled out the cart of mallets and colored balls.

"I'm glad Maxwell took in Stanley." Frances reorganized the displaced equipment. "I think Nita would be pleased with the arrangement."

"They do seem to have taken to one another." Ada rolled the set to the door.

Frances held the door open.

Alison Vaughn sprinted along the sidewalk toward them in jeans and a Willowdell staff shirt. The activities director, in her mid-thirties with auburn hair and brown eyes, smiled. "Hello, ladies. Can I help you with that, Miss Whittaker?"

"No, thank you, dear. It has wheels."

"Have a good one." Alison bounded off.

Ada turned to Frances. "Where do you want to set up?"

"Close to the lake. Maybe we can get a breeze." Frances raised a brown-spotted bare arm and shielded her eyes. She pointed toward the willows. "Over there."

Once they'd placed their stakes in the ground and the wickets approximately regulation distance apart, Ada took a moment to delight in the beauty of the lake. Its gentle, silver waves shimmered in the noontime sun.

"Oh my, what a glorious picture."

"Glorious and deadly." Frances took aim at the first ball.

Ada remembered their days growing up together on the farm in Somerset, Vermont. A lazy Sunday afternoon often meant challenging one another to a game of croquet. Two years her senior, Frances had been her best friend and competitor.

"Drat." Frances's ball rolled down the knoll into the hedgerow. "I hope there's no poison ivy in there."

"Leaves of three, let it be, Fanny," Ada teased. She hadn't called her sister Fanny since childhood.

Frances made an opening in the hedgerow and stepped through, searching the ground. A moment later, she bent down. When she straightened, she did not hold up the runaway ball but a narrow, rectangular object that glistened when angled toward the sun.

Meriday sat in his office, his size twelves on his desk, his hands clasped behind his head. It had been ten days and thirty-two interviews since Nita Beavers's death, and still he had no evidence indicating who or what sent the woman into the water.

The coroner determined the victim died from drowning. His findings regarding the blow to her head were inconclusive.

So, with no convincing evidence of foul play or any discovery of motive, Meriday saw no option but to declare the woman's death accidental.

He picked up her file. Deputy Bidwell's research on her revealed Mrs. Beavers retired from her position as Director of Nursing nine years earlier. She did not move into Willowdell until five years ago, when her son passed away and left her sufficient funds to pay the entry fee and the monthly rate for many years to come.

A tap sounded on his door. He clomped his feet to the floor. "Yep." He smelled the burning of an empty coffeepot left on the heat. He jumped up and shut off the coffee maker.

Ada Whittaker opened the door. "That kind young man at the desk told us to just knock."

"Miss Whittaker." He spoke through tight lips.

She entered with Frances Ferrell close behind, and again Meriday wondered over the difference in these two sisters. He returned to his chair.

"My sister found something that may be of interest. And you did say to let you know if we saw something or heard something. We did. So, I had Gwen bring us around. She's waiting in the car."

He tapped his fingers on the armrests of his chair.

"Gwen wanted to get out of the house for a while, anyway. Janet is too frequently interrupting the workmen with plates of cookies and sandwiches." Ada rambled while Frances dug around in an oversized shoulder bag. "And of course, Gwen is most anxious to have the job completed. I'm afraid it has caused considerable friction between her and Janet."

Mrs. Ferrell pulled out a small, silver object and placed it on his desk. "I found it in the hedgerow a few yards from where Nita fell in the lake."

He scowled at the dog whistle.

Ada said, "We believe someone used it to lure Stanley to the lake and, subsequently, Nita to her death."

He stifled the urge to advise these ladies to visit Hobby Lobby and purchase a few dozen cross-stitch kits to keep them busy. He stood and walked them to the door. "Thank you for bringing it in."

"Will you be checking it for prints?"

Mrs. Ferrell touched her sister's arm. "I believe they would be mine."

"Oh, yes. Of course." Ada gave a slight nod and stepped toward the door. "We must be more careful with the next clues we bring."

Meriday closed the door behind them and dragged his hands through his hair.

6

After a meander around the square with Stanley, Maxwell dropped onto a bench beneath a shade tree. He stuck his foot through the loop handle of the dog's leash and pulled it up to his knee. Never again would Stanley run off. Not unless the dog could drag one hundred eighty pounds.

The cocker sprawled out on the grass at his feet.

Maxwell scanned the gardens scattered over the square while a breeze played with the nearby lilac bushes and twirled their fragrance under his nose.

"Maybe I should take up gardening, Stanley. I doubt if I would find meaning, but at least my hands would be doing something besides stuffing food in my mouth."

Ada Whittaker waved and walked toward him.

"The lilacs smell wonderful," she said as she arrived. "I wish they would last all summer."

Maxwell slid over. "Good things rarely last."

Ada sat beside him, her smiling blue eyes heightened by the blue of her straw hat. "I saw you sitting here. I hope you don't mind my intrusion." She reached down and petted Stanley's red-brown fur.

"Not at all. I enjoy your company. Yours and your sister's." Ada Whittaker and Frances Ferrell frequently strolled the sidewalk around the square, and lately he'd found himself looking for them. They were kind, engaging, intelligent women.

"How are you adjusting to life at Willowdell?" Ada asked.

"It's taken me a while to get used to a slower pace. To shift gears from the busyness of ministry to ..." He shrugged. "To not sure what."

"It can take time. But it's important you not stay in neutral too long."

How did she know he had stalled? He definitely couldn't go back, but neither could he move forward.

He'd heard that Ada offered unsought advice, but he didn't mind. He appreciated anyone who spoke the truth in this day of namby-pamby. This day of intimidation. Guilt tactics. Seeker-friendly sermonettes. He forced out the air he'd been sucking in during his mental rant. What did he care, anyway?

He recalled the newspaper article praising the new pastor.

"I met Selma Potter. Gladys dropped in and brought her daughter. I'm ashamed to confess, I found Mrs. Potter somewhat wearing."

"Mm, yes, Selma Potter. We are both members of the board at Stonecroft Resort. Selma, I've found, is best taken in small doses."

"They ate all my brownies."

Ada smiled, and the fine lines around her eyes drew together. She chuckled, then she put a hand over her mouth to stifle her laughter. "Maxwell, you need something more substantial than brownies. You need a good home-cooked meal."

"Gladys said I need something to interest me. She recommends bingo."

"Then join Frances and me for supper this evening. Afterward, we'll all go to bingo."

His chest tightened. Panic played in the back of his throat.

"What is troubling you?"

He forced a reply. "I've tried to keep to myself. Avoiding people. Not taking on their concerns." He gave a slight shrug. "The people I poured my life into turned their backs on me. I taught them and cared for them. Visited them when they were sick. Prayed over them. Married and buried them. For thirty-five years. Then they voted me out. After all I had done for them."

He looked down at Stanley when his eyes threatened to mist.

"I don't believe for a minute you did all that for your congregation."

Startled by her candor, he turned to her.

"I believe, and tell me if I'm wrong, but I believe you did all that for the Lord. And he has not turned his back on you."

Her words stung like a slap. But she was right. Everything he had done had been done for his Savior, not merely for the people he served. He swallowed. His voice cracked when he said, "What time is supper?"

Wendall Compton shuffled about the bingo tables. Pushing ninety, the lanky, white-haired man paused and frowned several times. From a folding chair along the side of the room, Ada caught glimpses of him through a small crowd of residents milling about and creating a sociable rumble.

The recreation center's walls were punctuated with

bulletin boards and laminated posters of instructions regarding the use of sports equipment, food and drink, dates and times of activities, and lost and found notices.

Frances whispered from the seat next to Ada, "Wendall lose something?"

A good share of his faculties, perhaps. Poor man.

Maxwell Bailey, with trim gray hair and eyes the color of dusk, sat beside Frances. The two hovered in quiet conversation, and Ada concluded they would make an attractive couple.

Angry voices rose above the din and seized her attention. Players waiting for the game to start backed away from the tables. Their chatter subsided while the argument intensified.

"Mercy." Ada adjusted her position to ferret out the source. Dorothy Kane and Gladys Blumm? What could be the matter?

Retired judge Burton Fausset stepped forward and stationed his short, round frame between the two women. "Now, ladies—"

"What are you going to do, smack your gavel?" Dorothy sneered. "Well, this isn't your courtroom." A blond, wiry woman of slender build, Dorothy wore purple-framed glasses on her pointed nose.

Judge Fausset opened his hands. "True enough, but I do have an opinion."

"I don't care to hear it." Dorothy lifted her chin.

Gladys yanked on a chair positioned between the two women. "You don't care to hear anyone who don't agree with you."

Samantha Milsap stood near them with her hands on her broad hips. "Please, Dorothy. Can't you share, this one time?"

"You know this is my seat." Dorothy hit the back of the chair with her fist. Her red face glowered six inches below Gladys's scowl. "I *always* sit in this seat."

"No more." Gladys shoved Dorothy into the arms of Judge Fausset.

Samantha gasped. "You can't be pushing people. I'm calling the police." She trudged to the door with her cell phone to her ear. Within minutes a siren could be heard, growing louder with the seconds until blue lights pulsed outside the windows of the recreation building.

Ada groaned at the necessity of intervention at a bingo game.

Two deputies, jaws set, wearing tan uniforms belted about with all their gear, strode to the cause of the disruption.

"She started it, officers." Dorothy pointed at Gladys.

"It's not fair. She always gets this seat." Gladys pointed to the ceiling. "It's right under the fan. Why should she be the one who gets to cool off? If she's too warm, she can take off that sweater."

Frances whispered to Ada and Maxwell, "Dorothy always wears that orange sweater. Syracuse orange. Her son played basketball for the Orangemen, probably over twenty years ago." Frances pursed her lips and lifted her penciled brows.

"You *both* can cool off at the station," Deputy Sloan said. He and Deputy Bidwell handcuffed the women.

Gladys and Dorothy glared at one another while the officers escorted them to their cruisers, citing Miranda rights. Samantha followed, her ankle-length cotton skirt swaying over her canvas flats.

A wave of suppressed excitement spread over the crowd.

Alison Vaughn bounded up the steps to the stage and tapped the microphone, sending a screech through the loudspeakers. When everyone looked at her with hands over their ears, she shouted with a wide grin, "Are you ready for some bingo?"

7

Dorothy Kane looked out her window well past the time when most residents had gone to bed. Hers were the only lights on.

She grabbed her swimsuit from the bottom drawer of her dresser then kicked the drawer shut. Ever since the police hauled her away two nights earlier, she wanted to kill Gladys Blumm.

Her best friend. What got into Gladys? Getting in her face. Demanding to sit in her chair. Gladys knew that was her chair.

Bully!

Tears came unbidden. She sniffed. Her nerves were frayed.

With no appetite and unable to sleep, Dorothy thought of going to Gladys and talking things over, but why should she? She did nothing for which to apologize.

She changed into the suit and wrapped herself in a coverup. No one would be in the whirlpool at this hour. Maybe the hot water would help her relax. She could feel stress eating up years of her life. She had to do something. She had to sleep.

She remembered the muscle relaxant prescribed to her

after Jordan died. She had trouble sleeping then too. She put on her glasses, went to the medicine cabinet, and rummaged through the pill bottles until she found the Diazepam.

Expired—five years ago. Perhaps a double dose would prove effective enough to take the edge off. She popped two tablets into her mouth and took a sip of water. Dorothy then tucked the latest Syracuse University alumni newsletter into her pocket and grabbed a towel.

When she opened the door of her bungalow, light fell across the welcome mat. There lay a small package, gift-wrapped with a beautiful orange bow. "Gladys?" Her chest pounded. Has her best friend been feeling badly too? There was no card.

Dorothy gently removed and folded the wrapping paper and tucked it into her pocket, along with the bow. Inside the plastic container were four large brownies enfolded in wax paper. Yes, the giver had to be Gladys. She knew Dorothy so well.

Anger dissipated, and she determined to thank Gladys in the morning.

With the package in hand, Dorothy entered the dimly lighted lobby and shambled down the quiet hallway toward the pool area. Minutes later, she slid into the hot currents. Her muscles began to relax and release days of resident tension.

She unfolded the newsletter and reached for a brownie.

———

Just before sunrise, Meriday stood over the corpse of Dorothy Kane. He rubbed his chin in a way that kept a hand over his mouth. The rookie beside him didn't need to know his stomach roiled.

Pulled from the water, Dorothy stared with vacant eyes at

the glass panels overhead. The straps of the orange swimsuit hung off her shoulders. Likely, she had swirled in the hot water until the timer cut off.

Floating on the water was an SU newsletter, and at the bottom of the tank lay a pair of purple-framed glasses. An orange coverup lay folded on a chaise, with shower sandals tucked under it. Near the spa's edge sat a plastic container lined with wax paper. Inside was one partial brownie.

"Coincidence, sir?" Bidwell asked while they waited for the coroner and the department photographer to again make their way to Willowdell.

"Probably." Meriday struggled to breathe in the humid atmosphere. The smell of chlorine stung his nostrils. "There's bound to be the occasional death in a retirement village."

"Maybe she had high blood pressure and stayed in the hot water too long."

Meriday turned at the sound of a crowd gathering outside the glass door opening onto the wide porch. "Bag everything, then get rid of the sightseers."

"Sir." Bidwell rolled up a shirtsleeve and retrieved the glasses and the newsletter, then bagged everything that belonged to the victim. His shirt dripped while he strode to the door to disperse the crowd.

Samantha Milsap entered from the door that led through the hallway to the lobby. "You wanted to see me, Sheriff?" She shuffled toward him in her canvas flats. Beneath the swish of her long, cotton print skirt he caught sight of a tattooed ankle bracelet of black cat charms.

"What can you tell me, Miss Milsap?"

The young woman glanced at Dorothy Kane and seemed about to upheave her breakfast. "Do we have to stand by her?"

Meriday guided the manager to a distant corner and had her sit down. "I understand you are the one who called this in?" He took out his notebook. Fred Albright broke through the crowd that still gawked near the door, along with the photographer and two EMTs. Meriday motioned Fred toward the body then turned to Samantha.

She chewed her lower lip.

"Go on," he said.

"I received a call from Alison Vaughn, our activities director, around 6:00 a.m. Alison is always the first one at the pool in the morning. She found Dorothy."

"You were in the office then, when she called you?"

"No, I was still asleep in my bungalow. Number thirteen."

He jerked his head. "You live at Willowdell?"

"Yes, Simon requires me to be on the premises at all times. If I need time away, I have Alison cover the front desk. It limits my free time, but it's worth it, being able to live here. And I love working here." Her pale face sobered. "At least I did until ..."

"After Miss Vaughn woke you with a phone call, what did you do?"

"That's when I called your office to report what Alison had told me. That Dorothy Kane was unable to get out of the whirlpool and would require your help." She smiled despite the mist in her eyes. "I think that was Alison's way of making it sound not so ... horrible."

"What can you tell me about the deceased?"

"Not much without checking my files."

"Can you think of anyone who would want to harm Mrs. Kane?" Meriday had seen no signs of foul play, but he couldn't discount the possibility.

Samantha stroked her rose-gold hair. "Well, you probably know about the bingo game three nights ago, when Dorothy and Gladys Blumm had a disagreement over a certain chair."

His deputies had fingerprinted the two and assigned them to separate interview rooms to intimidate them into behaving like proper elderly women. After a brief questioning and some make-them-sweat time, Meriday had his deputies return the women to Willowdell in separate squad cars.

He dismissed the property manager after advising her to hold off on contacting the family until the coroner made his initial finding, and not to discuss this matter with anyone. He walked back to the body laid out on the cement inches from the whirlpool.

Fred removed his latex gloves and pushed his dark-rimmed glasses more snuggly up his nose. "Likely an allergic reaction. I'll get a copy of her medical records and do an autopsy."

"Right." Meriday gave the paramedics room to work. They placed Dorothy Kane's body in a bag and strapped it to a gurney. When they left the pool area, Deputy Bidwell stepped closer.

"Chief, if this Kane lady experienced an allergic reaction, why didn't she get out of the water when she first felt it coming on—to take a pill or something?"

"Why do you think she didn't?"

The rookie shrugged. "She couldn't?"

"Yeah." Meriday peered at the retreating body bag. "And it's our job to find out why she couldn't."

8

Tuesday morning, Maxwell Bailey's heart pounded against his chest while he read the *Ontario Times* report on the cause of Dorothy Kane's death. He tossed the paper aside, gave Stanley a treat, admonished the dog to be good, and closed the door to his bungalow behind him.

The sun peeked above the horizon over the lake, yet lights had been on for quite some time at number eight. He hurried across the square, surprised by a sense of purpose. He rapped lightly, careful not to upset the swag of white tulips.

Frances opened the door. She looked fully prepared to meet her day, complete with makeup and jewelry. Her slate-colored eyes sparked and a smile swept over her face. He silently praised God that he'd gone into town for a haircut and no longer moped about like a slob.

"Good morning, Max."

He greeted her then said, "May I talk to you and Ada? I need advice."

The air in the bright kitchen held the comforting fragrance of recent baking. He took the seat Frances offered.

"Just in time to sample my banana bread." Ada smiled beneath her pinned-up ivory hair. An apron circled her waist. She positioned three teacups and a pot of tea on the glass-topped table, along with napkins and a plate of sliced banana bread. "Mother's recipe has always been our favorite."

He hadn't enjoyed banana bread since before his Lois passed.

Frances poured tea into the cups. "What's on your mind, Max?"

He placed a slice of bread on the small plate Ada had set in front of him. "Have you seen the paper? Dorothy died from an allergic reaction to the peanut oil in the brownies found near the whirlpool."

Ada joined them at the table. "Yes, we read the article."

"It puts me in a bit of a quandary." Maxwell shifted his gaze between them.

"Why is that?" Frances sipped her tea.

"The day after that incident at the bingo game—the argument between Dorothy and Gladys—well, Gladys knocked on my door and asked if I had a brownie mix on hand." He scanned the counter. "Do you have any butter?"

Ada set the butter dish and knife before him then returned to her chair.

"Gladys told me Dorothy liked brownies, and she thought she would make them for a peace offering." He took a bite of the buttered bread. "Mm. Very good."

Ada smiled and edged the plate of banana bread closer to him.

"Apparently," he said, "Dorothy and Gladys were grand friends before the battle over the chair."

"They were." Frances set down her cup. "I was surprised things escalated between them to the point the police had to be called."

"Well, I'm pleased that Gladys took that step toward reconciliation," Ada said. "Let's hope Dorothy accepted her gesture, and they got matters righted between them before she met her sad demise in the whirlpool."

Maxwell took another slice of banana bread. "My fear is, Dorothy did accept. And that's what killed her."

Ada's blue eyes grew wide. "Oh, mercy. I see what you mean."

Frances's face paled. "You think Gladys intentionally gave Dorothy brownies made with peanut oil? Would Gladys even know Dorothy had a peanut allergy?"

With open hands, he asked, "Is having a deadly food allergy something a woman would share with a close friend?"

Frances and Ada looked at each other knowingly.

Ada turned back to him. "Gladys may have forgotten about Dorothy's allergy. Her intentions may have been completely noble. At our age, we do forget. And sometimes we forget important things."

Maxwell nodded and reached for a third slice, then flushed with embarrassment. He withdrew his hands to his lap. "That's why I'm reluctant to volunteer any information. If I say something to the sheriff, I may be pointing a finger at someone totally innocent."

The sisters stared at him, seeming to struggle for an answer. While waiting, he took that third piece and picked up the butterknife.

Later that morning, Meriday parked his brown cruiser with the word *Sheriff* stretched out on both sides of it in front of number five, Dorothy Kane's bungalow. He had one mission—find out who gave Dorothy Kane the deadly brownies.

He wanted to believe her death resulted from unwitting happenstance, but experience had taught him the folly of assumption.

Deputies Bidwell and Sloan pulled up beside him. They would start with a thorough search of the victim's property.

He stood on the sidewalk with his phone to his ear while his deputies lingered nearby. "This is Sheriff Meriday. We need access to Dorothy Kane's bungalow." Heat slowly spread through his body, then flashed. "She's barely cold. Who told you to do that?"

Meriday shoved his phone back in his pocket. "Mrs. Kane's bungalow has been cleared. The manager had the audacity to tell me that if I thought the place was a crime scene, I should have said so before now."

He blew hot air. "Sloan, go around back. See if anything got left behind. Check the trash. Check every trashcan at Willowdell. I want to know who has made brownies recently. Bag whatever you think could be evidence."

"You got it, Chief." Gray-haired and about to retire, Sloan moved with a slower gait than the eager rookie, but Meriday knew him to be well seasoned and thorough.

He scanned the area. A few residents dawdled about, chatting on porch rockers, reading on a bench, or walking a dog near the woodlot. Someone had to know something.

"Bidwell." Meriday pointed toward the hill. "Start with the back bungalows. Interview everyone. Find out all you can about Dorothy Kane. If someone wanted her dead, we need a motive."

"Chief." The deputy took long strides toward the bungalows lodged farther up the hill away from the lake.

Ada Whittaker scuttled up the sidewalk toward him. The sun beat down. He swiped his arm across his forehead, well past the mood for meddlesome tabbies.

She stopped in front of him. A purple straw hat shaded her crinkled eyes. "If you intended to search Dorothy's cupboards for evidence of peanut oil, I would suggest you have your deputies check the dumpster at the shipyard."

"Why would I do that?" He clipped his thumbs to his belt.

"The movers were here early this morning, and that's where they take everything. To the shipyard, not the dumpster. Just the small stuff goes in the dumpster, not the furniture. If there is a bottle of peanut oil there, you can run the prints." She narrowed her eyes. "It may be the only lead you have."

Is that what that was?

She scurried away.

Amateurs. Meriday turned, rubbing his mustache.

A man stared out the front window of number ten, a green bungalow with a frog flag stuck in the ground near an azalea bush.

A moment later, the door opened in response to Meriday's knock. A slightly puffy man with neatly trimmed gray hair appeared in khaki shorts and an untucked print shirt. After introductions, Maxwell Bailey led him inside.

Nita Beavers's cocker spaniel met Meriday at the door and sniffed his pant leg then returned to what seemed to be the dog's usual hangout in front of the fireplace.

Looking about, Leo Meriday knew he had entered a bachelor's pad. No bric-a-brac. Plain walls. A stack of paper plates on the counter. Clothes on chairs and newspapers stacked on the floor near a recliner. Three remote controls on the coffee table.

He noted with envy through the open door of the hall closet the handsome set of golf clubs parked in a corner. He'd like some time on the course himself. Maybe if he wasn't spending so much time at Willowdell.

"Can I get you anything?"

"Water would be great." Meriday pulled out a kitchen

chair, brushed off some crumbs, and eased down his two hundred and twenty pounds.

Bailey handed him ice water in a paper cup, then sat across the table with his own cup of water. "What can I help you with, Sheriff?"

"Have you made any brownies in the past week?" Meriday wondered at the older man's lack of surprise. Most people, he thought, would find the question odd.

"Yes, I have. Since I've acquired Stanley"—Bailey motioned toward the dog—"I seem to have visitors most every day, checking in on him. I keep brownies on hand. They're cheap, easy to make, and most people like them." Bailey interwove his fingers in front of him on the table.

"Dorothy Kane ever visit you?" Meriday pulled out his notebook.

"No, Mrs. Kane has never been here." The cup shook slightly when Bailey lifted it to his lips.

"Do you use peanut oil in your brownies?"

"No." He went to his pantry and returned with a bottle labeled *canola oil*.

Meriday opened the bottle and sniffed. About to stick his finger in the bottle, he paused. "Do you mind?"

"Not at all."

The sheriff tasted the oil on his finger. He dipped again and licked his lips. Definitely not peanut oil. He set the bottle aside. "Do you know of anyone who would have it in for Dorothy Kane?"

Bailey spoke hesitantly. "No. But I should probably tell you, the morning after Dorothy and Gladys Blumm had their disagreement at the bingo game, Gladys came by. She lives in the gray house next door." Bailey looked down at his hands. "Well, Gladys asked if I could spare a brownie mix. She knows I keep them in stock."

Meriday put a fisted hand on his hip. "Could you?"

Bailey bobbed his head while staring at his cup. "Gladys knew Dorothy liked brownies, so to make up with her,"—he lifted his head—"to let bygones be bygones, she wanted to extend a peace offering."

"A rest-in-peace offering?"

Blood drained from the face of the frog-flag man.

Wonder if he will croak. Meriday stifled the twitching of his lips.

Meriday walked across the grass to number nine, the gray bungalow next to Maxwell Bailey's. It was mid-May, but a wreath of plastic Easter eggs hung on the front door. After his knock, he scanned the dozen or so potted plants and counted eight windchimes that clinked out annoying tings and twangs in the slight lake breeze.

A tall, sturdy woman with wire-rimmed glasses perched atop a pinned-up mound of yellow hair opened the door.

"Mrs. Blumm? I'd like to ask you some questions, ma'am."

She stepped out on the porch, closed the door behind her, and pointed to a cushioned chair. "Take a load off." She parked herself in a rocker.

He sat and took out his notebook. "When was the last time you made brownies?"

The woman jerked back. "You planning a policemen's bake sale?" She pulled a bobby pin out of her hair and scratched an apparent scalp itch, then replaced it.

"Please answer the question."

"Can't say I recall. Don't make them very often."

"Didn't you recently obtain a brownie mix from Mr.

Bailey?" He watched her pale brown eyes for any flicker of falsehood.

"Yep. Thought I'd take some to Dorothy. Appease her with a batch." She grimaced. "Wish I had now. Her being dead and all."

"Are you saying you didn't make brownies and give them to Mrs. Kane?"

"Well, I got thinking about it, and it made me mad all over again." Mrs. Blumm tossed her arms around while she spoke. "Dorothy could have let me sit in that chair. If she hadn't been so selfish, I never would have been dragged down to your station like a criminal. I'm surprised you didn't post my picture on mugs dot com."

Meriday looked away and scratched his ear. Turning back to her, he asked, "Did you know Dorothy had a peanut allergy?"

"Of course. So did a lot of people. Whenever Dorothy wasn't sure of something she wanted to eat, she'd stop and ask."

The woman obviously didn't ask when she received the container of brownies. Or someone lied to her. "Do you have peanut oil in your house?"

"No, but you're not looking without a search warrant." She pushed off with her feet and set her chair rocking at a resolute pace.

9

In the study at Ada's peach-colored Victorian, Gwen Dunbar peered through her reading glasses at the spreadsheet and tapped her fingers on the desk. She would have to disclose the facts eventually. She had gone way over budget, and the workmen still weren't finished.

She heard Janet humming and suspected the cook was carrying another tray up the stairs. Gwen whipped off her readers and leaped up.

"Stop right there." Gwen stood with her hands on her hips.

Janet turned midway up the staircase, holding a plate of cookies. "The boys are hungry."

The two contractors working on Ada's bathrooms for the past two weeks were hardly boys. "Get down here. Take that plate back into the kitchen. Those *boys* are behind schedule because they spend way too much time stuffing Miss Ada's food into their mouths."

Janet glared at Gwen and moved slowly down the steps, her bottom lip curled. She paused in front of Gwen. "Jesus said whatever we do for others we do for him."

"Jesus could feed five thousand people with a budget of two fish and five loaves."

Late that afternoon, Sheriff Meriday moved to the window of his office and stared out at the quiet village street of Sackets Harbor. Coffee dripped into the pot on the burner and filled the small office with its welcome fragrance.

Deputies Bidwell and Sloan waited near his desk. They had just given an account of their time at Willowdell. Trashcans held nothing incriminating by way of peanut oil or brownies, nothing that would indicate an intentional assault on Dorothy Kane. Nor did Bidwell ferret out a motive from any of the residents he interviewed. Dorothy Kane had not been well liked, but she had been tolerated.

"Go out to the shipyard. Search the dumpster."

Bidwell asked, "What are we looking for, Chief?"

"I have it from a questionable source that Dorothy Kane's pantry may have been dumped there." Meriday walked to the coffee pot and filled his ceramic bulldog mug. "Bring back anything labeled oil. And I don't have to tell you, be careful of the prints. We need to verify, first off, that Dorothy Kane herself did not make those brownies. If she did, then we'll know someone intentionally swapped out her oil for peanut oil."

"And if there's no peanut oil?" Sloan asked.

"Then someone else made those brownies, and we need to track down how they came to be in Mrs. Kane's possession. With that information, we should be able to determine if her death resulted from tragic accident or murder."

Wendall Compton stirred and craned his neck off the pillow. "That you, Magpie?" A stream of moonlight filtered through the curtain into the otherwise dark room. Wendall shoved off the covers and tucked his feet into the slippers by his bed.

He found the rear door open and shuffled outside. Wind rising off the lake whipped at his pajamas while he scanned the stars. An owl screeched from deep within the woodlot behind his bungalow.

"Hoot. Hoot." A breezed tossed the tops of the pine trees.

Someone touched his elbow.

"Where've you been?" Wendall stepped off the patio. "Did you hear the hooter?"

He felt the tug on his sleeve.

Wendall shambled along behind the shadow that led him into the woods. "I'll show you that old hooter."

Deeper and deeper into the darkness, he followed. Pine needles crunched beneath his feet and pricked his ankles. He shivered with the rustle of the leaves. Oak trees creaked in the wind.

Again, the owl screeched. The shadow led.

"Hoot. Hoot." He searched the highest branches with an eagle eye. "I'll find you, you old bird."

Ada stepped out onto the porch of her sister's bungalow the next morning and gazed across the square. Maxwell Bailey moved about Gladys Blumm's porch with a watering can.

It had been nine days since Dorothy Kane's death, and although Ada had heard no official word on the matter, other than that the woman died from a reaction to peanut oil, she had heard plenty of speculation as to how it happened. Tongues flapped, and fingers pointed to Gladys Blumm.

Unable to bear the sideways glances and whispered accusations, the poor woman had shuttered herself away behind closed blinds and drapes. If it were not for Maxwell Bailey, Gladys's many potted plants would have suffered from the lack of attention.

Ada could understand why he did not want to point the sheriff in the direction of Gladys Blumm. Maxwell knew the potential for darkness to settle over his neighbor. A darkness from which he himself had recently begun to emerge.

The sound of vehicles grabbed her attention. The sheriff's car pulled up to the administration building, followed by two cruisers.

"Frances," Ada called into the bungalow. "Frances, come here."

Her sister came to the screen door holding a mascara wand. "What is it?"

"The sheriff is here again." Ada looked down the square. "He's going into the lobby with two deputies. Come on. Let's find out what's going on."

"I'm not going anywhere until I finish my makeup."

Her sister's insistence that no one ever see her without makeup nearly drove Ada to her knees. She muttered while she paced, "Must be a phobia."

Finally, Frances appeared looking as if she stepped out of a salon.

They entered the lobby undetected and hovered quietly near the door. Simon Hilton sat at his desk, chewing his lips while the property manager gave an account to the sheriff and two deputies.

"Wendall's home health aide found him gone when she arrived to prepare his breakfast and get him ready for the day." Samantha checked her watch. "That was about an hour ago. We've had our staff looking for him but without success."

"What can you tell me about Mr. Compton?" Meriday opened his notebook.

Samantha read from the manilla folder in her hand. "Eighty-seven years old. Some signs of dementia. The aide visits him daily, but no one stays with him at night."

Deputy Sloan sent a chilling look of censure to Simon Hilton. "Always looking out for the resident's best interest."

"You just need to find him," Hilton shot back. "If it should get in the papers that we misplaced one of our residents, it will negatively affect my election bid."

Meriday scowled and turned to Samantha. "We will issue the Silver Alert and get the media involved. You will need to contact his family."

Hilton raised a hand. "Do we have to do that just yet? Perhaps we'll find Wendall, and it won't be necessary."

"He listed no living relatives." Samantha closed the folder. "There's no one to contact."

Ada raised her eyebrows at Frances then tipped her head toward the door. Outside she whispered, "Did you hear that? Wendall has no living relatives."

"Neither did Nita or Dorothy." Frances glanced back at the lobby door, her brow crinkled.

"Come on." Ada grabbed Frances's arm. "We need to check out Wendall's place before the sheriff gets there."

10

Ada and Francis crept around to the back of number sixteen, the yellow bungalow in the upper row on the north side of Willowdell, and slipped onto the patio. Wendall's property nudged close to a woodlot.

"If he went into the woods," Ada said, "it's likely no one would have seen him. Especially in the night or early morning hours."

The bungalow's back door stood open.

"Stand guard." Ada stepped over the threshold.

Frances called in a hushed tone, "Remember, don't touch anything."

The bungalow smelled of camphor. A coat and sweater hung on hooks just inside the door. Below them, a rubber mat held a pair of slip-on shoes with the heels smooshed down.

Ada prowled about the kitchen. Clean counters. No dishes in the sink. The stove disconnected. A microwave. Inside the refrigerator, milk, eggs, the usuals. Frozen dinners in the freezer. Cold coffee maker.

She moved to the bedroom. Bed unmade. A robe draped across a chair. No slippers. No pajamas.

Frances called to her. "I hear voices."

Ada's heart banged in her ears. She had to get out. But she hadn't yet checked the bathroom.

"Hurry."

Ada sensed the panic in his sister's voice, but she refused to leave without a peek in the medicine cabinet. After a quick scan of the pill bottles, she scooted back to the patio.

Frances grabbed her arm, and they ducked around the corner.

"Hello, ladies. Speed-walking?" Maxwell Bailey held Stanley on a leash.

Before Ada could think of an explanation for their being out of breath, Maxwell's cell phone pinged.

He read the message on his phone. "Silver Alert. Eighty-seven-year-old male missing from Willowdell. Possible dementia."

"Wendall Compton," Ada said.

"The man at bingo who seemed to be looking for something?"

"Yes, and I'm afraid he is in his pajamas and slippers. I didn't see them anywhere."

Maxwell shaded his eyes. "You went into Wendall's bungalow?"

"I didn't break and enter. The back door was open."

"Did you find anything that would indicate what happened to him?" Frances said.

"His kitchen hadn't been used this morning," Ada said. "He must have gone out sometime in the night."

Maxwell frowned. "I hope not. The wind chill dipped low last night."

Frances reached into her pocket. "I found this on Wendall's patio, under the window."

Maxwell studied the necklace. "That looks like Selma Potter's necklace. The clasp is faulty. Maybe it fell off."

"What connection could there be between Selma and Wendall?" Ada said.

"I hope none," Maxwell said. "More rumors along that line could put Gladys on a ledge."

Ada prayed the gold chain had no bearing on the disappearance of Wendall Compton. She would not want to explain how they obtained the evidence.

"Whoa," Frances said, "let's first find Wendall."

"You're right," Maxwell said. "I hope he's okay." He tugged the leash to prod Stanley.

Frances walked beside him. "I hope he's found soon."

Ada followed. "I hope he's found alive."

Sheriff Meriday issued the alert within minutes of speaking to Samantha Milsap and Simon Hilton. Personally, he didn't care for either one. Hilton seemed a pompous punk. And Miss Milsap, blindly devoted to the man, would simply parrot her boss.

Within an hour, first-responders, deputies from neighboring precincts, firemen, and volunteers from Willowdell and the village of Sackets Harbor were coordinating efforts to find the wandering Wendall Compton.

Meriday stood at the top of the knoll, looking back at the square. News crews had arrived and parked along the lane. Simon Hilton skulked toward them, smoothing his hair and beard. He stopped and spoke to Samantha Milsap, who bore down at his heels. Her face fell before she turned and slogged back to the lobby.

He moved toward the lake and the dredging crew.

Maxwell leashed Stanley, hoisted a light backpack of supplies, and set out to join the search.

When he reached the woodlot, Ada and Frances called for him to wait up. He turned to see Frances in jeans and a flannel shirt, and Ada in a denim skirt, button-up blouse, hiking boots, and a pink straw hat. They each carried a small knapsack and a thermos bottle.

His heart sank. He didn't want them to go into the woods. The risk of separation and getting lost was too great. When they arrived beside him, he tried unsuccessfully to send them back.

"Then stay close together. We don't want to inadvertently sidestep anything important." Maxwell had an ulterior motive. He intended to keep watch of Ada. He feared, in her zeal to solve the mysterious disappearance of Wendall Compton, she might grow impatient and forge ahead on her own and get disoriented in the dense forest. As for Frances, he felt oddly protective and wanted to keep her close.

He led the women into the woods with an emerging sense of duty, the sense an army sergeant must feel when leading the charge. His interest in the people and happenings outside his four walls had crept unbidden, yet instinctively, back into his soul.

Maybe Gladys had it right, and there is life after retirement.

He hoped there would be life for Wendall after his wanderings.

Maxwell quickened his steps and called the old man's name.

The sun arced stealthily overhead while they tramped over rotted leaves and broken limbs, crossed narrow creeks, and stepped over hollow logs. The darkness and density of the forest deepened, and the air held the heavy scent of pine.

Ada and Frances stuck by him, despite receiving several scratches from the bushes. The humidity, coupled with the exertion, made it difficult to breathe. Frances's hair lay matted from her continual swipes at it with sweaty palms.

Wendall's name resounded faintly in the distance, informing Max the old man had not yet been found.

"Max, let's stop a minute," Frances said. She and Ada rested on a log and opened their thermoses.

Maxwell dropped the leash, opened his thermos, and poured a sampling of water in the cap for Stanley. After a sloppy guzzle, Stanley's ears perked. His nose twitched. A rabbit raced over the leaves, and Stanley darted. The dog ignored the command to come back.

"Stay right here," Maxwell told the women, then he hurried in Stanley's direction.

Ada raised her voice. "We're right behind you."

Leaves crunched behind him until Frances squealed.

He glanced back.

She waved him on. "Just a pricker bush."

He fell with a crash. Pain seared his shin.

Frances and Ada rushed toward him while he worked himself into a sitting position and leaned against a tree. He grimaced and brushed aside debris to see the roots of the old maple that had tripped him and jerked back, reeling at what he saw.

A slipper dangled from Wendall's foot.

11

The following morning, Sheriff Meriday and Deputy Bidwell entered Wendall Compton's hospital room. The old man had a large bandage over his forehead, blackened eyes, bruised cheeks, and cuts and scratches on the parchment skin of his hands.

Pneumonia made it difficult for Wendall to breathe. "Magpie?" Wendall wheezed and searched Meriday's face.

The sheriff shifted his stance, not sure how to answer.

Wendall's bloodshot eyes focused on Bidwell standing at the foot of the bed. "Did you see the owl?"

Bidwell looked at the chief and lifted his shoulders.

Meriday cleared his throat. "Did *you* see the owl, Wendall?"

"Hoot. Hoot. Funny old bird." He chuckled and gasped for air.

"Did Magpie take you into the woods?" Meriday bent closer to Wendall's slightly blue lips. "Did someone take you to see the owl?"

The old man's cough triggered the intrusion of a nurse,

who simply pointed at the door. They'd get nothing more today.

"I feel bad for the old guy," Bidwell said as they walked toward their cruisers. "He's lucky someone found him."

"Yeah, but he's got a fight with that pneumonia."

"You think someone led him into the woods?"

"I don't know how much merit we can give to anything he said." Meriday opened his squad car door. "Milsap said Compton doesn't have any relatives, but he sure talked like he did. We need to find this Magpie."

Four days later, Maxwell Bailey pulled his golf bag out of the closet. He hadn't touched the clubs since he moved into Willowdell and hadn't played golf since his elder board banished him to an early retirement.

He needed a distraction. The news of Wendall Compton's death triggered anew the images of the old man lying face-down on the damp forest floor.

Perhaps Frances could use something to take her mind off the poor old chap.

A half hour later, he drove his golf cart to the course with Frances beside him and Ada and the clubs in the back seat. Frances looked comfortable in khaki capris and a navy-blue golf shirt, and Maxwell felt comfortable with her.

Betrayal no longer stung. Light had dispelled his darkness, and the depression that weighed down his spirit had lifted. A ditty spun off his thoughts. *O retirement, where is thy sting? O resentment, where is thy victory?* He stifled a snicker.

They stopped to begin the course.

"You two go ahead," Ada said. "I'll scoot up into the

driver's seat and be your Uber guy." Her blue eyes sparkled beneath the brim of the red straw hat.

They were at the eighth hole when a golf cart shot over a rise and descended on them at full speed. Ada sat in their cart with her phone to her ear.

"Ada, watch out," Frances yelled. "Luty Mae's coming."

The speeding golf cart missed Ada's cart by inches and continued toward Frances and Maxwell.

"Be careful," Maxwell shouted at the driver.

The woman appeared no bigger than a girl when she whizzed past them, narrowly missing Frances. She cackled with laughter and continued unfazed over the green.

Ada trotted up beside Frances, her legs trembling. "Mercy. What could that woman be thinking? She nearly ran you over."

Frances pressed her hands against her stomach. "That's the problem. She hasn't been thinking right since she suffered a stroke a few months back."

"Somebody needs to take away her golf cart." Maxwell placed a ball on the tee. "Before someone gets killed."

———

Assured Miss Ada had avoided the renegade golf cart, Gwen Dunbar hung up the phone. She had been given an assignment. Ada wanted her to find out all she could about Nita Beavers, Dorothy Kane, and Wendall Compton. Locate any living relatives and search for anything they may have had in common, like mutual acquaintances, memberships, hometowns, or occupations in their earlier years.

Janet stuck her head in the study. "Were you talking to Miss Ada? When is she coming back? Those bathrooms have been done for days now."

"Not until the bodies stop dropping." Gwen went on to

explain Ada's particular concern for her sister's safety. "She's determined to stay with Frances until the threat, in whatever form that may be, has passed."

Janet sat her slightly plump frame on the Victorian sofa and furrowed her brow. "They should both stay here."

"I agree." When Janet stopped feeding the handymen, it took no time at all for them to complete the reformation of the bathrooms, leaving Gwen in a less combative mood. "They found the man who went missing dead in his hospital bed this morning."

"That's sad." After a moment of silence, Janet added, "We should start sending sympathy cards. It could be a whole new ministry for us."

"For you." Gwen reviewed the list of names. "I've been assigned the ministry of surfing the internet for information on the residents who died recently, to see if I can find anything that would link them."

Janet's deep brown eyes lit. "What can I do?"

Gwen placed her chin in her hand and tapped her lips. "Get my laptop off the shelf over there. With two of us working at it, we might find something."

Janet jumped up and started toward the shelf. "Oh, wait. I'll get us some coffee, then we can feel like real detectives." She left the study for the kitchen.

"Chocolate chip," Gwen called, knowing Janet would not return without cookies.

Frances stepped off the porch three days later with an oversized bag hung over her shoulder. "I'm taking the bus into the village. Dryden's is having a sale on their summer line."

Ada looked up from weeding the flower bed along the front

of the porch. Frances would always shop when she wanted to escape something unpleasant. She opened her mouth to speak, then paused to consider her words. How could she convince Frances to stay alert to her surroundings without creating more anxiety for her?

Ever since Wendall Compton had been found in the woods, Ada harbored the fear that her sister, too, could be in danger. Until she could determine why the residents of Willowdell were dropping like octogenarians at a line-dancing contest, Ada intended to keep close watch of Frances.

"I'll change and go with you." She climbed to her feet and brushed the dirt and grass from the front of her denim skirt.

"That's not necessary. I know you don't care for shopping. Besides, the bus will be here in a minute." Frances walked toward the front gate.

Ada looked after her, trying to quell the panic rising in her chest. "Fanny?" she called. Her sister turned back to her. "Do be careful."

Frances smiled and waved, then disappeared around the bend.

12

Two hours later, Ada opened the front door in response to an impassioned rap and found Miriam Kroft with a pack of brochures in her hand. Her black bouffant reminded Ada of a bygone day. "I'm afraid my sister has taken the bus into town. I don't expect her back for some time."

"Please advise her of the upcoming primary." She held out the paper face and broad smile of Simon Hilton. "Mr. Hilton has ordered a shuttle bus to take residents to the polling station. The bus will run every two hours so everyone should be able to take advantage of the courtesy."

"Oh, my, that's generous of him." Ada was repelled by the candidate's apparent expectation that his residents would cast their vote for him. After all, she doubted he would provide transportation if he thought the residents would vote for his nemesis. "How very selfless of him."

Miriam Kroft's birdlike, raisin-brown eyes sparkled with the pride of a mother for her promising son. "Since the primary is not for three more weeks, I will stop back a couple more times to remind you."

Ada took the brochure. "I'll let Frances know you stopped by." *If I can remember without being reminded two more times.*

The woman grinned and trotted away.

Minutes later, Ada sat at the kitchen table perusing the brochure and sipping lemonade. The front door sprang open, and Frances fairly flew into the bungalow.

"Mercy, Frances. What's the matter?"

She set her shopping bags on the counter. "I ran into our attorney at Tin Pan Galley."

Ada poured a glass of lemonade and handed it to her. "Drink this and calm down. How is Neil?"

Neil Tibbs, one of Sackets Harbor's most sought-after bachelors, held the position of board chairman at Stonecroft Resort in addition to being a respected attorney.

Frances took a sip then said, "He told me Gwen contacted him about the people on your list. Dorothy and Nita and Wendall. She asked if he represented any of them."

Ada raised her eyebrows. "Did he?"

"No, but he's disturbed by the upsurge in deaths at Willowdell. He's particularly concerned for Judge Fausset. Apparently, the judge mentored him."

"Yes, they are close. And with the judge having retired here, I understand his concern."

"Here's the exciting part. Neil told Gwen he would look deeper and try to find out the names of the executors of the deceased's estates."

"Wonderful. He's very good at that sort of thing." Ada recalled asking her attorney to research a few individuals before. His off-the-record detective work had proven invaluable in solving the scandal at Stonecroft.

Frances sobered and her smile disappeared.

Puzzled at the sudden change, Ada asked, "What is it?"

"He also cautioned me about jumping to conclusions. He said the deaths could have been accidental, and he doesn't want us casting aspersions or spreading suspicion."

"That sounds like Neil. He deals with facts and has little use for conjecture. Unfortunately, we have neither at this point."

"He's right. What if Nita Beavers did trip on something and fell into the water? She could have hit her head on a rock and not been able to get out." Frances opened her hands. "I assumed she'd been pushed, but I didn't see anyone."

"Yes, and Dorothy could have gotten ahold of the brownies through completely innocent means." Ada often countered her suspicion that a murderer resided in their midst with this very reasoning. Yet, every time she landed on the side of accidental death, another body would turn up.

Frances reached again for her glass. "Wendall likely wandered off by himself. His death can be traced to the failure of his care coordinator to see that he had twenty-four-hour supervision."

"I agree, Wendall should never have been left on his own."

Frances tilted her head. "Maybe we should leave the reasoning behind these deaths for Sheriff Meriday to figure out."

Ada had no intention of waiting on the sheriff. She needed to know the common link between the deceased residents, and if that link extended to Frances. Until she knew Frances to be clear of danger, she would do everything she could to find the truth, with or without the sheriff.

Three weeks had passed since Nita Beavers's body lay motionless on the shore of Lake Ontario, and still Leo Meriday remained clueless. He rubbed his mustache, then the nape of his neck, then went to the coffeepot and poured another cup.

Late into the evening he studied the reports on the recent deaths at Willowdell. So little to go on. Again and again, he reviewed his notes.

Nita Beavers. Dorothy Kane. Wendall Compton. Drowning, allergic reaction, pneumonia. Okay, so the old man died of natural causes. But did someone lead him into the woods intending to abandon him there? Compton talked like he'd gone into the woods to show someone an owl. Did he go alone?

The sheriff had spoken to the staff psychologist and learned that in Wendall's state of dementia, the old man could have imagined someone with him and wandered alone into the woods. In light of the other two deaths, however, Meriday was not inclined to dismiss entirely the idea of foul play.

He picked up the report on the victims.

Wendall Compton. Eighty-seven. Wife Arlotta, deceased at age seventy-two. Son, Marcus, also deceased. Vietnam. Before retirement, Wendall had been a professor of ornithology at Cornell University. "I can see why he would go off at the hoot of the owl." Compton's ear was tuned to a bird call like a mother's ear is tuned to her baby's cry.

Nita Beavers, seventy-four, widow. Prior to retirement, director of nursing. Son, Dr. Thom Beavers, deceased with no children. His assets went entirely to his mother. Nita moved to Willowdell just over five years ago.

Dorothy Kane, sixty-five, a New York State employee with the DMV, retired at age fifty-five. A widow twice over. First husband, a software developer, died in China three years into their marriage. Second husband, Albert. Father of son Jordan Kane, who played for the Syracuse Orangemen and later for the NBA.

Jordan Kane suffered a heart attack on the court. His estate went to his parents. Albert Kane had been a basketball coach at the junior college in Watertown prior to his death in a motor-cycle accident six years ago.

Meriday rubbed his chin. That's a lot of money left on the table. In the case of Compton, he had no living relatives listed. Who was handling his estate?

Frances moved about the kitchen, opening and shutting drawers and cupboards.

Ada paused her dust rag. With the open floor plan, she could see Frances staring into the pantry with her hands on her hips.

"What are you looking for?" Ada said.

"Have you seen my box of Hegler chocolates?"

The chocolates were Frances's one indulgence that she allowed herself once a day, and she took the indulgence seriously.

"Did you check the hall table?"

"Yes. I received a shipment yesterday, and I thought I left it on the table in the entryway, but the box is gone. I can't find it anywhere."

Ada tossed the dust rag and joined in the search. She walked to the desk in the dining room and spotted a paper issued by the main office advising of the next inspection date. Frances never left papers about. She held it out to her sister. "Did you leave this here for a reason?"

Frances scanned the paper. "I didn't put it there. Samantha must have brought it down to us. She usually does."

"She didn't give it to me."

"She didn't give it to me." A dawning swept over Frances's face. Her dark gray eyes flared. "Samantha Milsap came into my house when neither of us were here? Would she have taken my chocolates?"

Ada sighed. "I suspect the girl would do about anything."

13

After leaving his office, Neil stopped off at Willowdell. He rang the doorbell at number thirty and waited for Judge Burton Fausset to answer. The judge's bungalow, one of eight which lined the hill, overlooked the lake.

"Neil. This is a pleasant surprise." The retired circuit court judge swung wide the door. "Hungry? I smoked a brisket today. Ten hours. Mighty good. Got plenty left."

The judge loved to cook, and he loved to eat. At five feet, six inches, his width seemed nearly to match his height. He wore a white goatee, and his white hair lay thin and smooth on his round head.

"Thanks, but Aunt Gracie is expecting me for supper."

Judge Fausset led him to a sitting area where bookshelves lined two walls. "Have a seat. It's been a while since you've stopped by."

Neil smiled and sat on the leather couch across from the recliner where the judge settled himself. "I recall a Sunday dinner not too long ago."

"Glazed ham, butter-slathered mashed potatoes, my own

yeast rolls. I remember." The seventy-year-old man's brown eyes twinkled. "Now are you hungry?"

Neil laughed. "You're killing me."

"Speaking in those terms, I'm sure you've heard about the tragic occurrences of late here at Willowdell."

"That's why I'm here." He removed his suit jacket and leaned forward. "I'd like your opinion on those deaths."

"Afraid I don't have one." The judge raised the footrest of his recliner. "All I know is what's been reported in the paper."

"You've lived at Willowdell for, what ... five, six years?" Neil took a small notebook from his pocket and turned to the names of the recent victims.

"That's right."

"What can you tell me about Nita Beavers, Dorothy Kane, and Wendall Compton?"

The judge narrowed his eyes. "You seem inordinately concerned. Any particular reason?"

Yeah, Judge. Your safety. Neil grinned. "I'm a lawyer. Lawyers ask questions."

"For a purpose." Discernment shone from the judge's eyes. "But I will tell you what I know. Wendall Compton was a good man, a kind man. Somewhat asea, if I'm to be honest. He'd wander about the place and sometimes mumble to himself. But all of us, I think, tended to watch over him. Apparently, more should have been done to keep him safe at night."

"Any suspicions of foul play?"

His mentor studied his face. "Is that what you have? Suspicions?"

"Maybe. It all seems outside the bounds of coincidence."

"I'll tell you what I can, but I don't believe Wendall's death to be anything but a terrible tragedy. The death of Dorothy Kane did give me pause. Likely because of her squabble with Gladys Blumm at the bingo game. However, I do not believe the rumors. I don't believe Gladys sought revenge—not over a chair."

"People have died for less."

The judge nodded. "True."

"Nita Beavers?"

He chuckled and shook his head. "Always after me to take care of my heart. Told me to stop eating meat. Apparently, she wanted me to stop eating altogether. It's cliché, but she meant well. Folks likely didn't appreciate her advice, that's all." The judge frowned. "The news of her death surprised me. Drowning, I mean. Nita was fit. Strong. I have no doubt she could have run a marathon. Just goes to show, doesn't it?"

After several minutes of discussing the residents at Willowdell, Neil rose, saying, "I better get home, or Aunt Gracie will send out the cavalry."

The judge left the recliner with some effort. "I suspect your aunt will have the cavalry on standby for years to come." He walked with Neil to the door.

"Do me a favor, Judge."

"Absolutely, if I can."

Neil placed his hand on the doorknob then paused and looked at his friend. "Until Sheriff Meriday gets to the truth about these deaths, promise me you'll be careful."

The judge lifted a hand in the Boy Scout pledge. "I promise to be ever vigilant."

Maxwell waited for Gladys to answer his knock. The Easter egg wreath, faded by the summer sun, still hung on her door. Minutes before, he had taken brownies from the oven and now held a warm paper plate covered with a napkin.

Earlier that morning he'd watered Gladys's plants, yet he

sensed the need to do more to offer his support. It had been three weeks since his neighbor asked for a brownie mix and two weeks since rumors drove her into seclusion.

He tried the doorbell. Still, no answer.

Maxwell gripped the doorknob. Finding the door unlocked, he peeked inside. The living room and dining room were shrouded in darkness. He entered. The air smelled stuffy.

"Gladys?" A tabby purred at his ankles. In the kitchen, Simon Hilton's face stared up from the brochure on the counter. Beyond the kitchen, down a hallway, a door opened.

Selma Potter appeared, rubbing her eyes. "Mr. Bailey?"

"Yes."

"I'm sorry. I fell asleep watching a movie with Mother." Selma approached, wearing an orange print muumuu. Bobby pins hung from the curl on her left side.

He glanced at her neck, which bore no necklace, and held out the plate. "I made brownies."

"That's kind of you. Mother hasn't had much of an appetite. Maybe these will tempt her to eat." Selma took the plate.

"May I see her? Perhaps I can read to her or pray with her?" The desire to minister had been stirring from its forced sedation. Truth be told, he had not enjoyed a moment of focusing solely on himself.

"Mother is refusing to see anyone." Selma set the plate on Simon Hilton's face.

"You're not wearing your gold necklace. I hope it didn't fall off somewhere. You were having trouble with the clasp."

"It's lost." She reached under the napkin and pulled out a brownie.

"Sometimes it helps to retrace your steps. Where were you when you last had it?" He wondered if she would admit to being on Wendall Compton's patio.

She waved her hand. "I know where I lost it. Right here. Spending my days with Mother, trying to cheer her, it must have fallen off. I'll come across it eventually. Besides, it's just a cheap little thing." She bit into the brownie.

"Perhaps you lost it around Willowdell somewhere. Maybe up along the upper bungalows. Walking there, perhaps."

"Why are you so concerned about my necklace?"

A flush swept up his neck and warmed his face.

"Oh, I know." She waved a hand. "You're a pastor at heart. I guess they can take the pastor out of the pulpit but not the pulpit out of the pastor." She smiled a condescending smile. "Sweet."

Ada woke to the ear-piercing screams of fire engines. She raced to the window. Red lights flashed against the black night. The clock on the nightstand read 02:27.

A tap sounded on her door, and Frances stuck her head in. "A fire on the hill."

Ada threw on her flannel robe and slid into her slippers, then followed Frances into the smokey night. They hurried across the dew-coated grass until they reached the upper row of bungalows.

Her heart pounded in her chest. She linked arms with Frances.

Flames shot from the garage roof of number thirty, the bungalow of Judge Burton Fausset.

14

Maxwell awoke. The screech of sirens twisted his stomach into a knot. He went to the window. Even with it closed, he could smell asphalt shingles burning.

Alarm shot through him.

He slid into his shower sandals and left the house in his lounge pants, slipping a sweatshirt over his head while he hurried toward the red flashing lights of firetrucks. He found Ada and Frances huddled among a few other residents, the breeze tousling everyone's hair.

Firemen atop a ladder wrestled that same wind and blasted water relentlessly on the flames that shot up from the roof of a garage.

He stepped in close to Frances and Ada. "Whose place?"

"Judge Fausset's." The orange blaze could be seen in Frances's eyes while she blinked back tears. "I'm frightened. The deaths, and then this. No one is safe at Willowdell."

He drew an arm around her shoulder and firmly held his hand against the soft velour of her robe. The need to protect welled up in him. He had to keep her safe.

Ada heard someone call her name. She turned to see Neil Tibbs striding toward her. Worry lined his face.

"Have you seen Judge Fausset?" he asked, his voice strained.

"I haven't seen him." She quickly added, "But I haven't seen any stretchers going into the ambulance either."

Neil stared at the fire, rubbing the stubble on his chin. "Maybe he's still in there."

"Don't jump to conclusions." Ada bit her lip and turned back to the fire.

"Five days ago, I told him to be careful. Who could have done this?"

Ada peered at him. "You think someone purposely—"

"No." He shook his head. "I don't know. With everything that's happened ..."

After what seemed like an hour, a fireman strode toward them, the neon reflectors of his jacket shimmering ominously in the darkness. His face, covered in soot and sweat, came into view beneath a streetlamp. He approached Neil.

"Are you Neil Tibbs?"

Neil sucked in a breath then said, "Yes."

"We're taking Judge Fausset to the hospital, but first he wants to see you."

Late the next afternoon, Neil left his office and drove to the hospital. He had spent the morning addressing his mentor's affairs according to the judge's instructions when he summoned Neil at the scene. He contacted the insurance agency and a fire restoration company, completed forms for the judge to sign, and spent some time on the phone with Samantha Milsap. Much depended on the fire marshal's report.

"How are you?" Neil approached his bed. The patient pushed a button on the rail and raised himself to a sitting position. When he did not answer, Neil pulled up a chair and sat. "What happened last night?"

The judge leaned his head back. His brown eyes searched the drop ceiling. "What difference does it make? It is what it is."

Neil puzzled at his attitude. "Could you have left a burner on, or perhaps your smoker, still hot, had been left too close to something flammable? Did you have any candles burning and forget to blow them out?"

Judge Fausset's head snapped up. "No, I did not."

The defensive tone startled Neil. The judge had never spoken a harsh word to him. Clearly, something deeper troubled the man.

Fear, perhaps? Fear of being monitored? Losing independence? If the fire started because he forgot to turn off a burner or unplug an iron or blow out a candle, would Willowdell limit his freedom?

Neil dropped the matter. He'd wait for the fire marshal to issue a report. "I'm glad you're going to be all right. You kept my stomach in my throat for over an hour last night. No one seemed able to tell me if you were okay."

"If you don't mind, I'd like to rest now. I appreciate you coming."

"Okay. Let me know if there's anything more I can do. I owe you a great deal and, more importantly, you mean a lot to me."

The judge acknowledged his words with a slight dip of his head. "Did Samantha say if there is a bungalow available? I plan on getting out of here soon."

Of course, the fact he had no home to go to would be weighing on his mind. "She told me there are currently no open bungalows, but with the demographics of Willowdell, one could become available at any time."

He scoffed. "Isn't that the truth."

"Miss Milsap did say she would move you to the top of the waiting list, and they are lining up a crew to rebuild the garage at number thirty. I hope in the meantime you will stay at Greenbrier Inn. Aunt Gracie has an unreserved room, and you're welcome to stay with us as long as you need to."

"That's fine." The judge closed his eyes and turned away.

Neil said his goodbyes and walked back to his car. His gut told him something more than temporary living arrangements worried the judge.

Likely, the same thing that had troubled Neil while he watched the garage at number thirty go up in flames. Judge Fausset may have been a target.

15

"The girls are right, Frances. You should stay at my house." Ada sat with her sister, Gwen, and Janet around the wrought iron table on the shaded back patio of the yellow bungalow. Tumblers filled with lemonade were before them, along with a sampling of pastries Janet had brought with her. "At least until the sheriff can get to the bottom of what's happening at Willowdell."

Gwen and Janet had told Ada about their pact. They would strive to get along if she and Frances would stay at Fairfield Lane until the nightmare at Willowdell ended.

After the fire at Judge Fausset's the previous night, Ada, too, urged Frances to leave the retirement village.

"I promise, I'll cook some of your favorites." Janet fanned herself with a leopard print folding fan. Her eye shadow and mascara deepened her already dark eyes. She wore a narrow scarf headband, and her gold hoop earrings swung with the movement of the fanned breeze. "We got the bathrooms fixed up all modern-like. And Gwen's done an amazing job decorating."

Gwen smiled at Janet and swiped a hand through her red frizz. "You were a big help."

Ada raised an eyebrow. Janet had been a challenge to Gwen throughout the ordeal. But she could detect no sarcasm in Gwen's praise. The two had committed to being civil with one another, yet Ada—knowing them as she did—doubted their cease-fire would last. Regardless, it would be best to sequester Frances away from Willowdell.

"The girls love to shop." Ada smiled at Frances, hoping she had spoken the magic word. "Why don't you pack a few things and spend some time doing girl things? Perhaps dinner and a movie."

"How about supper at the Primrose?" Janet's eyes lit up.

Gwen asked, "What kind of movies do you like? I'm sure we can find something that will take your mind off everything here."

"I can't leave Ada alone. I won't." Frances picked up a watering can and began to water a fern.

"She's coming too." Janet looked at Ada, expecting cooperation.

Ada shook her head. "I won't leave until I'm confident Frances will be safe here."

Gwen's mouth dropped open. "But what about you?"

"I'm not worried about me. Whoever is behind the mayhem is targeting the residents." Ada had no proof the perpetrator would limit his or her targets to the residents, but she had to convince her sister to leave Willowdell. She turned to Frances and spoke firmly. "I want you to stay with Gwen and Janet on Fairfield Lane."

Frances moved to the potted plants with her watering can. "We're in this together. Besides, I don't want to leave Max. He could be in danger too."

"Max?" Gwen and Janet spoke in unison with a glance at each other.

Ada knew her sister and Maxwell Bailey enjoyed each other's company, but she'd had no idea Frances had grown so fond of the former pastor.

As if cued, Maxwell Bailey stepped around the corner of the yellow bungalow, wearing shorts and a print shirt. "There you are." A smile covered his face and sparked his dusky eyes.

"Hi, Max." Frances immediately perked up. She introduced Gwen and Janet. "They are trying to convince me to stay with them at Ada's home nearer the village."

Janet scooted her own chair over and made room for Max. He drew a chair up to the table for himself and sat down beside her.

His face sobered. "It might be best. That fire last night did nothing to reassure me that all is well here."

Frances returned to her chair. "But what about you? You're in danger too." She gave him a napkin and slid the basket of muffins and cookies toward him while Janet poured his lemonade. "It's not just women being targeted."

Maxwell studied the pastries and selected a variety. "They all look so good."

"That's the problem," Ada said. "There seems to be no common thread. The victims differ in sex, age, status." She turned to Gwen. "You found no link at all?"

Gwen shook her head. "Other than being residents here, none."

"What if there is no common link?" Maxwell looked about the group. "Could we then assume the deaths were accidental?"

"Or that the victims were randomly targeted?" Gwen brushed red curls from her face and glanced at Janet fanning next to her.

"Then anyone could be a target." Janet closed her fan, apologizing to Gwen.

Frances's voice trembled, "If there is no rhyme or reason—"

"There's a reason." Ada's brow crinkled. "We just have to find it."

Sheriff Meriday leaned over a narrow table along the wall of his office, going over the reports on the Willowdell deaths with Bidwell. They could find no commonality among the three victims.

He straightened and exhaled. "I wonder if we haven't been going about this all wrong."

Bidwell looked at him. "Sir?"

"Maybe there isn't a connection." Meriday moved to the coffeepot. "Say the Beavers woman really did trip on a tree root, topple into the lake, and hit her head on the rocks." He filled his mug. "Simple. Case closed."

"And the old man wandered out on his own in search of the owl."

"Right. Just bad luck." Meriday sipped his coffee then dropped in his chair. "The Kane woman—there's no evidence her death was anything but twisted circumstances."

"If Dorothy Kane's death was an accident—of sorts—wouldn't someone come forward and explain how it happened?" Bidwell sat on the edge of Meriday's desk.

The sheriff sent him a look, and he leaped off.

"Not if they didn't realize their role in the matter," Meriday answered.

"Do you want Sloan and me to search the dumpster again?"

"What I want is thirty-two search warrants." Meriday smacked down his mug and splattered coffee over the blotter.

A knock sounded.

"Yeah," he yelled at the door.

Neil Tibbs appeared. "Got a minute, Leo?"

"Have a seat." He waved him in and dismissed Bidwell. Meriday interlocked his fingers over his stomach. "What's on your mind?"

"The fire last night at Willowdell."

"I'm waiting for the fire marshal's official report. Initially, it looks like the judge left a soldering iron plugged in. Must have been using it at his workbench before he retired for the night. It took a few hours to burn a path to the rags he'd used with some sort of solvent."

Tibbs shook his head. "The judge is meticulous. Leaving rags around, not putting the iron back in its place, that doesn't sound like him."

Meriday knew Judge Fausset well and knew Tibbs to be his protégé. He wondered if Tibbs simply couldn't accept the fact the judge was aging and likely becoming forgetful.

"Someone could have broken into the garage," Tibbs said, "and set the stage for that very thing to play out after they were far from the scene."

"Is that what you want to believe?"

Tibbs leaned forward. "Consider everything that's been happening there."

Meriday placed his elbows on the desk, "Look, I'm going to level with you. There is something going on at Willowdell. I'm not saying the fire was arson or wasn't arson, but I will say it wouldn't hurt to keep an eye on your friend."

"The judge will be staying at Greenbrier Inn for the time being. He should be okay there. One other thing. Have you any idea who is handling the estates of the deceased?"

That had been a question looming in his own mind. One that would require a search warrant to answer—a search warrant that had so far been denied. "What got you wondering along that line?"

"Gwen Dunbar. She asked me to look into it for Ada Whittaker."

"I should have known that Whittaker woman would have her nose in this somewhere."

"I'm sure she's just concerned for her sister." Neil rose and moved toward the door.

"Frances Ferrell. Yeah," Meriday followed him, "I'm concerned for her too. If she's telling people she saw someone push the Beavers woman into the lake like she tried to tell me, someone might actually believe her."

Tibbs turned. "What are you saying?"

"I'm saying you'd better convince that nosey parker to get her sister away from Willowdell—today."

16

Three days later, Ada placed her purple straw hat on her head. She expected Maxwell Bailey to arrive at any moment.

She had finally convinced Frances, with Maxwell's help and Neil's persistent urging, to temporarily move in with Gwen and Janet. With five people working her over, Frances finally acquiesced when Ada and Maxwell promised they would keep watch over each other.

Today, they had plans to play golf. Of course, Maxwell would have to understand that Ada knew nothing of the sport, and he'd be spending his morning teaching her how to hold and swing a club.

The doorbell rang. Ada grabbed her tote bag holding her water bottle and cell phone and swung open the door.

"Good morning, Miss Whittaker." Miriam Kroft stood on the porch welcome mat, a pack of Simon Hilton brochures in her hands. Her fingernails had been painted a bold red. "Ten more days until you can cast your vote." Her red lips parted in a grin. "New York deserves a man like Simon Hilton in the state senate."

Ada looked up at the whine of an approaching golf cart. "I'm aware of the primary. Now, if you will excuse me, my ride is here."

Miriam Kroft hustled toward Maxwell Bailey. "Oh, Mr. Bailey. I hope you will make your vote count for Simon Hilton. New York State deserves a man of his ... well, his stamina."

Maxwell frowned as the woman held a brochure out to him. "I've seen the political ads on TV, Mrs. Kroft, and it doesn't sound like Simon Hilton would be good for any state, much less New York. Besides, the only ones who need stamina in New York State are the taxpayers. Have a good day."

Minutes later, Maxwell hovered over a golf ball, about to tee off, when a golf cart screamed over the knoll and whizzed past them. The driver squealed and laughed and raced away.

"Mercy." Ada put a hand over her heart. "It's that Luty Mae Mears again."

Maxwell glared at the woman's retreating cart. "Something should be done about her."

Luty Mae sat on the sofa in the dark, unable to sleep. Restlessness had plagued her since that last stroke. She grew stir-crazy with her mind trapped in a body that struggled to respond to her commands. Even now, she ached to drive her golf cart over the course and enjoy the thrill of freedom.

But she did not like the night.

Luty Mae's hands trembled while she clicked on the lamp beside her and poured wine into the juice glass on the coffee table. Disregarding the splatter, she focused on the pill bottle in front of her and wondered if she had taken her meds.

Just to be sure, she took another pill.

After two glasses of wine and feeling drowsy, Luty Mae turned off the light and nestled down into a throw blanket. She drifted to sleep, trying to remember if she had again forgotten to eat supper.

Luty Mae stirred, confused, not knowing how long she had been asleep. Did she dream the noise, the creaking of the screen door? She struggled to open her eyes, to sit up.

A sliver of moonlight streamed into the living room.

"I saw your light on earlier, Luty Mae. Not able to sleep?"

She squinted into the shadows.

"I was concerned that perhaps you forgot to take your medicine. Did you?"

Luty Mae recognized the voice and remembered she had eaten supper. Had she taken her pill? She allowed the hands to help her sit up and took the pill offered with a drink from the glass held out to her.

"It's a beautiful night. I thought you would enjoy a ride around the golf course in the moonlight. Doesn't that sound fun?"

"Will you go with me? I don't like the night."

"Of course. Let me help you."

Arms lifted her and placed her in the front seat of her golf cart.

The cart whirred, and the fresh air revived her spirit. The cage opened.

She recognized the golfing green, and adventure bubbled up from her belly.

The cart stopped. Suddenly it jerked and shot across the grass, weaving and spinning, out of control. A cold wind scraped her bare arms.

She tried to scream, but the gusts off the lake robbed her of breath. Gasping, her small chest heaved. Her heartbeat thrashed in her ears. She grasped at the night.

Pain seared through her body.

Darkness fell.

Just before dawn, when the first shade of blush swept the purple sky, Ada dressed and went to the kitchen to make herself a cup of tea. She stood over the sink and began to fill the teakettle from the tap.

Sirens stabbed the air and nearly stopped her heart.

She set the kettle down with a clang, grabbed a sweater and a hat, and hurried out the door to number ten.

Maxwell stood on his porch while police cars entered the retirement center and turned down the lane that led to the golf course.

"What happened?" Dread welled up in Ada's chest.

"I don't know. Let me take care of Stanley, then we'll go see." Maxwell opened the door to his bungalow and called Stanley while he reached for a leash.

Minutes later, Ada walked beside Maxwell in silence toward the pulsing blue lights. A small crowd shuffled about the knoll that overlooked a sand trap while two deputies unrolled yellow tape that read, POLICE LINE DO NOT CROSS.

Her heart pounded in her ears.

An ambulance arrived, eerily unannounced.

Ada and Maxwell exchanged glances.

Death had again come to Willowdell.

17

Sheriff Meriday swallowed back the angst invading his gut. Fred Albright stood beside him waiting to examine the crumpled body pinned beneath the golf cart in the sand trap. Someone was acting like a death collector at Willowdell, and Meriday needed to stop them.

The sputter of a Farmall tractor filled the early morning air when two Willowdell maintenance men arrived. A few men could lift the machine off the victim, but Meriday had no intention of letting the crime scene be trampled more than necessary. One man alone would secure a chain to the tipped cart.

Minutes later, the tractor pulled the cart to an upright position and off the body bystanders identified as that of Luty Mae Mears.

She lay on her side, dressed in a sleeveless gingham nightgown, her head twisted at an awkward angle, her short hair—like her face—a muted gray. She couldn't have weighed more than a hundred and ten pounds.

While the sun struggled to reach through the mist over the lake, the coroner examined the corpse, and the photographer took pictures. The sheriff's deputies searched the area, careful not to disturb any possible evidence that might shed light on the tragedy.

Meriday gave an investigative scan of the ground surrounding the sand trap. He walked the area in search of footprints in the dew leading away from the pit. The sound of snapping latex turned him around. He waited for Fred to reach him.

"Neck is broken." The coroner pushed his dark-rimmed glasses up the bridge of his nose. "Been four, five hours at the most."

Meriday shook his head. "She drove out here in the middle of the night, dressed like that."

Fred motioned for the EMTs to take the body, then turned back to him. "This is getting to be a habit, Leo. A bad one. Any idea what's going on here?"

"When do too many incidents stop being accidents?"

"Maybe we both need to take a closer look. I'll run some tests." The coroner picked up his case and moved with slightly slumped shoulders toward his vehicle.

Samantha Milsap emerged from a small crowd at the top of the knoll and stood behind the yellow ribbon.

When Meriday reached her, he drew her aside.

"I knew this would happen." Samantha ran her chubby hands down the front of her long skirt while she watched the paramedics load the body of Luty Mae Mears into the back of the ambulance. "We've had several complaints about Luty Mae driving on the green like a crazy person. Nearly running over people. Laughing."

Simon Hilton blustered from the crowd, his face red with a

sheen of sweat on his cheeks and forehead. He gripped Saman-tha's shoulders from behind and moved her aside. "Sheriff, you've got to keep this out of the papers. The election is days away. I can't have any more negative publicity. You've got to see to it."

Meriday glared at the owner of Willowdell. "Any idea, Mr. Hilton, why Mrs. Mears would be driving a golf cart around the green in the middle of the night?"

"The woman's wires shorted out. What else can be said?"

"It could be said that you don't take very good care of your residents."

Hilton threw his hands in the air. "I can't be responsible for these people. They're stubborn. They're set in their ways. You can't tell them anything. So don't blame me for any of this. Just keep it out of the papers."

Ignoring Samantha Milsap's appeal for a ride back to the office and her attempts to catch up, Hilton dropped into his metallic blue golf cart and drove away.

"Chief." Bidwell called to him from the sand trap, waving for him to come down. When the sheriff arrived, the deputy pointed to an end post from a croquet set lying in the sand. "There are marks on the base of the golf cart's seat, and the pedal has some odd markings. The stick could have been used to hold down the accelerator."

A punch landed full force in Meriday's gut. Someone inten-tionally sent the woman on the ride to her death.

Sloan approached him. "This was under her body."

He recognized the gold foil of a Hegler chocolate. "Bag everything. Let's try to get some prints." He left his team to finish up at the site and started up the knoll.

Ada Whittaker held down her hat and crouched under the police tape.

His blood pressure shot up. "There's a reason we string yellow ribbon, Miss Whittaker. And it's not to keep my deputies in."

"I understand, but I felt it important for you to know Mrs. Mears had suffered a stroke some months back, leaving her left side weak. When the cart started to tip, she likely would have fallen out, unable to catch herself, depending on how fast she traveled. And Luty Mae liked to drive fast."

He narrowed his eyes. "Your sister been on the golf course recently?"

"A few days ago, but not recently." She studied him with intelligent blue eyes. "What did you find?"

"A candy wrapper. Hegler."

"Oh, my. Yes, I can see why you would ask. Frances received a new shipment, but it went missing. You see, she thought she had left the box on the hall table and I'm sure she had, but she couldn't find it anywhere. Then I found a report that we assumed Samantha had placed on the desk. Of course, we both leaped to the conclusion the girl had taken the box of chocolates from the bungalow at that time."

He scowled. Ada Whittaker was the only person he knew who could say so much and yet so little.

"My point is," she continued, "someone took advantage of Luty Mae's vulnerability. They chose her because of her physical and mental weakness. Whoever set this drama in motion believed—based on Luty's previous behavior with her golf cart —the tragedy would be deemed accidental."

"Chose her?" He cocked his head.

"It's a possibility, I'm afraid." She looked sadly at the spot where Mrs. Mears had spent the last few hours.

Meriday crossed his arms. "Now, why would someone *choose* her to die?"

"That is the question, isn't it?"

He rubbed his chin, the bristles reminding him he hadn't yet shaved, the call waking him before dawn. "And you think Samantha Milsap took your sister's chocolates?"

"I dare say. However, that does not mean she alone ate them. Anyone could have taken a piece from the box."

18

Early the next evening, Gwen sat with Frances and Janet at the Primrose Restaurant. Crystal chandeliers hung low from the high ceiling, casting a warm light over the red marbled carpet. Elegant white cloths covered the tables laid with crystalware and linen napkins and centered with short-stemmed white roses.

Gwen and Janet had sensed Frances growing impatient in her exile and believed the cause to be worry over Miss Ada and Maxwell Bailey. Whatever the reason, they agreed an evening out might help.

Well into the meal, Frances said through pursed lips, "Why do they always have televisions on in restaurants now? It's so loud I can barely hear our own conversation. And those annoying campaign commercials are getting on my nerves."

Gwen glanced at Janet. The televisions were positioned in the bar section, a good distance from the dining room, and the volume had been set for those near the TVs. The two sections were divided by a plethora of plants and greenery that muted the sound considerably.

"They'll be over soon." Gwen said.

"One week until the primary." Janet squeezed lemon into her sweet tea. "Simon Hilton can promise anything he wants, but I have no intention of voting for him. He's failed to protect the residents at Willowdell. Why would anyone believe he would do any better for the residents of the state?"

"I agree." Gwen brushed a hand through her runaway curls. "Willowdell is supposed to be a continuing care community. But the fact that Wendall Compton could get lost in the woods at night, and Luty Mae Mears could drive her golf cart without restrictions, proves it lacks the appropriate safeguards for their residents."

"Exactly," Janet said.

Frances set down her fork and fingered the beads of her necklace. "It doesn't seem like Sheriff Meriday has made any progress in finding out the truth. Were they all tragic events of happenstance, or is there a murderer on the loose? Does he even know?"

"He could just be holding his clues close to his badge," Janet said.

"What clues?" Gwen asked. "Are there any clues?"

Frances pushed aside her plate, still half laden with linguini. "Well, there is the dog whistle."

"Dog whistle?" Janet's full face crinkled.

"I found it in the hedgerow, not far from where Nita fell in the lake."

"I don't get it." Gwen set down her water glass. "How can a dog whistle be a clue?"

"Ada and I think it's possible someone used it to lure Stanley to the lake, knowing Nita would follow. Then they pushed her in."

Gwen would have found that scenario hard to believe if not

for the subsequent deaths. She no longer arbitrarily dismissed anyone else's theory.

Janet drew a miniature muffin out of the basket. "There's the gold necklace you found on Wendall's property. I doubt it belonged to Wendall."

"Selma Potter told Max she lost it when visiting her mother."

"The village gossip isn't the most reliable source for truth," Gwen said.

"Maybe Selma Potter is telling the truth. What if Gladys found it and wore it to Wendall's?" Janet popped the last bit of the muffin into her mouth.

Frances shook her head. "Gladys has been holed up in her bungalow. Unless she sneaks out at night."

"If that's all the sheriff has, I can't blame him for not having solved the puzzle." Janet browsed the dessert menu.

"Well, we never told him about the necklace."

Gwen waved for the server. "Too bad there isn't a way for you and Miss Ada and Sheriff Meriday to compare notes."

"Personally, I don't think the man cares too much for anything Ada or I could contribute. But we probably should let him know about the necklace."

"That could add to the suspicion already swirling about Mrs. Blumm." Janet spoke with a raised eyebrow.

"Yes, I'm worried about that too." Frances placed her oversized bag on her lap. "It's hard to know what to do."

Janet set aside the dessert menu. "What do you say to a movie?"

"Yes, let's." Gwen took the check from the server.

Frances grabbed it, saying, "Okay, but no murder mystery."

The sun sat low in the western sky, and Max had just finished watering the potted plants on Gladys's porch. He poked his head inside the front door of her bungalow. "Gladys?"

Silence.

He had called out to her every day since Selma met him in the kitchen and took the brownies off his hands. He had yet to determine if Gladys still lived there—or if she lived anywhere.

He stepped inside. A cat swirled about his flip flops. He nudged it aside with his foot. "It's me, Max."

At first, he'd cringed at his neighbor calling him *Max*, but when Frances Ferrell began to call him Max, he started to like it. He found it comforting, somehow. Like he had a friend.

"Go away." He turned toward the distant voice of Gladys Blumm.

"We're all worried about you." He moved past the sofa cluttered with newspapers and unfolded laundry and crept down the hall.

"Not everybody. Not those peddlers of lies that say all manner of evil against me."

He paused outside the closed door. "I'm worried about you."

"Huh! You're the one that sicced that sheriff on me. Telling him I gave brownies to Dorothy."

"Are you decent?" He hoped so. "I'm coming in."

"Stay out."

"Here I come, ready or not." He slowly turned the doorknob and peeked inside. Gladys sat upright in a recliner, wearing a nightgown. An afghan covered her legs. "I want to talk to you."

Her hair laid about her shoulders, and a word-find puzzle book rested on her lap. Her glasses hung on her chest from a string around her neck. She did not invite him to sit down, but neither did she kick him out.

She stared straight ahead, apparently with a mind to ignore him.

With a silent prayer for wisdom, he pulled up a rocking chair and sat. He wanted to help this woman get back to the business of living her life.

"How were the brownies I brought to you last week?" he said.

"Don't talk to me about brownies. I never want to see one again."

"I'm sorry."

She turned and glared at him. "Why did you tell the sheriff I made brownies for Dorothy? I borrowed the mix from you then changed my mind and never made them. Check my pantry, you'll see. In fact, take the box back with you. I don't even want the mix in my house."

"Okay. Is there anything I can do for you?"

"Yes, you can find out what happened to Dorothy." Tears coated her dusty brown eyes.

"I don't know what did happen to Dorothy, but I know you had nothing to do with her death."

"That said, you can leave." Gladys sniffed and picked up the puzzle book.

Hunger pinged his stomach. He stood and slid the rocker back into place. "I'm deep-frying chicken wings tonight. I'll bring some over."

He moved down the hallway toward the kitchen.

Gladys yelled, "None of that hot sauce. Sets my innards on fire."

Maxwell smiled. He opened the pantry door to remove the despised brownie mix. He shuffled cake mixes, crackers, soups, sauces. Yet, the mix eluded him.

He squatted and reached to the back corner of the bottom shelf. His fingers froze.

Behind the apple cider vinegar and ranch dressing stood a bottle of peanut oil.

19

Neil spent the next morning meeting with clients and compiling briefs. After lunch, he turned his attention to the one matter that had been weighing on him. He opened a desk drawer and pulled out a legal pad. On it were the names of the residents who had recently met with tragedy at Willowdell. He hoped to make a connection that would indicate cause.

In his practice, greed came through his queue more than any other motive. Defending clients from nuisance lawsuits, defending victims of white-collar crimes, even defending small businesses from IRS harassment. Greed lay at the root of them all, the love of money and the quest for power.

With this in mind, he reviewed what he knew of each victim, whether of accident or foul play, but soon stalled. Other than the public information he gleaned online, which is not always accurate, he obtained little usable material on the deceased residents.

"What I need is the names of their executors."

The phone rang and his secretary informed him Ada Whittaker and Maxwell Bailey stood in the outer office. Did he have a moment to see them?

Neil opened his office door and greeted them.

Maxwell Bailey wore a white dress shirt and dress slacks. They shook hands and Neil motioned toward the leather chairs positioned in front of his desk. "Please, take a seat." He waited until they settled, then returned to his desk.

"Thank you for seeing us." Ada removed her hat. "I know you must be terribly busy."

Neil remembered seeing Mr. Bailey at the fire, standing with Ada and Frances Ferrell. He didn't think much of it at the time. Several of the Willowdell residents had gathered. He wondered why the man had accompanied Ada to his office.

"We have information that may be relevant to the investigation," Bailey said, "but we're hesitant to give it to the sheriff. We need to know if we are required to do so by law." He glanced at Ada.

"Yes," she said, "because what we have could cast suspicion on an innocent person."

"What information do you have?"

Bailey reached into his shirt pocket then placed a gold necklace on Neil's desk. "The necklace belongs to Selma Potter."

"My sister, Frances, found it on Wendall Compton's patio."

"Are you suggesting it's evidence, that Selma Potter could have been involved in some way with what happened to Wendall Compton?" Selma sat on the governing board of the resort, and Neil was familiar with her somewhat manipulative ways, but he could not imagine the wife of the newspaper editor being involved in anything nefarious.

"We are suggesting nothing," Ada said. "We simply need guidance. Should we tell the sheriff?"

Neil tilted his head. "When and how did your sister find this necklace?"

Bailey's eyes darted to Ada.

She blushed. "I went through Wendall's bungalow while Frances stayed outside on his patio. That's when she happened upon it."

"Ahead of the sheriff?"

Ada glanced at Bailey.

Neil leaned forward and intertwined his hands on the desk. "You clearly went into Wendall Compton's house after you learned he was missing, before the sheriff got there."

"I wanted a quick peek, that's all. Don't worry, Neil. I didn't touch anything, and the back door was wide open."

Neil closed his eyes a moment and slowed his words. "You entered a home where a crime may have been committed. Ahead of the police."

"No crime had taken place in Wendall's home."

"But you didn't know that at the time of entry." Neil lifted a hand. "Okay. Let's stop there. If there is the remotest possibility the necklace is important to the sheriff's investigation, you have a responsibility to turn it over to him."

He glanced at the clock, placed his hands on his armrests, and consciously stopped himself from tapping his fingers.

His visitors rose, and Ada picked up the necklace. She said, "Have you found anything on the executors of the estates?"

Neil walked with them toward the door. "I'm at a loss there. I could contact some of my peers, but they are under no obligation to share any information. The reality is, an executor can be anyone, anywhere."

Mr. Bailey spoke to Ada. "When we go to the sheriff, let's ask if he can get a search warrant to view the decedents' records and find out who gets their money."

Ada looked up at Neil. "Is that something you can do?"

"No, I'm not officially involved in the investigation. And I'll remind you both, neither are you."

———

Ada waited with her cell phone to her ear for Janet to answer her call, while Maxwell drove toward the sheriff's office.

Janet answered with her usual chirpy voice.

"Janet, I need your help. I want you to come to Frances's house for a couple hours, but you must come alone, and you must not tell Frances or Gwen where you are going."

Janet gasped, then spoke with a muffled voice, "When?"

"This evening."

"Okay, I'll send them to a store in Watertown right after supper. When they're gone, I'll be over."

"I'll text a list of items you *must* bring with you."

20

S heriff Meriday waited for the judge's secretary to hang up, then slammed the phone down. His petition to search the records at Willowdell had been denied. He flashed to his feet and stormed about the office, rubbing the nape of his neck. "Politics."

Bidwell stood near the door, unmoved by the chief's rant.

"Judge Nelson said it's not a good time. What does he think, there is a good time for murder? That twit running for the senate and his high-up muckety-mucks can't be interfered with right now."

"The owner of Willowdell?"

"Yeah, Sir Simon Hilton. Nelson said Hilton's old man is some bigwig in DC. Something to do with the State Department." Meriday crashed back into his chair. "Says there's not enough evidence of foul play."

"What about the croquet post? The inspection of the golf cart proved it had been used to lock down the accelerator. Any fingerprints?"

"Lots, all smudged."

"What about the toxicology report? The amount of mir —something."

"Mirtazapine."

"Mixed with alcohol." Bidwell stepped closer to Meriday's desk. "It proves Mrs. Mears would not have been able to get in the cart on her own, doesn't it?"

"According to Fred Albright, it does. Someone had to have helped her onto the cart. Yet that's not enough to move Nelson. Not until after the primary, anyway. He doesn't want to 'unduly influence voters.'"

"So where do we go from here?"

"Back to Willowdell." Meriday leaped up. "We interview everyone. Somebody knows something. It's up to us to get it out of them." He flung open the door.

Ada Whittaker and Maxwell Bailey made a wall in front of him. Bailey's hand hovered in the air, about to knock. Meriday pushed past them.

"We have evidence," Ada said.

He stopped, growled, and marched back into his office and plunked down at his desk. At times like this, he struggled to be a servant of the people.

Deputy Bidwell advised them to take a seat, then closed the door and stood with his legs pronged and his thumbs tucked into his belt.

Meriday looked at the old woman and the frog man. "Well, what is it?"

"My sister found this on Wendall Compton's patio." Ada placed a necklace on the desk in front of him.

"Your sister seems to have the nose of a bloodhound."

Ada's chin lifted slightly. "We are fairly certain it belongs to Selma Potter. Selma did say she lost hers, and Mr. Bailey did see her wearing one like it."

"It probably means nothing," Bailey added, "but because it

was found on Wendall's patio, we thought it best to bring it to your attention."

Meriday peered at Ada and leaned back in his chair. "Just when did your sister find it on Wendell Compton's patio?"

"The day Mr. Compton went missing, I believe. I get my days a bit muddled."

Yeah, right. The old woman's mind was as sharp as her ferret nose.

Bailey piped up. "You were asking me about peanut oil. If I had any in my pantry. Did you happen to ask Gladys Blumm that question when you interviewed her?"

No, I'm stupid. He drew a breath and said, "Mrs. Blumm denied having any."

"Then someone is trying to point the finger at her. I found a small bottle in Gladys's pantry, half gone. But the thing is, Gladys leaves her door unlocked. Anyone could have planted the bottle there."

Ada opened her denim tote bag and lifted out a bottle in a Ziploc bag. She held it out to Bidwell. "You'll want to check this for prints."

The deputy looked at the chief, then took the bag at his nod.

Bailey turned to the sheriff. "I handled the bottle carefully, gripping the bottom with a paper towel."

"We believe the necklace, too, was planted. Again, to point the finger at Gladys."

Frogman nodded. "Whoever placed the peanut oil in Gladys's pantry likely found the necklace at that time and then placed it on Wendall Compton's property, hoping you would find it and trace it back to Gladys."

Meriday clasped his hands behind his head. He narrowed his eyes and stared at Ada. "There's one thing you haven't explained. How is it your sister, and not my deputies, found the necklace on Compton's property?"

Bidwell shifted his stance.

"The important thing, Sheriff," Ada said, "is to find out who is trying to frame poor Gladys Blumm."

"Sorry, Miss Whittaker. I'm not ruling out Gladys Blumm. I'm not ruling out anyone. Not Bailey, here. Not you."

She stiffened.

Frogman cleared his throat. "Uh, if you don't mind me asking, will you be requesting a search warrant, or whatever it is you need in order to look over the records at Willowdell? Specifically, to find out who the decedents named as executors?"

"Yes," Ada said, "it so often comes down to money, don't you think?"

Meriday brought his arms down with a smack on his armrests. *No, it comes down to politics.*

That evening, hearing a car and expecting Janet, Ada went to the window.

Janet got out of her red Volkswagen convertible and raised the top. She reached into the back seat and pulled out a small duffel bag.

"Did you bring everything?" Ada asked, when Janet entered the kitchen.

"Yes, just like you said," Janet whispered.

"You don't have to whisper, dear. But you do have to keep this between us for the time being."

Ada led the way to the guest bathroom and sat in the chair she had placed before the large mirror. She took the bobby pins out of her hair and let her ivory locks flow about her shoulders. "Cut it short. A bob, I think they call it."

Janet stood behind her and stared back at her in the mirror, her mouth open and the whites of her eyes wide within the setting of midnight shadow and black mascara. "No, ma'am. No, ma'am. If you are saying what I think you're saying, uh-uh. No way."

"You must listen to me. I'm counting on you." Ada had feared this. But Janet had to help her. She spoke sternly to the mirror, "Cut my hair and cut it short. Did you bring the dye?"

"I didn't know you wanted this for yourself. I thought you wanted them for ... well, I didn't know why you wanted them. But not this. This never entered my mind, and you got to put it out of yours."

"I intend to find out why people are dropping dead at Willowdell." Ada worked to control her rising voice. "My sister could be in danger."

"But how is this"—Janet waved her hands behind Ada's head—"going to help you do that?"

"I can't tell you anything more. I don't want you to be an accomplice."

Janet gasped. "Are you going to commit a crime?"

Ada turned in the chair. "Take those scissors and start cutting. You have to hurry, before Gwen and Frances get back and find you gone and start asking questions."

Janet fumbled with the towel and dropped the clip while trying to secure a make-shift drape around Ada's shoulders. She retrieved it and fixed the towel in place then picked up the shears. Repeatedly blinking, she alternated between pursing her lips and chewing them until wisps of ivory littered the bathroom floor.

Ada closed her eyes and swallowed hard. She had never

worn her hair short and cringed at the final image in the mirror. But she had no choice.

"Now mix the dye."

"Oh, Miss Ada. I can't. The dye is dark. Real dark. You don't want your hair dark. I cut your hair like you said, but don't make me color it dark."

Ada drew in a deep breath, resolved. "Don't miss a strand." She had never used color on her hair. God gave her the color he wanted her to have, and who was she to think she could improve on his handiwork? But considering the circumstances, she believed God understood completely.

21

Night had descended on the Willowdell retirement village. Ada, dressed once again in Frances's black sweatpants and long-sleeved black shirt, spied out the land from among the weeping tendrils of a willow near the square.

Just after eleven, Samantha Milsap left the administration building and shuffled along the walkway toward her bungalow. She disappeared beyond the recreation center.

Ada dashed toward the lobby door and slipped inside.

Although dimly lit, the lobby remained light enough for a late-night rambler to catch sight of her. If anyone *should* happen to spot a woman moving surreptitiously about the lobby, it would take some doing to convince the sheriff they had seen Ada Whittaker in short black hair and dark clothing.

Crouched, she crept to the door of Simon Hilton's office and gripped the handle with a latex-gloved hand. Relieved to find the door unlocked, she entered and quietly clicked it shut.

Using the flashlight on her cell phone, Ada scanned the office.

Desk in the middle of the room. A bookshelf. A family snapshot. File cabinets along the back wall. She moved to them and shined the light on the labeled drawers.

Nita Beavers's name on a manilla folder had been highlighted and was easily located. Ada quickly shuffled through it and could find no listing of a power of attorney or even an emergency contact. She did see, however, that Nita had paid an entry fee of ninety-six thousand dollars, refundable pro-rated up until five years of residency.

A highlighted tab identified Dorothy Kane's file. No relatives listed. No attorney or executor listed. Dorothy's agreement had been signed nearly six years earlier. She paid an entry fee of eighty-nine thousand for the smaller bungalow.

Ada studied the paragraph near a checked box. Dorothy gave her consent for her legal matters to be handled, at no cost, by the attorneys for Willowdell. Ada replaced Dorothy's file then rechecked Nita's contract. Maybe she missed that section. There, too, was the checkmark authorizing Willowdell's attorneys to manage Nita's legal affairs.

Voices sounded in the lobby.

Her stomach lurched. She shut off the light.

"I want to check the answering machine." Ada recognized the pert voice of Alison Vaughn.

She ducked under the desk and held her breath while her mind slipped to worst case scenarios should she be caught. If Simon Hilton was orchestrating the residents' deaths, he could easily arrange hers. Without her signature hairstyle, could her body be identified?

"Never mind that now. Simon wanted these flyers up today." *Miriam Kroft?* "If I didn't have to spend all day in Watertown—"

"Why did you go to Watertown?"

"I had to fix your uncle's mess-up. Again. He seems completely incompetent when it comes to anything online. He either sends the right shipment to the wrong address or the wrong shipment to the right address. Grab the Scotch tape, and let's get these announcements up. I'm exhausted and want to get to bed."

"But everyone knows about the shuttle bus," Alison said. "You've been to every home, how many times?"

"It's what Simon wants."

"Mother, why do you kowtow to that man? Daddy ought to put his foot down."

Mother? Strange no one had ever mentioned Alison as the daughter of Miriam and Duncan Kroft. Ada thought about it. How else could an activities director afford a bungalow at Willowdell?

"Your father has never had the backbone to put his foot down."

Alison chuckled. "Lucky for you."

"Enough out of you."

The voices faded and left Ada with the sound of her own heart pounding in her head. She crawled to her feet, tiptoed to the door, and placed an ear against it. They had gone. She had to get out. Alison could return to check Hilton's messages.

Through a crack in the door, she scanned the area. Believing herself to be alone, she stole to the lobby door and sprinted down the sidewalk to number eight.

Ada sat in the living room and watched the clock, hoping to give Miriam and Alison time to post the notices throughout the facilities. She wanted nothing more than to collapse in her bed, except for one thing—to make sure Simon Hilton found nothing amiss in his office. For that, she had to return Nita's file to the file drawer.

The investigation could be ruined if Hilton was to find the files of the deceased had been searched. If he held any responsibility for the tragedies at Willowdell, he would be much more vigilant about his activities and more protective of his records.

———————

Maxwell woke when Stanley's legs landed on his back. He turned over and clicked on the bedstand lamp. "Do you know what time it is?"

The cocker spaniel's black eyes begged for action.

"Okay, okay." Maxwell swung his feet out of bed and slid them into his shower sandals. "I don't understand why your timing has to be off like this."

Stanley whined near the front door.

Maxwell grabbed the leash, without turning on any lights, and walked Stanley to the dog park. Moonlight streamed through the woodlot silhouetted against the night sky. While the dog sniffed every inch of the area, Maxwell scanned the square, the lake, the woods, the stars, and the square again.

He caught movement.

A person dressed in black sneaked along the front porch of the main building. When the door to the lobby opened, he caught the outline of a woman with short dark hair entering.

"That's strange," he mumbled.

Walking Stanley back home, his thoughts of the woman persisted. Was she a resident? He'd never seen her. Maybe she was wearing a disguise. What if she was orchestrating the deaths?

His chest tightened. The thought of Frances becoming a victim compelled him. He couldn't let it go. He had to check it out.

With Stanley settled back into his dog bed, Maxwell clipped across the square and entered the administration building's eerily quiet lobby with the dexterity of a cat burglar. His eyes darted about in search of the black-haired stranger.

Where could she be?

He remembered the pool and the body of Dorothy Kane. Adrenaline pushed him forward while he paddled over the carpeted lobby. Outside the glass door reading POOL, Maxwell cupped his hands around his eyes and peered into the dimness. Night lights glistened over the blue water of the indoor pool. He detected no other movement.

The slight sweep of a door opening drew his attention. He scurried toward the lobby, arriving in time to see the dark figure slink out the door.

Maxwell raced outside. The woman trotted down the sidewalk and leaped onto the porch at number eight. He gasped. Ada could be in danger.

Adrenaline kicked in. He charged down the sidewalk with a sense of moving in slow motion. Images of what might be happening sent fear like a dagger through his chest and cut off his air. What would he do when he got there?

He needed a plan.

He'd wrestle the woman to the ground. But could he? He'd put on so much weight over the past several weeks trying to fill the void left by—

Focus.

Ada alone mattered now. He had to save her.

Sweat formed on his forehead and upper lip. Something moved in his peripheral vision, but he dared not pause.

Lord, help her. Help me.

Maxwell's legs felt weighted when he stepped onto the front porch of Frances's bungalow. He put his nose to the window.

The woman in black leaned over the kitchen sink.

What had she done to Ada?

Max grabbed his cell phone and called 911.

———

Duncan Kroft stood with the refrigerator door open, searching for a late-night snack. He grabbed a carton of strawberry yogurt, despite Miriam's claim it contained too much sugar, and a spoon, then stepped out onto his porch. Crickets chirped beneath a sparkling black sky while a subtle current touched Miriam's irises and sent their fragrance swirling in the air.

He ducked with a sigh into the chair tucked in the corner and relished the seclusion and undisturbed respite. Here he had a few moments to himself without having to listen to Miriam's yapping. What'd Solomon say? *A nagging woman is like a continual dripping in a bucket.* That was Miriam. Drip. Drip. Drip.

Duncan had never wanted to move to Willowdell. He was a country man. A simple man. He cared little for the upper-crust snootery his wife craved. Miriam reveled in associating with elitist snobs like that ladder climber, Simon Hilton.

Oh, there were a few people he liked here. Take Wendall. He wasn't a bad egg. Sure, the old guy was picking up speed on a downward spiral and probably should have had his independence brought down a notch. But hey, you got to go sometime. Better you go free.

Duncan lifted the empty yogurt carton to the night sky. "Here's to you, ole buddy. And to freedom. Rest in peace, my friend."

Just then, he caught sight of a figure—a woman dressed in black, scampering down the sidewalk. She entered Frances Ferrell's bungalow. Moments later, a man rushed from the office's lobby and plodded down the sidewalk in flip-flops.

Duncan stood. He snickered into his mustache when the man leaped onto the same porch. "Bailey, you old fox."

Ada arrived back at her sister's bungalow too upset to sleep. She had returned to Simon Hilton's office and discovered Nita's file was no longer on the desk. She checked the file cabinet and found the folder missing. Someone had removed it.

She wondered if Alison Vaughn had returned to Simon's office to check for messages. But surely if Alison had seen the folder on the desk, she would have returned it to its proper place in the drawer.

Perhaps Alison believed Samantha left it out and was holding it for the sole purpose of bringing the infraction to Simon Hilton's attention. Ada winced. She hoped Samantha would not be chastened.

She stood at the sink and filled the kettle for tea.

Footsteps sounded on the porch.

She jolted and turned, her heart pounding in her chest. Maxwell pressed his face grotesquely against the window. She gasped with a hand over her mouth. *What could be the matter?*

She opened the door. "Mercy. You startled me half to death."

He stood speechless, staring at her.

Ada remembered her appearance. Her ears burned.

"Why are you—" The horns of Sherwood Forest blared from his cell phone. A sheepish look swept over his face when he answered. "Uh, no, ma'am. No emergency. But thank you for checking."

She sighed at the ripple effect of her actions.

Over steaming cups of tea, Ada explained the reason for her

change in appearance and her search of Hilton's office. "I have to protect Frances."

"*We* have to protect Frances."

"I worried about her living alone and finally convinced her to move to Sackets Harbor," Ada said. "Now look. I've put her in danger."

"You can't blame yourself for Frances being at risk. But I agree, we need to do whatever it takes."

Ada furrowed her brow. "We have to follow the money. I'm convinced of it. Both Nita and Dorothy had checked the option on their lease agreements for free legal services through Willowdell attorneys."

"I remember the option on my lease." Maxwell stirred sugar into his tea. "I declined. I'm too cynical to trust attorneys I haven't personally vetted."

"No doubt some residents would think it a wonderful benefit, provided the firm operates by ethical standards."

"What if the lawyers for Willowdell don't operate by ethical standards?"

Ada straightened her shoulders. "That's where we come in."

22

A light rain tapped on Ada's umbrella while she power-walked along the trail leading into the woods and away from the senior village. The belt around her waist held a bottle of water and her cell phone. Her dark hair was tucked under a turban and topped with a purple straw hat.

She had slept fitfully after her adventure in the early morning hours and arose sluggish when she awoke at 8:00 a.m. A stimulating walk would be just the thing to pass the time before Janet could get away from Frances and Gwen with a bottle of ivory hair dye.

Humidity weighted the air, and the odor of mold and mildew rose from the rotting leaves that blanketed the forest floor. Along the trail she moved, praying and meditating on things above and on things of the earth.

She prayed for Frances. Until Sheriff Meriday could determine if there was a murderer at Willowdell, and arrest him or her, Frances—and every other resident—could be in danger. She prayed for Leo Meriday and his deputies.

The sprinkling stopped. Ada paused and folded the

umbrella then moved on. She came around a bend and jerked
to a halt.

A voice sprang from deep within the woods.

She listened but could not make out the man's words
above the thumping of her heart. Droplets from the leaves
overhead plunked on her hat while she stared in the direction
of the irate voice. Who could be out here in the middle of the
forest?

Two people who did not want to be seen or heard?

Should she investigate?

A quarter mile from the bungalows, and likely no one had
seen her take this trail. If something unfortunate should
happen ...

The confrontation could be important to the case.

Ada stepped off the trail and skulked toward the voice then
tucked into the wet branches of a blue spruce.

The voice rose. "How many times have I told you? ... Ship
it!" The voice faded, along with the crunching of footsteps on
twigs and leaves.

Ada attempted to follow unheard. Quietly stepping around
bramble bushes and over fallen logs, she came to the northern
edge of the woods. The lake, a few hundred yards ahead,
rippled in the emerging sunlight.

At the whirr of a golf cart, she ducked behind a large oak
tree then peeked around it to catch a glimpse of the driver.

A twig snapped behind her.

Unable to obtain a search warrant to access Willowdell's
records, Leo Meriday focused on the death of Dorothy Kane. He
stood outside the door of the gray bungalow and waited for

Gladys Blumm to respond to his knock. A light breeze sent the windchimes into a dither of clinks and twangs.

He knocked louder then shifted his stance and caught sight of the frog man coming out of his bungalow with the dog on a leash.

Bailey paused on the sidewalk. "She won't answer."

"Why is that?" Meriday said.

"Gladys doesn't want to see anyone. Not since Dorothy's death. People were spreading rumors, saying Gladys gave Dorothy the toxic brownies intentionally." Bailey shrugged. "Guess Gladys couldn't face them anymore. Not when they're thinking she might be a murderer."

"Maybe she is and maybe she isn't. My job is to find out. I need to talk to her."

Bailey stepped up on the porch and secured the dog. "The door isn't locked, but I'd better go in and let her know you're here."

Meriday expanded his chest, then stepped aside.

The retired minister opened the door and stuck his head in. "Gladys? It's me, Max. Are you decent?"

Meriday rolled his eyes, then followed Bailey inside.

The place smelled stale. The rooms were dark, except for the bit of light filtering through the kitchen curtains. A cat lay curled in a cushioned rocker in the living room.

They moved down a hallway until Bailey stopped outside a closed door.

"Gladys? The sheriff is here."

"What does he want?"

"We're coming in." Bailey opened the door, and Meriday could see the elderly woman sitting upright in an easy chair, wearing a bathrobe over her nightclothes. A red plaid blanket was draped over her knees.

Gladys removed her reading glasses that hung from a string around her neck and set aside the newspaper crossword.

Meriday stepped around Bailey. "Ma'am, I have a few more questions for you."

"Did you find Dorothy's killer?" Gladys eyed him accusingly.

"That's why I'm here."

"You won't find no killer here."

Bailey poked his head around him. "The sheriff has some questions about the peanut oil found in your pantry."

Meriday thought the man had left. "I'll take it from here, Mr. Bailey. You can go."

"Max stays. He's my witness to police harassment."

"Ma'am, I'm not—"

"And what's this about peanut oil in my pantry? I never use peanut oil in anything. Dorothy and I spent a lot of time together, and she's had many a meal in my home. I'd never use anything I knew would harm her."

Despite not being invited, Meriday lowered his frame into the nearby chair and relieved his feet of his weight. "From what I understand, you were very angry with Mrs. Kane. Perhaps you didn't intend for her to die, but to make her suffer a little."

"If Max found peanut oil in my pantry, someone put it there." Gladys reached for a glass of water and knocked some pills off the nightstand.

Meriday bent and picked up the bottle labeled sleep aid. "Having trouble sleeping?" He wondered if a guilty conscience kept the woman awake at night.

"They're good for my nerves."

"What's wrong with your nerves?"

Gladys stiffened and jutted her jaw.

When she refused to answer, Meriday pulled a small

plastic bag out of his pocket and held up the gold necklace. "Ever see this?"

Gladys swiped at the hair hanging about her shoulders. "Can't say I have."

"Why can't you?"

She locked her arms over her chest. "I won't say another word until I speak to Jackie Senak."

Meriday took out his notepad. "Is she your attorney?"

"Sheriff," Bailey said, "may I have a piece of paper?"

If it will get rid of you. He tore a sheet out and gave it to him. "May I use your pencil?"

"You may not."

Gladys Blumm handed off her pencil. "Yes, she's with the firm of Bigelow and Senak."

Bailey spoke while he wrote, "The firm provides free legal services for the residents of Willowdell."

"They say it's free," Gladys sniped, "but the residents pay for it in their fees. You'd have to be a dupe to believe the vultures give anything for free."

Meriday pulled on his ear. "About those fees, how is it you can afford to live at Willowdell?"

The kitchen door slapped shut.

A high-pitched voice called out, "Mother? I brought you a tuna sub. I'll scrape a little tuna in kitty's dish. I saw the sheriff's car parked near the square. Probably found another body. I hope the bully doesn't come around here harassing you anymore."

Selma Potter stepped into the room carrying a paper plate holding a sandwich and a dill pickle. He recognized the woman with chin length, light brown hair, pin-curled at the temples. Her face flushed at the sight of him, nearly matching the red of her loose-fitting dress.

"Mrs. Potter." He tipped his head. The wife of the newspaper editor had over the years successfully maneuvered herself onto nearly every board and committee in Sackets Harbor.

"I don't appreciate you hounding my mother. Rumors are flying. People are whispering and insinuating Mother is some sort of killer. And no wonder, the way you keep showing up at her door. Can't you see Mother isn't well?"

"Calm down, Selma," Gladys said. "The sheriff is leaving."

Meriday held up the gold necklace. "Is this yours?"

Her chubby hand trembled when she handed the plate to her mother. "Where did you find it?"

"Answer the question."

Selma gave a little stomp. "Yes, but how did you get it?"

Bailey answered. "Somebody found it on Wendall Compton's property the day he went missing."

"I'll handle this, Bailey." The preacher didn't know when to leave. Guess that's why they had to show him the door of his church. Meriday turned back to Selma. "Any idea how your necklace would come to be on Wendall Compton's patio?"

"Don't answer that, Selma." Gladys bit into the dill spear.

23

"Mercy, Mr. Hilton," Ada placed a hand on her stomach, "you gave me quite a start."

"It's not wise to go off the trail. There's twelve hundred acres of dense woods. You may not make it out again." Simon smiled at her. "Let me give you a lift back to the square. We can have a chat."

Reluctantly, she allowed him to carry her umbrella and lead her out of the woods and along the short stretch of grass to his golf cart.

Seated beside him, she asked, "What was it you wanted to talk about?"

He drove slowly over the well-worn path that wound along the lake. "I'm curious. Why were you so far off the trail?" His blue eyes sparkled when he tossed her a smile. "It looked to me like you were hiding behind that tree."

"Oh, mercy, no." Ada drew a draught from her water bottle. Her mouth had gone suddenly dry. "Are you aware that right here along the southern shore of Lake Ontario we have one of the best bird-watching regions in the country?" Ada scouted the tree line and scanned the lake. "Especially at this time of year. You see, the lake serves as a natural barrier to north-bound birds. They tend to habituate these woods and hedgerows right here along the southern shore."

"I wasn't aware."

"I had hoped to see a golden eagle."

Simon entered the blacktopped lane that led to the square. His smile vanished. "What did you see?"

"I didn't see anything, but I did hear something."

He parked and eyed her. "What did you hear?"

"I heard a man's voice. An angry voice. And I heard a few words. *Ship,* for one. You were referring to the shipyard, perhaps?"

His smile returned along with the sparkle in his deep-blue eyes. "Wow. Busybodies. Well, you got it wrong." He shifted toward her. "I'll be honest with you ..."

Here it comes. Ada believed when someone started a sentence with these words they were about to lie. She waited for it.

"I ordered another shipment of yard signs ten days ago. Now the printer says they won't be ready to ship for three more days. That's too late. The primary is Tuesday." His face tightened. "I have no patience for incompetence. Everything is too important."

"Why is it so important for you to win the election? You're already a successful man." She tilted her head and quickly reached to hold her hat in place. Her heart raced. She suddenly feared that in her trekking through the woods, a brunette wisp may have escaped the turban. She resisted the urge to check.

"Not successful enough to suit my father. He's with the State Department in DC. He's a powerful man. He's some-body." He swallowed visibly. "And he expects me to be somebody."

"And you believe you will be somebody in the state senate?"

"For a while. Then my father will expect more. Chandler Hilton always expects more." He sat silent for a moment, then told her to get out.

Ada walked toward her sister's bungalow convinced that beneath Simon Hilton's arrogant, type-A personality there hid a boy quite unsure of himself.

The sun had dried the morning's sprinkling, so Gwen returned to deadheading the petunias near the porch, and Frances went to the back yard to hoe around the tomato vines.

The lace curtains in a front window moved in Gwen's peripheral vision. Janet peeked out. The cook's odd behavior last night seemed to carry over to the morning. Janet sent her and Frances to Watertown to pick up a specialty lemon extract. Gwen had hoped to get a lemon meringue pie for her troubles, but as yet no pie had been produced.

Moments later, Janet hustled down the porch steps with a plastic bag tucked under her arm and her imitation alligator handbag over her shoulder. She wore ratty lounge pants and a baggy T-shirt that should have been in the rag bag.

"Where are you going?" Gwen said.

"Errands." Janet tossed the bag into her Beetle.

"Dressed like that?" Gwen placed her garden-gloved hands on her hips. "And what about our lunch?"

"In the fridge." Janet plunked in the front seat and without a glance pulled out of the driveway.

Frances came around the corner of the house. "Where's Janet going?"

"No idea."

"I'd like to go to the bungalow today to check on Ada."

Gwen removed her gloves. "Let's go now. We'll take lunch with us. I guarantee Janet has made plenty. And we can leave a note for her should she return before we get back."

"Wonderful. We can surprise Ada."

A knock sounded on the front door of Frances's bungalow, and Ada gave a sigh of relief. Janet had arrived to change her hair back to its God-intended hue. She trotted toward the door and through the swag glimpsed a tan shirt and brass badge.

"Oh, mercy," she muttered. She turned tail toward her bedroom, replaced the turban over her dark locks, then hurried to the door.

"Good morning, Sheriff. Won't you come in?"

"Miss Whittaker." His steel-gray eyes narrowed.

"Is something wrong?"

"I have a few more questions for you and Mrs. Ferrell."

She offered him a seat. "I'm sorry, Frances isn't here. Would you like a glass of lemonade?"

"No, thank you." He sat on the edge of the sofa. "I've just come from Gladys Blumm."

Ada sat in an adjacent chair. "Oh?"

"Selma Potter showed up. Seems the necklace is hers. But I couldn't get any more out of her. And of course, Mrs. Blumm claims someone is trying to frame her."

"Were there any prints on the bottle of oil Mr. Bailey found in Gladys's pantry?"

"None. That tells me someone planted it there. Or," he lifted a shoulder, "Gladys wiped the prints herself to make it look like someone is attempting to frame her."

"Yes, I see what you mean."

His face tightened, and he drew his brows together. "What do you know of this preacher, this Maxwell Bailey? Could he have planted the oil?"

"Everyone is suspect, I suppose. But Maxwell, I believe, tries to do the right thing."

"What's with his interest in Gladys Blumm? They seem pretty chummy."

"He is merely being a good neighbor. Watering her flowers. Taking her an occasional meal."

"Nothing more?"

"You mean, a hidden agenda?" Ada sighed. "Yes, that is so often the case, isn't it? But Mr. Bailey has a great deal of understanding and compassion for Gladys. You see, Mrs. Blumm has too much pride to face people right now, and Maxwell has recently been in a similar place. I believe he sincerely wants to help her."

The sheriff gave a slight nod. "When will your sister be in?"

"She's staying with Gwen and Janet—and I hope, out of harm's way—until we can ascertain why there are so many deaths here at Willowdell."

"We?" Meriday scowled. "Miss Whittaker, if there is a death collector roaming Willowdell and he or she gets wind of your meddling, you could be putting yourself in danger."

She stiffened. "I don't intend to do anything *but* meddle while my sister is in danger. Now tell me, will you be speaking to Simon Hilton?"

"Any particular reason why I should?"

"I heard him in the woods this morning ranting at someone. I have no idea who. If you should talk to him, I suggest you ask him about the warehouse at the old shipyard."

A car door slammed.

Oh, mercy. Her stomach twisted. She stood, asking, "Is there anything else?"

"No," he lifted himself off the sofa, "that's it for now."

Janet burst through the door. "I got your hair color." She stopped short and threw a hand over her mouth when she saw the sheriff.

He greeted Janet and stepped outside. Ada closed the door after him and discovered the reason he seemed puzzled when he first arrived. Her reflection in the glass revealed that a short black strand had been sticking out of her turban the whole time.

24

Samantha Milsap's bungalow smelled of cats, and no wonder. Meriday counted four of them prowling about the neo-Gothic living room where he sat waiting for Willowdell's front desk clerk to finish her phone call and come out of her bedroom.

Framed pictures of cats and castles hung on merlot-red walls. A black vinyl couch and chair, wrought-iron side tables, one holding a Wuthering Heights video case, and a chrome bookshelf—holding more snapshots of Simon Hilton and cats than books—filled the small room.

When Samantha opened the door to return to the living room, Meriday glanced up and caught a glimpse of a Simon Hilton political poster on her bedroom wall. He rubbed his chin. What would she do for Hilton? The owner of Willowdell seemed the sort of man who would take advantage of the Miss Milsaps of the world.

"Sorry to keep you waiting." She plodded to the straight-backed chair across from him, her rose-gold hair tied up in a sort of messy pile, revealing a tattoo on the side of her neck—a deep red heart with a black arrow through it.

"As I said, I took a couple hours away from the front desk this morning to take Heathcliff to the vet." She pointed to the shorthair in the cat bed in front of a dated twenty-four-inch television sitting on a tray table.

He disliked cats, but still, he hoped the TV wouldn't fall on the unsuspecting creature. He opened his notebook. "How long have you known Simon Hilton?"

"I've been working here a couple years."

"You didn't know him prior to your employment at Willowdell?"

"Right."

"How is it you came into the position of property manager? Running a place like this is a lot of responsibility, and you're only ...?"

"Twenty-five. Yeah. Miriam Kroft put in a good word for me. I worked at the shipyard in the office before it closed."

Meriday wondered how Miriam Kroft could have that much influence with Simon Hilton. "Do you have a degree in business management?"

She smiled. "No, but when I interviewed, Simon said I would be perfect for the job."

"I see." He glanced at his notepad. "I understand one of the benefits you provide your residents is that of free legal services. Tell me about that."

She ran her hands along her thighs, smoothing the lap of her long print skirt. "What is it you need to know?"

"What specific services do the attorneys provide for those who sign the contract?"

"Simon probably could help you with that. My job is to go over the lease with potential residents and get their signature on all the forms, assign the bungalows, and if they want, set up laundry and housekeeping services. Stuff like that."

"You advise the potential resident of free legal services, but you don't actually detail what those services could be. Is that right?"

"I don't, but an attorney comes out and meets with each resident who opts in."

"Do most of the residents sign up for this service?"

Samantha Milsap squinted, her full cheek rising to hide one eye. "I'd say maybe a third do from the start. Some will switch later on to take advantage of the benefit."

"Do you tell the residents they are assigning a new Power of Attorney when they sign up for this service?"

"I wouldn't know anything about that."

A loud bang hit against the front door.

Samantha jumped and blinked rapidly. With a hand over her bosom, she waddled to the door.

Meriday heard it open.

"I said you could have two hours to take your stupid cat to the vet. Not two and a half hours. I've got an election to win. I can't be answering the phone along with the senseless questions of mindless residents. Why are you not back at the desk?"

Simon Hilton.

Samantha's answer came, low and repentant. "Sheriff Meriday had some questions."

Meriday stood and moved his quarterback frame to the door. "Is there a problem?"

Hilton, dressed in a light-gray suit, confronted him, his face hardened. "If you are asking specific questions about Willowdell, our employees are not authorized to speak on these matters."

"Are you authorized?"

"I am." Hilton lifted his chin.

The sheriff placed a hand on the doorknob. "Then I'll meet you in your office when I'm done here, and that's when Miss Milsap will be back at her post."

Hilton spewed at the girl, "Mind how you go," then spun and stormed off.

Her ears turned red. "I'm sorry. Simon is under a lot of stress."

He's going to be under a lot more stress if I ever get that search warrant.

Janet tossed the plastic bag onto the counter in Frances's kitchen and removed hair color, latex gloves, combs, clips, and a towel for Ada's shoulders. "I'm sorry, Miss Ada. The sheriff is on to you because of me."

"He's no such thing." Ada sat in the folding chair she had taken from the hall closet. "I thought it best to work in the kitchen. The lighting is better, and I want you to make sure every hair is covered."

"Copy that." Janet clipped the towel around Ada's shoulders, pulled on the gloves, and mixed the dye. When she reached for the comb, the kitchen door opened. She yelped.

Ada peeked around her cook. Her stomach tightened.

Gwen and Frances stood inside the door holding a small cooler, their eyes wide and their mouths agape. Gwen moved closer and looked down at her. "Please tell me you are not Ada Whittaker."

"Oh, Miss Ada," Janet said, "I thought they were working in the yard. I didn't know they were coming here. I swear. I never said anything."

Frances slid onto a bar stool at the counter. "Why? You treasured your hair."

Ada admonished Janet to get on with it then answered Frances, "I went under cover. But no worries. I kind of like my hair short." Ada would never confess to her sister how it struck at her heart to see her hair lying on the bathroom floor. Yet, she would willingly make whatever sacrifice necessary to protect her sister.

While Janet sectioned her hair with the intensity of a brain surgeon, Ada detailed the exploits of the previous night and the early morning hours, in which she played the part of a brunette investigator.

"Mercy, it felt thrilling. Until Miriam Kroft and Alison Vaughn came into the lobby, and Alison said she wanted to check for messages in Simon Hilton's office. I thought my heart stopped—except I could hear it banging in my brain."

Gwen used the Keurig and made Frances and herself each a cup of coffee while Ada went on.

"But God be praised, Miriam talked Alison out of it. Frances, did you know Alison is Miriam's daughter? The things you find out when you hide under a desk in a dark room …"

"No, I didn't know. Why would they be there at that time of night?"

"Simon had given Miriam the job of posting notices, letting everyone know about the bus he arranged to take residents to the polls next week." Ada wiped a drip of dye from her ear with the edge of the towel.

"To vote for him, no doubt." Gwen poured hazelnut creamer into her coffee.

"Did you get a chance to look in the files?" Frances said.

"I had time to check Nita's and Dorothy's, but no others. When I glanced over their lease agreements, I found where they agreed to the option of free legal services through Willowdell's attorneys. Maxwell obtained the name of the firm from Gladys—Bigelow and Senak."

"I remember now." Frances reached for the creamer. "My lease offered the same option. But since I have Neil Tibbs for my attorney and my son for executor, I opted out."

"Speaking of Neil ..." Ada said. "Gwen, would you get in touch with him and ask him to find out what he can about that law firm?"

Gwen pulled out her cell phone. "Could Willowdell's attorneys assign themselves to act as executors of the deceased residents' estates?"

"Legally," Ada said, "I suppose they could."

"That's not right, even if it is legal." Janet squirted the balance of the dye on Ada's hair and worked to saturate each strand.

"I'm afraid there are a great many things that are legal but not right," Ada said.

Frances took sandwiches out of the cooler. "Think about the opportunity for corruption. Nita, Dorothy, Wendall, Luty Mae. They each likely had an impressive estate."

"And in the files that I checked," Ada said, "there were no relatives listed in the next-of-kin section."

"Someone's collecting all that money." Janet set down the empty bottle and checked the clock.

"Money isn't the only collecting going on." Ada reached for a sandwich. "Fred Albright is racking up quite a collection at the morgue."

Neil drove to his office, leaving his aunt with the judge and a thousand-piece jigsaw puzzle spread over a card table in the front room.

He had received Gwen's text asking if he knew anything about the law firm of Bigelow and Senak. An uneasiness about the matter hovered throughout his evening meal. He decided to find out what he could.

He unlocked his office door and flipped on the lights. At his file cabinet, he retrieved Frances Ferrell's file and reviewed her lease. He studied the wording on the contract and searched for contact information for the firm. He found none. How would a resident get in touch with them?

And why had he never heard of this firm in the nearly twenty years he had been practicing law? Clearly, they were not from this area.

He turned to his computer and began a search for the elusive attorneys. After several minutes of searching, he glimpsed the mention of an attorney in Syracuse by the name of Raymond Bigelow, the representative lawyer for the buyer in a commercial real estate transaction.

Neil dug deeper. Bigelow represented Ontario Developers, the buyer of the defunct shipbuilding company and its twenty-eight acres abutting the shore of Lake Ontario in Sackets Harbor. The seller? Duncan Kroft.

25

The following morning, Meriday returned to Willowdell. When he left Samantha Milsap's bungalow the day before, he'd made the decision to hold off on his interview with Simon Hilton. Considering the man's ire had already been raised, the exchange would prove counterproductive. Besides, if Hilton harbored information about the deaths at Willowdell, Meriday hoped the man would have a sleepless night fretting over the impending inquiry.

He entered Hilton's office and found the candidate standing over two stacks of yard posters on his desk.

"A little late to get those out, isn't it?"

Hilton bellowed, "Of course it's late. They shipped late. The printers said they would try to get fifty more signs to me by the fifteenth. They failed."

Meriday parked his frame in the chair by the wall and took out his notebook. "I have a few more questions."

Hilton stiffened his jaw, making his trimmed, dark beard appear tighter. "I understood you'd been ordered to cease with your distractions until after Tuesday's primary. I don't have time for this investigation of yours, this constant annoyance."

"I agree, murder can be a distraction. And an annoyance."

Hilton's blue eyes flashed. "Murder? What murder?"

"Dorothy Kane's. And possibly Nita Beavers's and Luty Mae Mears's. Wouldn't doubt if someone had a hand in Wendall Compton getting lost in the woods too."

"That's ridiculous." Simon Hilton scoffed. "Old people die. They fall. They forget. And quite often, they are just plain foolish. The Mears woman, for example. Wacko, that's what she was."

"If you believed Mrs. Mears to be mentally incompetent, why did you allow her to live on her own? Isn't it the responsibility of Willowdell—in other words, your responsibility—to periodically evaluate the mental and physical condition of your residents? Ensure they are provided with the appropriate level of care?"

Hilton's nostrils flared. "Not me, personally. I have people to do that. You can't put any blame on me."

"Sit down, Mr. Hilton. Answer my questions."

The vein in Hilton's neck pulsed, and his face flushed. Finally, he landed with a rebellious thud in the chair behind the desk.

Meriday reviewed his notes. "Tell me about the firm, Bigelow and Senak."

The face on the sprawled posters appeared confident, but the face peering at him blanched. Meriday could practically hear the gears churning while Hilton scavenged his brain for an answer. "What do you mean?"

"They represent Willowdell? Handle legal matters for the residents?"

His smile appeared forced. "Oh, yes. We have contracted with the firm to provide the benefit of legal services to our residents. If the resident so chooses. There's no pressure, and it is completely optional."

"And completely free."

"To the resident. But not to us. As I say, we have a contract. And, as with any business, we pass the fees along to the residents. The cost is tucked into their entry fees."

"So, the service is not free." Meriday studied the cocky young man who tried to project a so-sure-of-himself image but failed miserably. "Everyone pays, whether they use your firm or not."

"They're not *my firm*. And there's nothing illegal about it. But I'll tell you what is illegal. Someone stole into my office under the cover of night. I found this slipped under my door this morning." Simon Hilton opened a desk drawer, took out a folded piece of paper, and handed it over.

Meriday read, "In the midnight hour, a woman with short, dark hair, dressed in black, entered your office. She's on to you."

"It has to be true," Hilton said. "I found a file folder under my desk. Samantha said she didn't put it there."

"Do you lock your door when you leave?"

"No. Samantha and Alison may need access, since all the important files are in here."

A woman with short, dark hair. A strand poking from a turban ...

Ada Whittaker told him to ask about the shipyard.

He shifted his weight. "What can you tell me about the warehouse at the old shipyard?"

Hilton's neck muscles stiffened. He pulled a business card out of his desk drawer and handed it to Meriday. "Any more questions, contact my attorneys."

The hostility seemed an overreaction to a simple question.

Unless the question proved too complex for the property owner.

"I have a campaign to run. The primary is just a few days away, and I have no time—nor the patience—for your investigation." Hilton rose and held the door open.

Meriday tucked the Bigelow and Senak business card into his shirt pocket and stood. He'd get nothing from those attorneys. Hilton would order them to stall the investigation until after the primary. Forever, if possible.

Outside the office door, he waited. Seconds later he heard what he had expected, Simon Hilton on the phone.

Alison Vaughn came around the corner into the lobby and slid up to the counter. "May I help you, Sheriff?"

He noted her medium length, wispy mahogany hair. It could pass for short and dark. He approached her. "Did you happen to come into the lobby last night?"

"Yes. My mother and I came in quite late. We placed notices on all the doors letting people know a shuttle bus would take them to the polling place Tuesday."

"Your mother?"

"Miriam Kroft."

Sheriff Meriday's mind immediately went to the rain forest. "You live with your parrots? I mean, parents?" His face flushed hot.

"No, I have my own bungalow. It's small, but sufficient for me."

"Still, it must take your entire salary to stay in a place like this."

Alison Vaughn's brown eyes danced while a smile revealed even, white teeth. "My employee benefit package gives me a reduced rate."

No doubt.

Deputy Byron Bidwell cleared his desk and prepared to leave the station. He and Sloan had worked overtime, and he could think of nothing but grabbing takeout and relaxing at home. He tucked his chair in and followed Sloan toward the exit, mulling over menu options.

His desk phone rang. He glanced at Sloan, then turned back to answer, while Sloan stopped at the door and waited.

"Sheriff's office. Deputy Bidwell."

The caller spoke with a muffled voice. "Stake out the shipyard."

"Why would I do that?" Bidwell copied down the caller ID.

The caller snickered. "Heard there might be something going on there tonight. Thought the sheriff would be interested."

"Who is this?"

The caller hung up.

Bidwell replaced the handset.

"What was that about?" Sloan asked.

"Somebody messing around."

Bidwell walked toward his cruiser no longer thinking about takeout, but the possibility that the call could have been a legitimate tip. He wondered if the gnawing in his gut could be *instinct*.

Sloan drove out of the lot.

Bidwell opened the door of his cruiser and slid into the seat. *Stake out the shipyard.*

The chief had sent him and Sloan to the shipyard a few weeks back to search the dumpster. Although they found nothing evidential at the site, something there had piqued the sheriff's interest.

He'd better check it out.

26

Maxwell Bailey pulled his Infiniti up to 4110 Fairfield Lane, parked, and walked the path through Ada's English garden to the porch of her peach-colored Victorian. Nerves jitterbugged in his stomach.

At the top of the steps, he inhaled and slowly exhaled while he brushed a sweaty palm over his jeans and smoothed his white polo shirt.

Janet opened the screen door before he could knock. A crock filled with petunias served as doorstop to the inside solid oak door. "Come in, Max. I'll let Frances know you're here."

"Great. Thanks." He followed her instructions to take a seat in the parlor. *Parlor? Does anyone have a parlor anymore?* He entered what he would call a front room or a sitting room, boasting two long windows open to the evening breeze.

He stood before one, breathing in the mixed fragrances of the garden he had just passed through. He had been too focused on himself and his attempts to calm his nerves to appreciate the blossoms at the time. He scanned the hydrangeas and peonies, wild rose bushes, and brilliant azaleas. Beyond the garden, pink and white roses intertwined the spindles of the wrought-iron fence. Lifting his eyes to the distance, he caught the ripple of the silver waves of Lake Ontario beneath a faint and rising moon.

Stirred by the beauty of creation, his senses filled with praise to the Lord. *Thank you for helping me to see light again. To see you again.* His days of darkness had grown farther and farther apart. Discouragement had gradually given way to hope.

This restored joy came not entirely because of the friendships forged over the past weeks, but because of his willingness to forgive his elder board. To let go of the past. He no longer avoided trips into town for fear of running into someone from the church. Maxwell had served the Lord to the best of his ability, and there was nothing of which he needed to be ashamed.

He sat in a wingback chair and placed his hands on the armrests.

The room seemed reticent of a bygone era. Cream walls. Polished hardwood floor. A chintz loveseat. A marble-topped, mahogany coffee table. A fireplace. Old books on the mantel, secured with brass bookends.

Maxwell rose to check the titles.

At the sound of light footsteps, he turned to see Frances, her eyes bright and a smile on her face. The strap of a small leather purse crossed over the front of her blue blouse, and a scarf had been tied to a beltloop of her white capris.

"Hey, Max. Are you ready for this?"

"For what?"

Her laugh seemed musical. "You called me, remember? Saying something about a walk along the lake."

"I did call you." He moved and opened the screen door for her. "It took all my courage too."

She laughed again. "I'm glad you found a sufficient supply."

Relief washed over him when he confessed his nervousness.

He knew well how much of his life in ministry had been lived on eggshells. Always keeping his emotions in check, his opinions to himself. Weighing every word before he spoke, in and out of the pulpit. That feeling of being watched. Judged. Held up to the light.

Maybe, just maybe, with Frances Ferrell he could be himself.

They traveled the marina road. Minutes later, he parked a short distance from the docks. In the twilight, they strolled the walkway along the shore while cruisers and trawlers tied to their moorings bobbed in the restless waters.

Frances paused and panned the landscape. "I'm looking for the warehouse where they used to build boats."

Maxwell tipped his head to the left. "The shipyard is down about a half mile. They built the boats in the fabrication building, and they used the warehouse for storage."

A breeze tossed her hair while she stared in that direction.

He stepped closer and pointed. "You can't see the warehouse from here. The road leading to the shipyard is beyond that clump of trees, where that semi-truck is turning off the main highway."

"The business is shut down completely, isn't it?"

"Right. The owner, I believe, sold the property after the company defaulted during the recession."

"Then why would the driver be entering the shipyard?"

"Maybe he's drowsy and needs a place to sleep a few minutes before he continues his run." Max's stomach growled. He'd left his bungalow too anxious for food. Now that dusk had fallen, the café beckoned. "Let's get something at Dockside."

"Shouldn't the headlights be on?" She stood with her hands on her hips.

Max sensed the end of their romantic evening.

Bidwell waited. For who and for what, he had no clue. He had entered the shipyard and parked behind a thicket just inside a woodlot, keeping his cruiser hidden, yet giving him a clear view of the warehouse.

The crumpled bag on the passenger seat had held a chicken sandwich and waffle fries. A large drink rested, nearly finished, in the cup holder.

Despite the breeze playing near the shore and in the tops of the trees, humidity had filled the car. Increasingly uncomfortable, Bidwell reached to flip on the air but stopped. A diesel engine rumbled.

A tractor-trailer prowled toward the warehouse, its lights off. There was no company name on the cab.

The driver pulled ahead, then backed toward the loading dock. A young man jumped out of the passenger seat. He unlocked the chain padlocked to a green steel door and went inside. Moments later, the overhead door creaked and crept open. He stood in florescent lighting, waving the driver back tight to the dock.

The engine shut down. The driver, an older man, got out and leaped onto the dock. For several minutes they loaded furniture into the back of the truck, the driver in the trailer and the younger man operating a forklift.

"I'm not getting this." Bidwell wiped the perspiration dripping down his temple with a napkin. Furniture wasn't typically on a list of stolen goods. He couldn't understand why the caller would tip off the police. "Suppose I better find out."

In descending darkness, he weaved through the brush toward the green door. He stepped inside and paused in the shadows playing on the gray walls. His breathing went shallow. Someone felt the need for him to be here. Why?

Placing a hand on his weapon, he moved toward the sound of the motor. He entered the open, well-lit area he had seen from his cruiser and waded through a sea of couches, chairs, beds, and tables.

The forklift driver froze at the sight of him. When color returned to his face, he shut down the motor and jumped to the concrete floor. "Something I can help you with, Officer?"

"You can tell me what you're doing." Bidwell placed both hands on his belt.

The driver stepped out of the trailer, his whiskered jaw set, his narrowed eyes steeled. He reached up to a button on the wall.

The overhead door crept noisily downward and shut with a final crash.

Bidwell straightened his shoulders and stood his ground, reminded that he was still a rookie and had failed to let anyone know where he had gone.

27

On the short drive to the road that led to the shipyard, Frances filled Max in on her previous excursion with Gwen and Ada. "The mover outside Nita's bungalow told Ada they were taking everything to this warehouse. We wondered who would claim her property, since Nita had no living relatives. That made us wonder who would benefit from her estate."

"You believed checking out the shipyard would tell you that?"

"What else could we do? We had to start somewhere."

Max failed to see why Frances and Ada felt they had to do anything, but he kept the point to himself. "So, you think when a bungalow is cleared out, everything is taken here?"

"It has to go somewhere, I suppose."

Exactly. The management at Willowdell had to store the stuff somewhere. The warehouse actually seemed the perfect place.

"Park over there, Max, behind those pine trees. We can't let anyone see us." Her nose nearly touched her window. Her hand gripped the door handle.

He cringed at the thought of scratches to his car but did what she asked. He parked and shut off the engine. "Why are we hiding?"

Frances opened her door and threaded through an area of tall weeds, then ducked under the branches of a pine tree. She beckoned for Max to join her.

"Okay," he mumbled to himself, "I'll play along. What could go wrong?" He followed her trail until he reached her. "You do know we're both wearing white."

"Shh." She pointed to the dock.

A forklift operator balanced a couch on the front end of the loader and disappeared into the back of the truck. He reappeared, and an older man in a sweat-soaked yellow T-shirt stepped out of the trailer. He yelled something to the younger man then went back into the trailer.

Frances whispered, "Those men are the movers who cleared everything out of Nita's bungalow the day after her death."

The men continued to load the trailer.

After a few minutes, Max spoke in a hushed tone, "Again I ask, why are we hiding in pine trees, spying on furniture movers?"

"It looks like they're clearing the warehouse."

They watched until the humidity grew suffocating for Max. Even the sweep of an occasional warm breeze brought no relief. He preferred the comfort of air conditioning. He touched Frances's arm and pointed toward the car.

"Wait." She pulled on his sleeve. "Look."

A sheriff's deputy stood silhouetted in the light. His hands on his belt.

Bidwell? Maxwell's stomach twisted. Why would he be here?

The man in the yellow shirt reached up and held his hand over a projection on the wall. The overhead door began a creaky crawl downward and closed.

The driver pulled out his cell phone.

"He's probably calling the boss." The young man stepped up beside Bidwell. "We're not supposed to talk to anyone, so maybe he wants to know should we talk to you."

"Who's your boss?" Bidwell took his notepad from his shirt pocket.

"You have to ask Tut." The kid pointed with his thumb toward the yellow shirt.

Bidwell wrote down the name.

Tut returned his phone to his pocket without having spoken to anyone and waved toward the kid.

Bidwell sensed sudden movement. A strong arm circled his neck. Panic rose in his chest. He struggled for his gun. He couldn't breathe.

The notebook slapped the floor.

The warehouse went dark.

28

Meriday stood at his office door and scowled again at the clock. Seven a.m. and Bidwell had yet to appear. The rookie always arrived early at the station. Today he missed roll call.

Sloan sat at his desk with a cup of coffee and a breakfast sandwich, scanning a Medicare Advantage site.

Meriday popped a couple antacids and moved toward him. "Sloan."

The deputy set down his cup and swiveled his chair around. "Chief?"

He kept his voice low. "Have you seen Bidwell?" He didn't need the office blabbermouths to catch wind of the rookie being AWOL.

"Not since last night. We both left here around eight."

He didn't need this stress. Or the upset stomach. "Did he say anything?"

"No. But he took a phone call. Something about the shipyard. But he didn't seem concerned."

Again, the shipyard. "Who owns the property out there now?"

"I heard some developer got their hands on it. I can find out."

"Do that, but first take a ride over to Bidwell's place and check it out. I'm going to the shipyard and look around. Let me know immediately if you hear from him."

"10-4."

Wearing a belt bag around her waist and a purple straw hat, Ada set out for a power walk along the upper trails. Her hat fit better and she felt cooler now that her hair had been clipped short. She no longer had that naked feeling she first experienced at the loss of her ivory nest.

Willowdell gossip floated the sighting of a stranger, a woman with short black hair, sneaking about the square in the midnight hours. But that's all it was—gossip. As yet no one suspected her, nor had anyone discovered her mission.

Ada stepped up her pace and rounded the outer row of bungalows.

A vehicle engine started. A small moving van pulled away from number three, the former bungalow of Luty Mae Mears. Nearly a week had passed since the death of the frail Luty Mae. Ada wondered who could be moving in and changed course.

Stacks of boxes nearly filled the garage. Perhaps she should introduce herself and welcome the new residents. She stepped inside the cool garage and picked her way around the boxes toward a door that likely opened into the kitchen and knocked.

Judge Fausset opened the door wearing a white tank undershirt and pants held up by red suspenders. "Oh, hello, Miss Whittaker. Is everything all right?"

Ada focused on his kindly face. "Yes, I thought I'd pop in and welcome you." She felt awkward welcoming a resident who'd been at Willowdell several years. "I'm glad you were able to secure a bungalow so soon after the fire." She looked around the garage. "It appears much of your personal property was spared."

"The firemen did a heroic job containing the flames. A little water damage and quite a bit of smoke damage, but Neil contacted a restoration company for me, then hired two guys and a truck to bring everything here. In the meantime, I've been staying at Greenbrier Inn."

"I hope you have help unpacking." The job could be quite a challenge for an elderly man alone.

"Neil will be by Saturday."

"Very good. Well, I won't keep you from your work."

"Stop by again. I'll smoke a beef brisket." His smiling brown eyes backed up his invitation. "Or perhaps smoked salmon?"

Ada closed the conversation politely and took her leave.

Outside the garage, a shimmer on the ground near a patch of hollyhocks caught her eye. She picked up the gold foil wrapper. *Hegler.* Sheriff Meriday had told her about a Hegler foil being found under Luty Mae's body. Did Luty Mae take Frances's box of chocolates?

Could the wrapper have been tossed there by the judge?

Or one of the movers?

More likely, it was dropped by the person who entered Luty Mae's bungalow the night she died, the person who unwittingly left evidence of their indulgence both here and in the golf cart, where the wrapper landed under Luty Mae's broken body.

"Stalking the judge?" Miriam Kroft stood on the sidewalk. Red lipstick outlined her crooked grin.

"Mercy, no." Ada approached her. "I stopped to pick up this candy wrapper I spotted near the garage." Ada held out the wrapper. "Have you ever tried Hegler chocolates?"

"Can't say I have." A subtle breeze from the lake failed to move Miriam's stiff bouffant, yet sprayed the air with the scent of Aqua Net.

Ada lowered her voice. "I heard the sheriff found one of these wrappers under Luty Mae's body."

Miriam rolled her raisin-like eyes. "Luty Mae, racing over the golf course while stuffing candy in her mouth. No wonder she tipped her cart. She could barely do one thing at a time, much less two. Excuse me. I have an appointment with my attorney."

Ada tilted her head. "I hope you're not having legal trouble."

A slight sigh escaped the woman's lips. "It's standard practice. Willowdell attorneys meet annually with each resident they represent. Now, goodbye."

Miriam turned, and Ada resumed her power walk.

Thirty minutes later, Ada rounded the bend and approached the square.

A woman with short, messy blond hair tossed a leather bag into the passenger seat of a Hyundai parked in front of the Kroft bungalow. She then jumped in and zipped toward the front gate.

A tingling swept up Ada's neck. She had seen that woman before.

Meriday drove his cruiser at a prowler's pace over the dusty lot, searching for anything that would clue him in on the whereabouts of his deputy. Weeds surrounded the boarded-up fabrication building. The current owner didn't seem to be in any hurry to develop the property.

He drove around to the back of the warehouse and parked. Beyond the overhead door stood a green steel door, chained and padlocked. He left his vehicle and strode to a small, dusty window and peered in.

Dark. Empty. Silent.

He walked the perimeter of the building.

What had Ada Whittaker been alluding to when she advised him to ask Simon Hilton about the warehouse? And that phone call Bidwell took last night, was that the reason he was absent today, or had something completely unrelated detained him?

A trail of matted grass led him to a dumpster buried in the tall growth. The putrid odor of rotting food stung his nostrils.

After a cursory search of the area, Meriday walked to his car.

He stood with his hands on his hips and scanned the horizon while a breeze off the lake swirled around him. Boaters on the far shore undocked their crafts and headed out into the rippling water like all the world could sing, unaware his deputy was missing.

He jolted at the ring of his phone. "Yeah?"

"His pickup is in the driveway," Sloan said, "but his cruiser is gone. I checked all the windows. There's no sign of him."

Meriday ended the call with an odd mixture of fear and anger. Did the kid get into something he couldn't handle? So many rookies thought they could manage calls on their own, then ended up doing something stupid.

He popped two more antacids and turned. The sun glinted off something tucked deep in the thickets. He squinted and shaded his eyes with his hand. His heart stopped. The reflection bounced from a side mirror of a cruiser.

He edged toward the vehicle.

At the open window, he leaned in. Nothing lay on the seat but a crumpled Chick-fil-A bag. Meriday opened the door and gave the cruiser a solid search. A sniff of the drink in the cupholder revealed lemonade.

He turned his attention to the ground around the vehicle. Matted, damp leaves gave no evidence of a scuffle. He moved deeper into the woods, walking circumspectly and calling Bidwell's name.

Each pause to listen yielded the rustling of leaves, the caw of seagulls, and the distant murmur of boat engines, but no response.

"Where could he be?" Meriday looked back at Bidwell's squad car.

Goosebumps lifted the hair on his arms.

29

Gwen and Frances relaxed with coffee on the porch of Ada's Victorian. The fragrance of cosmos swirled in a cloudless blue sky. Frances related the story of her time with Max the previous evening at the warehouse. "When the overhead door closed, we didn't know what to think."

Janet stepped out of the house holding three placards fastened on sticks. "Here you go, ladies. I stayed up late last night working on these. Let's start in front of the school, where they will be setting up the polling booths."

Gwen read the signs aloud, "Silence Simon, Halt Hilton. Save Your Mother, Save your State. Value Life, Vote Blythe." She scowled at Janet. "Are you crazy? And what do you mean, *save your mother?*"

"No, I'm not crazy. I'm angry. Simon Hilton is responsible for the deaths of those residents." Janet flung an arm in the direction of what Gwen could only assume to be Willowdell. "We need to stop him from getting anywhere near the state senate."

Frances held up a hand. "Now, I don't think in all objectivity that we can blame Simon Hilton for the deaths at Willowdell."

Janet plopped down in a porch rocker, brooding.

Gwen brushed a hand through her frizzed red hair. "Look, just don't vote for the guy. You don't have to get all political."

Janet jumped up and glared at Gwen. The placards slid to the floor. "And that's the reason this state is in terrible shape. People like you who don't vo—"

"What do you mean, people like me?" Gwen leaped to her feet. The rush of blood heated her face. "I'll have you know, I have voted in every election for the past ..." She paused while she mentally counted. "Twenty-five years. Not that it matters. Upstate voters have to put up with taxation without representation, and that is why—"

"Whoa." Frances stood between them with raised hands.

"What is going on here?" All three turned. Ada marched up the path. "Mercy. I heard you bickering from way down the street."

Sheriff Meriday reached inside the open window of Bidwell's cruiser and unlatched the trunk. His stomach roiled while he moved to the back of the vehicle and lifted the trunk lid.

He exhaled noisily. Nothing there that shouldn't be.

Again, he looked toward the warehouse and stared at the steel door barred with chains. Could Bidwell be inside? Sweat broke out on his forehead and under his arms. He grabbed the deputy's bolt cutters and lifted a high-powered flashlight from the trunk then marched toward the green door.

Within minutes, the chains clanked to the ground.

The air inside the warehouse felt cool, yet damp and

smelled faintly of turpentine and wax. He paused and listened and was met with an eerie silence.

He scanned the walls with his flashlight and located a light switch. Florescent lights flickered to life overhead. Why hadn't the power been cut to the abandoned building?

Something lay on the floor near an overhead door. The tap of his boots echoed through the building as he strode across the cement floor.

Bidwell's notebook. His jaw tightened.

Meriday picked it up, flipped a few pages, and checked the last entry. *Tut.* "What is that supposed to mean?" A noise caught his attention. He strained to identify the source of what sounded like a soft growl.

Silence.

He shoved the pad into his pocket then walked to the office near a set of stairs and opened the unlocked door. A flip of the light switch revealed a cot tucked into a corner, its mattress worn and bare. A cardboard box near his feet held rolls of red packing tape. He kicked it aside and stepped to the cluttered desk.

His head jerked up at the sound of scuffing overhead.

Upstairs?

He left the office, crept up the stairs, and panned the shallow loft with his flashlight. He moistened his lips. "Bidwell?"

A moan sounded from the far end of the loft. Hair stood on the back of his neck. The moans grew louder as Meriday's boots tromped a fast-paced rhythm across the wooden floor.

Deputy Bidwell lay on his back, his hands and ankles taped to a rafter. Red packing tape covered his mouth and circled his head. The lump in Meriday's throat dissolved. Despite the opened snap, Bidwell's service revolver remained snug in his holster.

Meriday took the jackknife off his belt and stooped, shaking his head. "I ought to leave you right here. Let you learn a lesson."

Beneath the layers of red tape, the wooden face cracked.

———

Ada informed Janet that she had every right to position herself in front of the school with a placard, and Gwen had the right to refuse, but neither had the right to be critical of the other.

She then pulled the two aside and reminded them of their promise. While Frances stayed with them, they were to refrain from squabbling.

Janet and Gwen quickly apologized to each other and to Frances.

The four women sat around the kitchen table, and Ada mentioned her visit with the judge. "I found a Hegler wrapper near Luty Mae's garage. And if you remember, the deputies found one under her body." She looked at Frances. "I know we've always suspected Samantha of taking your box of chocolates, but finding these foils causes me to question our assumption."

"Alison Vaughn?" Frances said. "She helps out in the office."

Janet squirted lemon in her iced tea. "Didn't you say Mrs. Kroft came around with brochures? She could have taken the chocolates."

"It doesn't matter who took the box," Gwen said, "it matters who ate the chocolates."

Ada nodded. "You're right, Gwen. Even if Samantha did take the box, anyone could have taken one or two pieces out of it."

"Or Samantha could have shared the box." Frances sipped

her tea.

Ada shook her head. "I can't see Samantha sharing chocolates. No. Gwen's right, we need to focus on who may have eaten the chocolates and tossed the wrappers, ignorant of the fact they were leaving evidence."

"You be a good boy, Stanley," Maxwell admonished the cocker spaniel. The dog stood by the front door, eyeing the leash hanging on the hook. "Stay."

Maxwell closed the door and looked across the square at number eight. The porch awning had not been lowered against the afternoon sun. Frances had not yet returned to Willowdell.

Bored and looking for something to do and someone besides Stanley to do it with, he tucked his hands into the pockets of his red shorts and sauntered toward the recreation center.

Duncan Kroft looked up from his stance by the shuffleboard court, leaning on a cue. "Hey, Max. How about a game?"

Maxwell resisted the offer. Shuffleboard had long been associated with the aged, and he resisted that aged part. He looked around the large room. Some women sat at a craft table, their hands busy, their chatter low. Another area hosted a quilting frame and several quilters stretching over it, gabbing.

He shrugged. *Shuffleboard it is.*

Duncan seemed to revel in his need to instruct him in the art of successful shuffleboard form, with the occasional dip into condescension. The man lunged and waited for the disk to stop. A grin spread over his face. Duncan leaned on his cue and spoke in a lowered voice. "Say, Max, I saw you follow some strange woman into Frances Ferrell's bungalow. Got a little something going on?"

The remembrance of Ada's night of espionage disquieted Maxwell. Then the full import of Kroft's words struck him. His eyes flashed. Rage raced through his veins.

"Duncan Kroft." Sheriff Meriday entered the rec center and stepped across the room with Deputy Bidwell not far behind.

Maxwell took a deep breath. The appearance of the tan uniforms stopped him from lifting a righteous hand. Wouldn't the folks at Westlake Community Church delight in that headline! *Former Pastor Fights Claim of Indiscretion.*

Duncan stammered, "Wh-What can I do for you?" His cockiness seemed to have slithered under the disk. He took a hankie from his pocket and wiped the eggshell mustache that huddled like a full defense under his large nose, then shoved the rag back into his pocket.

Meriday stood close to him. "You placed a call to my office last night."

He shook his head, trying to deny the statement without a voice.

Bidwell stuck a small note under Duncan's nose. "The caller ID links to your cell phone."

Duncan Kroft forced a chuckle. "All right, I called."

Meriday glared. "Why did you tell us to check out the shipyard?"

"I was clearing brush from the walking trails when I heard Hilton's golf cart near the edge of the woodlot. He heads into the woods sometimes to make a private phone call." He lifted his shoulders. "So I followed him and listened. When he said something about the shipyard, I figured he needed watching."

Meriday scowled. "Tell me about those two men."

"What men?"

Bidwell moved in. "The men who forced me to spend the night in the warehouse, bound and gagged with packing tape."

Maxwell raised his eyebrows. Is that what happened after

the overhead door closed? He had no inkling at the time that the deputy could have been in danger. If anything, he'd wondered if Deputy Bidwell played a role in the operation. But a kidnapping would explain the two-inch strip of irritated skin across the deputy's face.

Duncan took a step back. "You're crazy."

Meriday's nose nearly touched his.

With a gulp, Duncan said quickly, "I'm just saying, I don't know anything about two men. If something illegal was going down, Hilton had to be behind it. That's all."

"Why the vendetta against Simon Hilton?" Meriday said.

"All he cares about is that stupid primary. He doesn't care that old Wendall died. Or anything about the others, either." Duncan lowered his head and mumbled, "He's a jerk."

Maxwell piped up, still a bit resentful of the man's insinuation. "Miriam seems to like him. Doing all that canvassing for his campaign. Putting up all those posters around the admin building." A hot flush sprang to his face. No one could know how he learned about the posters.

Meriday tilted his head toward him, and Maxwell feared he might ask him a question, but the sheriff turned back to Duncan Kroft. "Did you happen to see a woman with short black hair enter or exit the lobby two nights ago?"

Maxwell swallowed hard.

Duncan glanced at Maxwell before speaking. "If you mean like between midnight and one, then yeah. I did. I let Hilton know too. Let him think someone's checking into his business. I figured maybe it'd rattle his skeletons."

"Why would he be concerned about someone looking into his business?"

"Check with Miriam. Like Max said, she likes jerks."

A twisted grin came to the sheriff's face. "Apparently."

30

Saturday arrived sunny and warm. Neil Tibbs sat on the shaded patio at Judge Fausset's new bungalow. He and the judge took a few minutes to rest from lifting and unpacking boxes. Sweat trickled down their temples.

Neil drained his tumbler of ice water then said, "I understand Duncan Kroft sold his shipyard to Ontario Developers. Do you know anything about that?"

Judge Fausset picked up the water pitcher and refilled Neil's tumbler. "Duncan had a good shipbuilding business there for decades. Then the recession hit and folks no longer considered a sailboat essential. That left Kroft with a lot of costly inventory. He had no choice but to let his employees go and get out from under the business. He was forced to file bankruptcy."

Neil rubbed his chin. How had the couple stepped out of bankruptcy into a premier retirement village?

"He took a hit on the sale price," the judge said. "He had to sell, and there were no other offers."

"So, the developer got a deal."

"Why the interest in the shipyard?"

"My interest is in the buyer's attorney, Raymond Bigelow, and the firm of Bigelow and Senak. They represent some of the residents here at Willowdell, and I promised I'd look into them."

His brown eyes narrowed. "Oh?"

"I hoped you were familiar with the firm and could assure me Bigelow and Senak are reputable attorneys." A growing uneasiness troubled Neil.

The judge shook his head. "I'm aware of the option on the lease agreement, but I've not heard of that firm."

Samantha Milsap opened the drawer beneath the lobby counter. She had been waiting for Simon Hilton to disappear behind his office door. The closer primary day drew, the more his rantings increased. She needed to calm her nerves with chocolate.

She lifted the lid of the little brown box and frowned. Did she eat that many? Of the dozen pieces, three remained. She chose one and removed the foil wrapper and popped the chocolate into her mouth.

Simon's door swung open.

Her eyes darted to him with her chew suspended.

"If Meriday comes around, tell him I'm not in." Simon cursed. "If I get my hands on those idiots ..." The door slammed.

She swallowed the drool that had filled her mouth and turned to see Frances Ferrell's sister standing at the counter.

Ada had stepped into the lobby while Hilton barked his order regarding the sheriff. She doubted very much Samantha would be able to keep Leo Meriday at bay, any more than she could keep a hungry dog out of an open refrigerator at a meat packing company.

"Good afternoon, Samantha. I understand Frances has a package."

The property manager waddled to the back room. She soon emerged with the replacement shipment Frances ordered from Hegler and placed the package on the counter.

"Frances's chocolates." Ada smiled. "Have you ever tried them?"

A pink, slow-moving flow washed over the young woman's face. She shook her head.

"I wonder, did Luty Mae Mears ever receive a shipment from Hegler?" Ada placed the package in her tote bag.

"I don't think so." Samantha slid a hand along her rose-blond hair. "Sometimes Alison distributes the mail. She might know."

"Does Alison also distribute the inspection notices?"

"No, that's my job. Simon insists I hand deliver the notices to the residents at their homes. He says they're more likely to remember the appointment if the notice is delivered in person. And too, some residents don't have email."

The lobby door opened, and Miriam Kroft grunted at Ada's greeting. Samantha's pale green eyes hurled daggers at the woman when she entered Simon's office without a knock. Hilton rose, and Miriam shut the door.

"Mrs. Kroft seems to be quite supportive of the candidate," Ada said.

"She wants him to win. We all do." Samantha slammed the drawer beneath the counter.

Monday morning Meriday stood looking over Bidwell's shoulder while the rookie scanned the mugshots of area thugs, hoping to identify the two men who seized him. Growing impatient with his deputy's lack of recognition, Meriday stalked back to his office.

He had to do something. He couldn't just stand still.

Earlier, he had called Willowdell to request Simon Hilton come to the station to answer a few questions, but Samantha Milsap informed him Hilton had gone to Watertown and had given her no indication when he would return. The tremor in the young woman's voice told a different story, but he let it ride.

Meriday refilled his bulldog mug and plunked down at his desk. He pulled out all the files and reports he had printed out relating to the deaths at Willowdell. He laid them out in order of occurrence.

A rap sounded, and Bidwell entered. "No luck, Chief. And I couldn't find any with the name Tut. They may not have a record. They didn't seem experienced in anything other than moving furniture and the use of packing tape."

Meriday leaned back in his chair. "What if Kroft is right, and Hilton is involved with the shenanigans at the shipyard? Could be Hilton ordered the movers to detain you."

"I think this Tut guy made the decision himself. He tried to place a call, but I don't believe he got through."

Meriday scratched his mustache. "Why commit a felony just to keep a cop from poking around while you move furniture out of a warehouse?"

"Drugs in couch cushions, maybe?"

He wondered if Bidwell aimed for a joke, but the young

man's poker face gave no indication of humor. But then, it wouldn't.

Neil Tibbs glided his BMW off Interstate 81. He followed the signs for downtown Syracuse and his GPS directions to Tryon Street.

Through an examination of the former shipyard's property deed at the County Court House, he'd found an address for Ontario Developers. He hoped through the developer to obtain information on the attorney who handled the sale and the firm representing Willowdell residents.

Driving at a crawl down the street, he searched the brick structures for number eighteen. He had to be close but saw no sign touting Ontario Developers. An unmarked door stood recessed in an alcove between a coffee shop and what looked to be a second-hand store. Number eighteen had to be in there.

Neil whipped his car into a parking space.

Older vehicles, rusted by years of winter salt spray, lined the opposite side of the street. Beyond them sprawled an overgrown lot, rimmed with broken chain link fencing and splotched with trash. He ran a hand through his hair. He had no choice but to leave his car, although locked, unattended.

A minute later, Neil stood at the top of a narrow staircase. Three doors skirted the landing, identified by small numbers etched in the frosted glass. He opened the door of eighteen.

Off to one side of the dim room sat a small, cluttered desk stacked with files. A larger—and neater—desk sat more central to the remaining space. Despite the office's somewhat depressing appearance, the air smelled like the towels fresh out of Aunt Gracie's dryer.

He heard water running, then all went quiet.

A woman emerged from an adjoining kitchenette. She sent him a smile when she spotted him. Her blond hair, stylishly short, framed her pretty face. She stepped toward him.

"May I help you?"

"I'm looking for Ontario Developers."

"We represent Ontario Developers." She held out a smooth, manicured hand. "I'm Jackie Senak."

31

Ada sat on Frances's porch sipping a lemonade. She wondered at the casualness of Miriam and Simon's relationship. Could Simon Hilton be Miriam's son? She squinted and tried to visualize Alison Vaughn and Simon Hilton side by side. Similar in build, but not in facial features or skin tone. But then, dissimilarity wasn't conclusive.

Perhaps Miriam was a family friend or a former neighbor. That could account for her familiarity with the owner of Willowdell. Likely, Miriam Kroft was simply all in with Simon Hilton's politics, and like Samantha Milsap said, wanted to see him win the primary.

Ada wished her sister were there to discuss the matter. It didn't seem right, Frances not being able to be in her own home. But until Ada could determine why the poor deceased were targeted, she would try to keep Frances from returning to Willowdell.

She looked across the square.

That's odd.

Gladys Blumm came out of the Kroft bungalow in a stealthy manner. She held something close to her chest and trotted up the sidewalk then ducked inside her own front door.

Ada had not seen Gladys for nearly a month. Not since that awful row at the bingo game, just days before Dorothy's body had been found floating in the whirlpool.

A moment later, Duncan Kroft came over the knoll in wet swimming shorts, whistling, "Yankee Doodle Dandy." A towel draped his bony shoulders. He carried his flip-flops.

Ada stepped off the porch. "Hello, Mr. Kroft."

His acknowledgment appeared forced. "Miss Whittaker."

"I'm glad I met up with you." She walked beside him. "I heard about your wife's collection of jungle birds. I've been eager to see them. Do you think Miriam would mind if I had a peek?"

"It's not the best time. As you can see, I'm dripping."

"I don't mind waiting until you change." Ada settled into a rocker on the front porch of number twelve. "I'll wait right here."

He rolled his eyes and went inside.

Several minutes later, Miriam Kroft ambled down the sidewalk studying a painting. Ada recognized the backing of one of the canvases the rec center supplied for resident artists. Miriam looked up when she reached her porch.

"Miss Whittaker, I didn't realize you were here. What can I do for you?"

Ada stood. "I've heard so much about your collection. I do so love the rainforest with its birds, its vibrant colors, and beautiful flowers."

"I'd love to show you." Miriam's face glowed. "I finished this ruby-cheeked sunbird today."

Ada viewed the painting in Miriam's hand. "Oh, my. What marvelous colors."

"You must see my buntings. I'm so proud of my precious ones." Mrs. Kroft opened the front door and led the way.

Ada entered the living room and felt ambushed by a Peruvian jungle.

Dozens of framed photographs of parrots, kingfishers, and tanagers nearly hid the dark green walls. Palm trees sheltered bamboo furniture. The tables held a glass menagerie of brilliant red, blue, and yellow birds. Chairs and a sofa were covered in a pattern of brilliant flowers.

"Oh, my." She followed her tour guide along a green carpeted path to a three-tiered shelf. "Mercy, they're stunning."

A satisfied smile spread over Miriam's face. "This is my bunting collection. They're simple little birds, but you're right, they are stunning. And they hold the most meaning." She picked up one. "Dunc gets one for me every year on our anniversary."

Her smile vanished. Alarm filled Miriam's raisin-like eyes. "It's gone. My blue bunting." She scavenged among the collection that nearly covered the shelf.

Mr. Kroft appeared, his shorts and shirt dry, his thick, eggshell hair slicked back.

Miriam shrieked at him, "What did you do with it?"

The red of Mr. Kroft's recently sun-kissed face deepened. "Why is it, whenever you misplace something, you accuse me of doing something with it? I have no idea what you've lost this time."

"My blue bunting. It's gone."

"Maybe it flew away." Duncan Kroft goose-stepped to the door and disappeared with a slight bang.

Yes, to number nine, the gray bungalow of Gladys Blumm.

Neil found the covert law firm without the glitz he had expected. Its shabbiness seemed more fitting for legal aid than for a firm handling multi-million-dollar clients.

"What can I help you with, Neil?" Jackie Senak asked.

He had introduced himself while accepting the offered chair. She settled behind the smaller desk. The office didn't exactly project professionalism, so he accepted the fact that she referred to him by his first name.

"I'm here about a property in Sackets Harbor." He had used the entire seventy-mile drive to think through his approach. "Ontario Developers, I understand, purchased the shipyard there."

"And this is of interest to you, why?" She leaned forward.

"I'd like to discuss the purchase of five acres with lake frontage." Neil knew, even if it were true, he could never swing the cost of one acre of lakefront property, much less five. After all, his practice was in Sackets Harbor, not Albany.

"Are you a doctor?" She targeted his financial position, but he had no intention of disclosing his vocation.

"My aunt's B & B is an aging Victorian, and with repairs and upkeep, the business sometimes struggles through the winter months. We believe we could increase tourist trade if we sold the current inn and rebuilt on the lake. You know what they say, location is everything." He smiled, hoping to evoke cooperation.

She turned to her computer and typed. After a short scan of the screen, she said, "There's no indication Simon Hilton will subdivide."

Simon Hilton is Ontario Developers?

"But if you'd like, Mr. Bigelow can present your offer." Jackie drew a yellow legal pad closer. "He's in Watertown this morning, but when he returns—"

"Can you present my offer?"

She eyed the larger desk. Her chin lifted slightly. "Mr. Bigelow and I are partners, but he handles most of the face-to-face with clients."

Neil detected a note of resentment in her tone.

She poised a pen over the paper. "What is your offer?"

Neil looked down and scratched his wrist. He then lifted his eyes to her and spoke with a softened tone. "Jackie,"—since they were on a first-name basis— "before I commit to a specific offer, I want to make sure I remember right. The property is assessed at nine hundred thousand. Is that right?"

The attorney again searched the screen. "One million, four hundred thousand. That's public information."

He knew Ontario Developers paid nine hundred thousand. That, too, was public information. That was a significant and immediate gain of half a million in value. He studied her face. She didn't act as though she had anything to hide.

"Did Simon Hilton and the seller, Duncan Kroft, make a second deal—off the record?"

She blinked rapidly and leaned back in her chair. Her blue eyes seemed to x-ray his façade. "Before we go any further, how does your aunt, who can barely eke through the off-season, intend to pay for five acres of lakefront property?"

He lifted his hands and remained silent, determined to keep his personal information out of the equation.

"Just who are you, Neil Tibbs?"

He placed his elbows on the armrests of the chair and steepled his fingers. "Who is Bigelow and Senak? What I see is a quasi law firm sequestered in a back alley, operating behind unmarked doors, and facilitating backroom deals."

She did not flinch. "What I see is someone pretending to be a legitimate inquirer, who is instead seeking private information on one of our clients. Regardless of your impressions, you know nothing about me or my partner or our practice. Therefore, you are in no position to pass judgment. And with wasting my time being the least of your infractions, I expect an explanation."

Neil tugged at his collar. Heat spread up his neck.

32

J ust after five o'clock, Ada approached Gladys Blumm's
bungalow with a warm casserole.

Selma Potter stepped off the porch. "Oh, hello, Miss
Whittaker."

"Hello, Selma. I made a little extra."

"That's kind of you." Selma came closer and lowered her
voice. Ada read the address on the small package Selma held in
her hands. "Truth is, I'm worried. Mother hasn't been out of
the house since all the gossip started over Dorothy's death. She
sits all day in her room doing word searches and crosswords."

Not all day—at least, not today.

"I've tried to get her interested in *Andy Griffith* reruns. She
used to love them. She'd laugh, even though she'd seen them
so many times she can recite Barney's lines. But Mother won't
allow the television on while Simon Hilton is running his
campaign ads." Selma flushed and fanned herself. "I need to
get home. You can leave the dish on the counter. The door isn't
locked."

Ada waved and waited for Selma to drive away, then

crossed over the porch. Windchimes trilled around her while she slid open the door. "Gladys? Ada Whittaker."

Late afternoon light filtered through the kitchen curtains into the otherwise dark living area. She listened. A tabby purred while circling her ankles. Ada found a spot on the cluttered counter to set the casserole dish. A brochure protruded from beneath a pizza box. Someone had drawn a Hercule Poirot mustache on Simon Hilton's face.

She raised her voice, "I brought a little supper for you."

Gladys's voice came from behind one of the closed doors down the hallway. "Leave it on the counter."

Ada did not intend to leave anything on the counter without a reward for her labors. She had determined to find out why the woman who had convinced everyone she never left her home had done just that—and likely returned to it with Miriam Kroft's blue bunting.

A rap jolted her.

Maxwell stood on the porch holding a plate covered with a napkin. Ada offered a quick thank you to God. If anyone could get her in to see Gladys, Maxwell could.

Ada called to Gladys while she opened the door, "Maxwell Bailey is here."

Maxwell's eyes sparked when Ada opened the door and greeted him. "How is Frances?" he asked, entering the gloom.

Before she could answer, Gladys yelled, "Send him away. If he brought brownies, he can take them with him."

"I need to talk to her," Ada whispered.

"Then we will. All her bluster is exactly that. Come on." Maxwell placed the paper plate of brownies beside the casserole and moved down the hall. "I'm coming in, Gladys. Ada is with me."

No reply.

Ada followed Maxwell into a small sitting room.

Gladys Blumm sat upright in a recliner with a blanket over her legs. She held an open newspaper in front of her face.

"Hello, Gladys." Ada took a seat in the rocker Maxwell had pulled up for her. "I brought a sample of my Hungarian goulash. I hope you enjoy it."

Gladys crunched the paper down onto her lap. "It's not spicey, is it? My stomach's a bit prejudiced when it comes to those foreign dishes."

Maxwell, seated in the desk chair, placed his hands on his knees. "Ada wants to talk to you."

"I'm sitting right here, ain't I?"

Gladys seemed a woman who spoke her mind without a hem or a haw. Ada took the same approach. "I saw you leave the Krofts' bungalow today with something in your hands."

"Hah!" Gladys slapped her hand to her lap and smacked the newspaper. "No holding back the horns. Right to the point."

"Did you take Miriam's blue bunting? Is that what Selma is mailing to Sheriff Meriday?"

"Well, what if I did, and what if it is? I'm not the only one sneaking around."

Ada wondered if Gladys could possibly be referring to her, but she chose to stay focused on her mission. "Why did you take it?"

Gladys pinched her lips tight.

"Gladys?" Maxwell said. "Why?"

"All right, I'll tell you. I have proof Miriam Kroft planted the peanut oil in my pantry."

Ada's stomach flipped.

"What proof?" Maxwell asked before Ada could get a word out.

"I found one of those political brochures, the ones Miriam Kroft has been peddling, on my kitchen counter yesterday.

That woman came in my house unannounced. And me, hiding out in this room, didn't even know an intruder had entered. So, I figure if that shrew would enter to leave a brochure, she would enter to plant evidence."

Ada exchanged a glance with Maxwell, then said, "But why send the bunting to the sheriff?"

"Stuck a note in it. Told him to investigate the owner."

Maxwell said, "But would Sheriff Meriday know who owns the bird?"

"I suspect he's made a trip or two to the jungle."

The next morning, Frances walked the full stretch of Fairfield Lane, crossed Market Square Park, and took an alternate route back to Ada's house. By the time she reached the stoop of the kitchen entrance, she had made her decision.

She found Ada's home pleasant and welcoming, and Gwen and Janet had worked hard at peacekeeping. Yet, her concern for Ada and Max had grown, leaving her anxious to return to Willowdell. She opened the back door.

The smell of lemon extract filled the kitchen, and Janet stood over a bowl stirring batter.

Frances went to the cupboard for a coffee mug. "I haven't heard of anyone being eliminated from Willowdell lately, so I'm going home today."

Janet paused the wooden spoon and looked at her wide-eyed. "That doesn't mean you'll be safe there. Sheriff Meriday hasn't made any arrests. Miss Ada would have told us if he had."

Their eyes locked in a battle of wills.

The door leading to the dining room swung open. "Good

morning, ladies. What's on the agenda today?" Gwen dropped her smile. "What's going on?"

Frances poured herself a cup of coffee. "I'm going home today. To stay."

Gwen glanced at Janet then sat at the table across from Frances. "That may not be a good idea."

"We can visit," Janet said. "We can spend all day with Miss Ada if you want. Do some fun things. Swim or play croquet. Or maybe cool off by the lake. I'll pack a lunch. We can take some of these lemon poppyseed muffins to Miss Ada."

Gwen looked somewhat pleadingly at Frances. "Let's do that."

"We can check on Max." Janet's face held the hope of having dangled the right bait.

Admittedly, Frances knew she had.

Max allowed Stanley to take his time sniffing the hedgerow around the dog park, until Ada's gray Volvo entered the Willowdell gate.

Minutes later, he left Stanley in front of the fireplace crunching on a Milkbone and crossed the square. The four women sat about the wicker coffee table on the porch. They invited him to join them. While he helped himself to a muffin, Frances poured a glass of sweet tea and set it before him.

Max noticed Janet abstaining. "Not having a muffin, Janet?"

"I'm on the Atkins diet."

Gwen rolled her eyes.

"Will you be taking the van to the polls today, Maxwell?" Ada asked.

"No, but I do intend to vote."

The next few minutes were spent discussing politics and what might become of Willowdell if its owner should win the primary and then his bid for a senate seat.

Janet expanded her fan and waved it in front of her face. "I still think Mr. Hilton is involved in whatever is going on here at Willowdell."

Duncan Kroft had nearly said the same when the sheriff confronted him at the shuffleboard court. That reminded him ... "Frances, the night we watched the movers at the warehouse, remember the deputy on the loading dock?"

"Yes, and I'd still like to know why a deputy would be there."

"I found out those two men bound Deputy Bidwell with packing tape and left him all night in the warehouse."

The women gasped.

Maxwell took another muffin. "The sheriff is trying to get a lead on them. I don't know if he's had any success." He looked up at the rumble of a small diesel engine. A fifteen-passenger van edged along the lane and came to stop near the administration building's entrance. The banner strung along the side of the van displayed Simon's name and face.

Miriam Kroft hustled out the lobby door with a clipboard. While residents began to line up for a ride to the high school to vote, the driver took a walk around the vehicle and kicked its tires.

Frances stepped to the porch rail. "The driver looks like one of the movers."

Maxwell joined her. His chest tightened at the recognition. "We need to call the sheriff."

"I'll call." Ada hurried into the house. She soon returned. "I left a message with dispatch to send him to the high school. He's out on a call."

Gwen grabbed her purse. "Let's go. Maybe we can meet the sheriff at the school and clue him in before the van gets there."

Maxwell knew the five of them would not fit easily into Ada's sedan, but he squeezed into the back seat with Janet and Frances. With Ada strapped into the front passenger seat, Gwen squealed out the gate and sped down the road.

33

The day after Neil returned from his trip to Syracuse, his secretary advised him Jackie Senak stood in the outer office. He went to the door with a rock in the pit of his stomach. He had not expected a second meeting.

Jackie had demanded an explanation for his visit to her office.

He'd explained his concerns for the residents at Willowdell, stating, "There have been several unexplained deaths. Some of the victims, possibly all, were represented by your firm."

Jackie had taken a few notes and unceremoniously walked him to the door with what he assumed had been a dismissal of the matter.

He drew in a slow, deep breath, then opened the door to his office. "Come in. Have a seat." She sat in one of the brown leather chairs, and he returned to his chair behind his desk. "I didn't expect to see you."

"I thought about what you told me. About the residents at the retirement village." She looked professional, wearing a light gray skirt and matching jacket. A subtle shadow deepened the blue of her eyes, and her lips and cheeks had been dusted with a pale blush. "I realized more fully what you were implying, and I don't want you or anyone to believe Mr. Bigelow and I do not act in our clients' best interest."

Neil gave her a slight nod.

"I reviewed Simon Hilton's personal accounts, along with the records of his real estate transactions. I found nothing illegal." She pulled a file from her leather bag. "I also did some research and found the four residents you mentioned were each represented by our firm. I found nothing amiss in their files. They signed the agreement authorizing us to handle all their legal matters."

"What about their estates? I understand they listed no living relatives."

"The information I have is privileged in its details, but I will tell you, their estates have for the most part gone to various charities. Minus our fees, and I make no apology for that." She pulled out a paper and handed it to him. "Our fees schedule."

He checked her ring finger, then checked himself.

The fees charged by Bigelow and Senak were comparable to the fees he would expect any attorney practicing in a metropolitan area to charge. Although when he recalled the location of their office, he wondered where the firm invested its profits.

"We charge the fees to Willowdell per our agreement with the owner, Simon Hilton. How he secures those fees from the resident is out of our control and oversight."

"You said 'for the most part.'"

"Yes, there are the occasional provisions for those who played a special role in a resident's life, for example a close friend, a beloved teacher, a church affiliation, etcetera. For my part, I spend time with each resident who signs on with our firm and make a thorough study of how they wish for their assets to be disbursed."

"I see." He handed the paper back to her. "You said something about Hilton's personal accounts."

She glanced to the side and bit her lip. Neil understood. If it came to Simon Hilton's attention that his attorney had disclosed information regarding his personal accounts without his authorization, her license to practice law could be challenged.

"I'm sorry," he said. "I'm not going to ask you to share anything you shouldn't. I won't place you in that position."

A slight curve of her lips made his pulse race. She returned the file to her bag and rose. "I will say this. Although Mr. Hilton's accounts reflect no illegal activity, they still may be something someone should look into."

Neil stopped his expression from revealing his curiosity and stood. "I appreciate you making the trip. And I appreciate whatever information you can give me." He walked her to the door. "Perhaps we could meet for dinner sometime. Unless you're married—or something."

She stiffened. Her eyes went cold. "My husband died in Afghanistan."

A knot caught in his throat. "I'm sorry."

She spit the words, "Everyone is sorry. Except the killers responsible." Her hands shook while she fumbled with the strap of her purse.

Neil felt like an idiot, causing her pain.

Jackie swallowed and shook her head. "I'm sorry. The frustration, the injustice is always right there, under the surface. The senselessness of it all."

He opened the door, resisting the urge to say he understood.

She reached to shake his hand. "Goodbye. I hope I have restored your faith in Bigelow and Senak. Please let me know if there is anything else."

He shook her hand and hoped there would be something else.

Ada scanned the parking lot at Sackets Harbor High School from the passenger seat of the Volvo but did not see the sheriff or his cruiser. She bit her lower lip. Did dispatch convey her message?

Near the glass front doors, Simon Hilton grinned his way around the voters, shaking hands and slapping backs in an obvious attempt to gain last minute support.

"Where's the sheriff?" Frances's tone reflected her own anxiety.

"What should we do?" Maxwell said from the backseat. "I mean, if the law doesn't show up?"

Gwen unbuckled her seatbelt. "We need a plan."

In silence, it seemed everyone searched their grids for a workable strategy to detain the driver until the sheriff or a deputy arrived.

Janet, wedged between Frances and Maxwell, shifted her weight. "Maybe we should put in another call for help."

Frances agreed. "To 911 this time."

Gwen got out her cell phone.

They turned their heads at the low rumble of an engine. Ada groaned within herself. *Where is the law? Did the governor defund the police in Sackets Harbor too?*

Maxwell opened his door and got out.

Frances leaned over Janet and looked up at him. "Do you have a plan?"

"Maybe."

Ada exited the car and stood beside him. "What do you think?"

"If you ladies could draw the driver away from the van and somehow keep him distracted, then I could at least keep the van from leaving. That might keep the driver from leaving."

The driver waited for the Willowdell residents to get out of the van, then he drove to a corner of the lot and parked in the shade. He walked back toward the school and sat on a bench beneath a maple tree.

Janet and Frances listened to Max's instructions then approached him.

Sheriff Leo Meriday entered the station, wiping his brow with a handkerchief. He hated domestic calls. The dispute that called him away had been resolved peacefully, but it left him drained.

His eyes swept the desks and cubicles. "Sloan, where's Bidwell?"

"Report of a fire at the shipyard. He went to check it out."

Meriday grumbled, "Again the shipyard." He entered his office and closed the door. On his desk sat a small box. After pouring himself a cup of coffee, he plunked down in his chair, sliced through the shipping tape, and opened the flaps.

"What the blazes?" A blue glass bird peeked out of a nest of napkins from a local pizza parlor. A scribbled line on one napkin read, "My owner is a murderer."

He had no clue to the sender, but he had no doubt of the owner.

Sloan entered with a tap on the door. "Meant to give this to you. The call came in about twenty minutes ago." His deputy handed him a note.

Female reports moving man driving van. High school. States urgent. Meriday scowled. "What does that mean, *moving man driving van?*"

"No clue." Sloan motioned toward the blue bird. "What's that?"

Meriday smirked. "That, Sloan, is a red herring."

Ada stood by the car watching Frances and Janet approach the mover.

Gwen stepped up beside her. "What if that man recognizes Frances from the warehouse?"

"Let's trust he didn't see her there." Ada turned to Gwen, feeling anxious. "What did the 911 dispatcher say? Is the sheriff on his way?"

Gwen crinkled her green eyes. "I didn't call 911."

Ada's heart leaped into her throat. "But I saw you on your phone. I assumed you were calling 911."

"But you already talked to the sheriff's office. I called the contractors." Gwen tucked her phone into the back pocket of her jeans. "There's a leak in the upper bathroom, and I just remembered. We left the house this morning on an impulse."

Ada looked toward the bench, fighting the panic rising in her chest. Janet worked to charm the driver with jokes and laughter, but the man would have none of it. He leaped up and hurried away from them into the school.

"Come on." Ada grabbed Gwen's arm. Seconds later, the four women entered the front doors and stood in the terrazzo tiled lobby, searching the crowd for the man Ada had spoken to outside Nita Beavers's bungalow, the man Frances and

Maxwell saw loading furniture at the warehouse, the man who detained and bound deputy Bidwell.

Max sat on a bench in the sun, bouncing a knee while Frances and Janet talked to the driver. It had been a long time since he looked under a hood, but how complicated could it be?

The driver had parked the van with the front tucked beneath an arbor of trees, leaving the hood hidden and yet accessible. Max waited for the opportunity and prayed for three things: the ability to render the van inoperable, God's forgiveness pre-offense, and the sheriff's swift arrival.

The stocky, unshaven driver shot off the bench and hustled toward the school. Ada and Gwen raced to Frances and Janet, and the four women entered the school on the man's heels.

Maxwell glanced over his shoulders, then sauntered toward the van. Feeling about, he found the latch and lifted the hood a few inches.

A queasiness invaded Ada's stomach. They were chasing a felon at her directive. A man who would bind a deputy with packing tape and leave him for who knew how long would not hesitate to attack them.

"Where did he go?" Frances scanned the halls with her hands on her hips. "In a voting booth?"

"Let's try the men's restroom," Janet said.

Gwen ran a hand through her frizzed hair. "This is ridiculous. Let's go outside and wait for the sheriff."

Ada heard muffled voices. She peeked around the corner

and saw the owner of Willowdell standing with the driver, his face no longer grinning but distorted in anger.

Hilton spit out the words, "I told you to get a different driver."

"Don't worry. That deputy won't be anywhere near here today."

"You better hope he stays away until you get these votes back to Willowdell and disappear." Simon Hilton stormed toward the gymnasium, where the polling booths were set up and a smile, no doubt, would spring to his face.

The mover entered the men's room.

"Come on," Ada said. "We have to keep him in there until the sheriff gets here."

Gwen crossed her arms. "How do you intend to do that?"

Janet and Frances abandoned Gwen and hurried to the restroom door behind Ada. Janet turned her back to the closed door and stretched out her arms and legs in the frame. "He won't get past me."

The door opened. Janet stiffened and stared wide-eyed at Ada.

The scraggy-faced man sneered. "What do you think you're doing?"

Frances stepped forward and spoke through Janet's upraised arms. "We're doing what you did to that deputy. We're detaining you."

"That's funny." The man's face did not reflect humor. Nor did the fire in his dark eyes convey fear. He shoved Janet into Frances, they stumbled into Ada, and the three of them tumbled to the floor.

Gwen gasped, and when the man hustled past her, she gave chase.

Ada, Frances, and Janet struggled to their feet and, ignoring the odd stares of primary voters, rushed outside. They arrived at the van, panting, and joined Gwen and Maxwell in remonstrating the driver while he tried in vain to start the motor.

The sheriff's cruiser pulled into the lot and, with a spurt of its siren, drew up behind the van.

34

The following morning, Neil left Greenbrier Inn and drove toward the sheriff's office. Rain pummeled his windshield while thunder rumbled in the dark clouds and lightning flashed over the lake.

As he drove along the marina highway, the smell of smoke filtered into his BMW. He followed the acrid odor into the shipyard, parked, and scanned the charred remains of what had been the fabrication building.

Boarded and abandoned after the closure of Kroft's business, the building had sat empty for nearly three years. What, after all this time, could have brought it to ashes?

Could the same person who set this fire have set the fire in Judge Fausset's garage?

Guilt made his gut wrench. He had come to believe the judge had been absentminded, yet staring at the ashes he wondered if he had labeled him unfairly.

"Yes, I know Simon Hilton won the primary yesterday. And I appreciate your position but—" Leo Meriday tapped his fingers on his desk while Judge Nelson argued on the other end of the phone line. Heat traveled up his neck. "I understand a possible fallout, but I still have an ongoing investigation into the deaths of four people at his facility. And frankly, I believe we have enough cause to warrant a search."

Bidwell stood near the door with his thumbs tucked into his belt. A rap sounded behind him. He opened the door, and Neil Tibbs stuck his head in.

Meriday waved him toward a chair and spoke firmly into the phone. "You have to agree some unhealthy stuff has been going on at that retirement village." He listened with a clenched jaw. "Look, Judge. No disrespect, but the residents signed up for assisted living, not assisted dying."

At last, the sheriff heard the words he had been wanting to hear for weeks. He thanked the reluctant judge and hung up wanting to shout hallelujah. Perhaps if he had been alone, he would have, but he simply said, "He'll sign."

Bidwell tipped his blond crewcut and left the office.

Meriday would swear a smile nearly emerged from the deputy's wooden face. He turned to Tibbs. "What's on your mind?"

"I hope that phone call will take care of the matter on my mind. I wanted to suggest a search of Simon Hilton's personal accounts. There may be a link to the deaths of the four residents at Willowdell."

"In what way?" Meriday stood and poured another stream of coffee into his bulldog mug. "Coffee?"

"No, thanks. I don't know exactly." Tibbs quickly added, "I'm not saying Hilton's directly involved in their deaths, but that he may have profited financially by them."

Meriday returned to his chair. "I can promise you our team

will go over every jot and tittle in that office for anything that would indicate a motive. And that includes Hilton's personal accounts. But even if Hilton profited, it doesn't mean he's guilty of a crime."

"Understood." Tibbs ran a hand through his hair. "There's one other thing. I noticed the fabrication building at the shipyard is now a pile of smoldering ash. What caused the fire?"

"Arson. Bidwell stayed at the scene yesterday for several hours."

"What's going on out there? The assault on your deputy and now arson."

"We have the man Bidwell identified as his captor. His name's George Tuttle. The taxpayers are currently providing him with room and board. He couldn't have started that fire. It's likely his partner did, but Tuttle's dropping no names."

"You do know Simon Hilton owns the shipyard, right?"

Meriday picked up a folder and scanned inside. "Ontario Developers is listed as the property owner."

"Simon Hilton is Ontario Developers."

Meriday felt a tingle at the base of his neck. *Interesting.* He tossed the folder aside, knocking the blue bird to the floor.

Tibbs picked it up. "I'm afraid its beak is chipped." He set it on the desk.

"Miriam Kroft won't like that." Meriday slid the incriminating napkin toward him. "She won't like it, either, when I tell her she's been fingered for murder."

Tibbs frowned at the scrawled message on the napkin. "Any idea who wrote it?"

Meriday chuckled. "The one woman who thinks she's clever. Ada Whittaker."

Ada knelt in the grass beside Frances's flowerbed, deadheading marigolds. She expected her sister to return later that day to once again take up residence in her own bungalow, and Ada wanted all to appear well tended.

Although no determination of foul play had been made regarding the deaths at Willowdell, the arrest of George Tuttle had brought both sisters some relief. They agreed Frances would return home with the stipulation that Ada would remain with her, until the sheriff had the person he referred to as the death collector in custody.

A scuffing sound caught Ada's attention.

Samantha Milsap sniffed while she plodded past number eight with her shoulders slumped and her head bent low. She continued dolefully toward the lake.

That was odd. The young woman should be happy. Simon Hilton won the primary, and he seemed likely to go on to win the seat in the New York State Senate.

Samantha sat on a bench nearly hidden by the weeping branches of a willow tree near the shoreline.

Ada felt compelled to check on the girl. She removed her garden gloves and climbed to her feet, brushing grass and dirt from her denim skirt. She walked prayerfully toward the lake. Samantha had issues, and Ada felt a few wise words fitly spoken could help her address them.

Not wanting to startle the young woman weeping with her face in her hands, Ada nearly whispered, "Samantha?"

Her head jerked up. She picked up the front of her skirt and dried her eyes and sniffed. "Oh, Miss Whittaker. Alison is in the office if you need something."

Ada slipped down on the bench and waited patiently for Samantha to collect herself. A minute later, the simpering stopped. All that could be heard were the gulls squawking as they glided in figure eights over the lake.

"I'm sorry." Samantha again dabbed her eyes with the front of her skirt.

"Something has upset you." Ada looked at her red-rimmed, pale green eyes.

"It shouldn't have. I should have known." Samantha gazed at the lake.

Ada tilted her head. "What should you have known?"

"He didn't need me. I tried to believe he did, to believe I was important to him."

"Mr. Hilton?"

"Yes. Simon. He played all sweet to Alison and that silly cow, Miriam. Saying they were his 'source of strength,' and without them he 'may not have won the primary.' Nothing for me. Not one word. I set up all the advertising. I fielded all the phone calls. I did nine hundred things he has no clue about, and I don't even get a thank you."

No doubt, Simon had no qualms taking advantage of Samantha's weaknesses.

"I'm a fool. A stupid fool."

"We all act foolishly on occasion, but that does not make us a fool." Ada sensed the opportunity to bring up an important matter. "No more than losing a box of chocolates makes someone a loser."

Samantha Milsap dropped her gaze to her feet and a moment later said, "I'm sorry. Simon really upset me the day I delivered Mrs. Ferrell's report. When I saw the box on the table ... well ... chocolate makes me feel better." Samantha looked at her. "I promise I won't do it again. Please don't tell Simon."

"I wouldn't think of it. But I will hold you to your promise."

"I'd better get back."

Not until Ada finished the interview. "Did you happen to share the chocolates with anyone?"

"No. But someone has been taking them. I keep them in the drawer beneath the counter in the lobby."

Ada's pulse raced. "Any idea who?"

"Probably that greedy Miriam. But I suppose Alison could have. Or the cleaners. Anyone really. I don't keep the drawer locked."

"Simon Hilton?"

Samantha again looked at her feet, and Ada knew the girl would continue to protect the reputation of her beloved scoundrel.

Maxwell led Stanley along the walking trail that wound through the woods behind the upper level of bungalows. He'd recently begun to bring Stanley to this least used trail and let him freely run and sniff and chase the wind.

Max paused a hundred feet in and removed the leash from the spaniel's collar. Stanley ran in circles, jumped fallen logs, and barked at squirrels while Maxwell sucked in the scents of pine, honeysuckle, and mold.

After a few minutes, Stanley returned in response to his call and submitted to the reattachment of the leash. Maxwell gave the dog a treat and ruffled his coat. "Good boy. The more you obey, the more freedom I'll give you."

"Yoo-hoo, Max." The screech hailed from somewhere within the woods. He turned, scanning the trees and bushes until he spotted Gladys beyond a cluster of cottonwoods, waving him over.

What is she doing?

He heaved a sigh. "Come on, Stan Boy. We better find out." They tramped over leaves and pine needles, dodged saplings and thornbushes, and arrived at the looming cottonwood where Selma Potter knelt on the ground in front of her mother.

Selma beamed up at him. "Look what Mother found."

"Don't touch it," Gladys scolded.

Max stepped closer. "What is it?"

Selma's eyes sparked. "A tape recorder. And there's a tape in it."

"Happened upon it when we were searching for raspberries." Gladys pointed to the empty plastic pail at Selma's feet.

"I thought you were determined to stay in your house," Maxwell said, eyeing Gladys keenly.

"The sheriff is finally looking where he needs to look. All eyes will soon be on the true killer, and the pointy heads won't be yammering lies about me anymore."

Maxwell gave a slight nod yet remained clueless.

"Get up now, Selma." Gladys looked to him. "What should we do?"

Selma rolled onto her hands and knees with a groan.

Maxwell dropped Stanley's leash and assisted Selma to her feet. While she brushed dirt off her knees, he considered Gladys's question. His first instinct said leave the tape recorder where they found it. Obviously, someone put it there for a reason. His second instinct left him curious about the reason.

"Well, Max?" Gladys said.

Selma fanned her flushed face. "Let's play it."

Maxwell shrugged, then picked up the hand-size recorder expecting the battery to be dead. He brushed it off and pushed *play*. A screech pierced the air and sent a chill surging up his spine.

Selma slapped her hands over her ears.

Stanley yelped until Max snapped off the machine.

"Other than giving one's nerves a jostle," Gladys said, "I

don't see the purpose in that. Let's go, Selma. I'm hungry. And bring the bucket."

Selma snatched up the pail and followed her mother through the woods back to the trail.

Max slid the recorder into the pocket of his cargo pants.

35

"Mrs. Kroft is at her art class, Sheriff." Meriday recognized the voice and turned from the front door of number twelve. Ada Whittaker stood on the sidewalk. Short strands of ivory hair jetted out from beneath her pink straw hat. "Mr. Kroft is likely helping out the maintenance department."

He stepped off the porch. "Perhaps it's best that I speak with you first."

"Oh? Why is that?"

"A little birdie told me you have information you need to share with me." The old woman gave him a puzzled stare, and he wondered if he had been correct in his assumption that she had been the anonymous sender of the bunting. "Didn't you send a package to my office telling me to investigate Miriam Kroft for murder?"

"Mercy." Her hand went to her throat. "I would never cast an accusation of that nature on anyone, and I would never interfere with your investigation in that way."

No, but you would in a dozen other ways.

"Sheriff?" Maxwell Bailey stepped out from around the corner of the Kroft bungalow. "I have something to show you."

Meriday crossed his arms over his chest. "What might that be?"

Bailey looked around and focused on Gladys Blumm's gray bungalow before saying, "Not here."

"Come sit on the porch. I'll pour lemonade." Ada trotted across the square.

A minute later, Leo Meriday sank into a cushioned chair on the front porch of Frances Ferrell's bungalow. His feet thanked him. He waited for Ada to bring the lemonade and Bailey to take his dog home and return.

Wonder what he's got. Better be something good. The investigation was going nowhere. Maybe his team going over the Willowdell records would come up with something. *A motive would be helpful.*

Bailey arrived, and Ada set a tray of drinks on the table. "What do you have, Maxwell?" She passed out the glasses.

He reached into his pocket and pulled out a tape recorder. "Gladys and Selma found this half buried beneath a pile of leaves in the woods behind the upper bungalows."

He pushed *play.*

The taped hoots and screeches of an owl smacked Meriday with the image of an old man in pajamas meandering deeper and deeper into the forest. "That's enough. Shut it off and don't touch it again." He turned to Ada. "Do you have a Ziploc bag?"

"You think it's evidence?" Her eyes wagon-wheeled with curiosity.

"Mr. Compton taught ornithology at Cornell University," Meriday said. "We've always believed he wandered into the woods in search of an owl. This tape may indicate someone deliberately used the sound of a screech owl to lure him, not merely into the woods but to his death."

"But who would know about his past profession?" Bailey said.

"Oh, my, everyone knows everything about everyone here." Ada frowned. "Does the tape *prove* malicious intent?"

"No." Meriday rubbed his chin. "But it certainly points that way."

She shook her head. "That poor man. Why would someone do such a cruel thing?"

"That is the question." Meriday picked up his glass and drained it.

With the evidence of premeditation bagged for the lab and refills of lemonade poured, Ada turned once more to Sheriff Meriday. "To answer your earlier question, I did not send the blue bunting to your office. I do, however, know who did. Gladys Blumm."

Meriday tossed his hands in the air. "Does she think I have time for games?"

"Now, now." Ada held up a hand. "Let me try to explain. Gladys has been sitting alone in her room for weeks, sulking over the suspicions and rumors people have spread about her. I'm sure she has imagined and contrived all sorts of possible scenarios."

Meriday noisily emptied his lungs.

Ada hurried to her point. "Gladys found the brochure regarding the primary and Simon Hilton's bid for the senate on her kitchen counter. Someone—I assume Gladys but perhaps Selma—had drawn a mustache on Simon's face. But that's neither here nor there."

The sheriff tapped his fingers on the table.

Maxwell chimed in. "Gladys believes Miriam Kroft entered her home, left the brochure on the counter, and planted peanut oil in her pantry."

"And Gladys believes that's when Miriam took Selma's necklace," Ada said. "Believing it belonged to Gladys, Miriam planted it on Wendall's patio for you to find. But of course, you didn't. Frances did."

A vein pulsed in Leo Meriday's neck.

"It's all conjecture, of course." Ada offered the sheriff more lemonade.

He declined and squinted at her. "Gladys Blumm sent the bird to my office?"

"I'm afraid so."

"And Mrs. Kroft had access to Mrs. Blumm's pantry?"

"Yes," Maxwell said, "but so did any one of the residents. Gladys never locks her door in the daytime."

The sheriff released a long sigh then rose and picked up the plastic bag. "Come down to the station. We need your prints to compare with any others that may be on this."

Maxwell nodded. "I'll be right there."

When Meriday drove away, Ada turned to Maxwell. "I call it providential, you being there when Gladys found the recorder."

"Either that or we are two of the biggest dupes in Sackets Harbor."

Ada peered at him. "What do you mean?"

Maxwell fidgeted with his glass. "Likely, Gladys knew I would be there. I've been taking Stanley to the upper trail every morning between nine thirty and ten for the last two weeks."

"You can't think Gladys intentionally placed the recorder there and wanted it to be found."

"To deflect suspicion,"—he lifted a shoulder— "maybe she did."

"What reason did Gladys give for being in the woods this morning?"

"Raspberries. Gladys wanted Selma to help her pick berries. But I've never seen raspberry bushes in that area. And their pail was empty."

Ada leaned back. "I don't like what you're saying."

"I don't like it either. But Gladys could have planted the evidence herself. The peanut oil. The necklace. The recorder. All in an effort to convince the sheriff she's being framed."

"But those deaths ... What possible motive could Gladys have?"

"I know, I know. I'm being stupid. I guess I'm getting paranoid." He flashed a smile that never reached his eyes. "I'm even beginning to doubt Stanley."

36

Two days later, while on her power walk, Ada collided with Alison Vaughn when they both rounded a bend that led to the golf course. Alison came from the opposite direction, staring at her cell phone and walking a copper-colored papillon on a leash.

"I'm sorry, Miss Whittaker. I got distracted wanting to post a picture of Annie."

Ada smiled at the dog. "Is she yours? She's very cute."

"No, she belongs to Judge Fausset. Her official name is Annie Oakley. He just got her. I guess he wanted a watchdog. You know, with the fire at his place and all. I'm trying to teach her to obey simple commands."

Ada wondered how Alison intended to communicate commands to the dog through text messaging. "I didn't know Willowdell provided dog training."

"The center doesn't, but when I saw how cute Annie is, I couldn't resist offering to walk her. I used to work at the animal shelter before I came here, and I have some experience training." Alison bent down and smoothed the papillon's coat.

"How interesting. I imagine training dogs could be quite rewarding."

"Yes. I loved it. But someone convinced me it would be more rewarding to work with the residents here."

"And is it?"

Alison's brown eyes darted to the left before saying, "It has its rewards. I'd better get Annie Oakley back to the judge. Have a good one." Alison and Annie trotted off and disappeared around the bend.

Ada regretted not asking if she had misplaced her dog whistle.

Frances Ferrell stepped out of the pool, draped a towel around her waist, and moved to a lounge chair. The sun streaked through the glass panels overhead and warmed her skin. She mentally relaxed every muscle, and tension reluctantly surrendered.

She closed her eyes and rested in the peace of having the pool to herself. Her thoughts drifted to Max, and her lips formed a faint and gentle smile. They had enjoyed some time together since her return to Willowdell two days ago—walking, talking. Sharing their stories.

A heavy door slammed and jarred her alert.

She leaned forward and searched the pool area behind her. "Hello?" No one answered. Goosebumps trickled up her arms. Someone had been there. She held her breath and listened. The water rippled near the pool's jet streams.

She grabbed her coverup and slipped it on while she hurried toward the locker room. The adjacent door marked *Maintenance Personnel Only* opened, and Duncan Kroft stood directly in front of her.

He gave her a quick scan. "Hope I didn't startle you."

Frances spun and bolted.

Ada stood at the counter in the admin building talking to Samantha Milsap until Frances burst into the lobby from the direction of the pool, her face drained of color.

"Mercy, Frances, are you all right? Didn't you bring clothes to change into?"

Frances passed by Ada and hurried away without a pause.

"I do hope she's not coming down with something." Ada looked out the lobby glass door until Frances reached the porch of her bungalow, then turned back to the counter.

"Maybe the exercise upset her stomach." Samantha placed a book of stamps on the counter. "It always does mine. Is there anything else?"

Ada leaned to the side and looked around Samantha to the open door of Simon Hilton's office. Two men in suits and a woman with sleek, blond hair stood, scanning files. "Mr. Hilton has had a great deal of company the last two days, but I've not seen *him*."

The manager stiffened. "If there's nothing else."

The woman stepped out of Hilton's office with her hands on her hips. "Miss Milsap." She spoke to Samantha's back. "We are still waiting on the records from Harbor State Bank. Please contact them again. Tell them to send a courier with the files now, unless they want the sheriff to pick them up. But remind them, it may not give their customers confidence to see the sheriff walk out of their bank with a box of records under his arm." The woman turned away.

Samantha blew a raspberry over her shoulder.

Ada ducked out the door.

Neil tapped his fingers on his desk and stared at his cell phone. He wanted to reach out to Jackie Senak but couldn't create a convincing reason for his call. The Syracuse attorney tended to see right through him.

Maybe that was the problem. Maybe he should be upfront and not try to manipulate matters. Embarrassment again swept over him when he recalled their first meeting.

"I could simply tell her the truth, the true reason for my call. That I'd like to see her. Get to know her. All she can do is hang up."

He reached for his phone. It rang before he could find her in his contacts. At the sight of the caller ID, he sucked in some air, held it to the count of four, and let it out.

"Hey, Jackie. I was about to—"

Her voice sounded muffled.

His throat tightened. "What's wrong? Where are you?"

37

Duncan Kroft spotted him in the corner of the library reading the day's edition of the *Ontario Times*. "Looking for advice to the lovelorn, Max?" The old man with the eggshell mustache snickered.

Having his space invaded and his peace interrupted, Maxwell folded the paper and tossed it back on the reading table.

"Up for shuffleboard?" Kroft said.

"No, thanks. I can't take defeat."

"I get it. How about archery? But I warn you, the wife and I have been getting some coaching along those lines. I boast not, but I'm pretty good at that too."

Maxwell glanced at the arrogant archer. He wasn't eager to spend time with Duncan Kroft, but he grew restless inside his four walls. Neither could he hang out at number eight all day. He stood. "Sure. Show me what a great marksman you are."

With a grin, Duncan smacked his back. "You're a brave man."

No, just bored.

Minutes later, Max waited while Duncan lifted his bow and took aim at a target approximately thirty yards away, his arm steady, his grip strong. The arrow flew straight to the bull's-eye. After five more shots with similar results, Kroft cackled like a shameless hustler. "Your turn."

Maxwell hesitated. He had not touched a bow or an arrow until this moment. Clumsily he placed the arrow on the bow and lifted it. He gave the area a quick scan in case he missed the target entirely. In the distance, Judge Fausset walked a small dog.

He lowered the bow. "I better not. I might hit the judge."

"Wouldn't be so terrible if you did. The old rot."

"Why do you say that?" Maxwell wondered at the bitterness in Kroft's voice.

"A few years back, when the economy flatlined, I had to sell my company. Forced into bankruptcy. The judge had purchased a couple boats from me over the years, so I asked him for advice." Kroft scowled at the dog walker. "When some developer wanted to buy the shipyard and the twenty-eight acres it sits on, Fausset advised me to take the offer before filing bankruptcy." He tipped his head. "Come on. I've had enough."

They gathered the equipment and walked toward the recreation center.

"That was a good thing, wasn't it? Selling the property first?"

"I took a huge loss with the selling price. But the only bid came from Ontario Developers." Kroft placed the archery equipment in its designated place and closed the door. "I found out later the two-faced Simon Hilton *is* Ontario Developers. Then I knew why there were no other offers."

"He's that powerful?"

"His father is. He's in the State Department." Kroft made a face. "What do you say to a stop at the café?"

"Sure." After decades of listening to people's problems, Maxwell could sense when a man needed to talk. He sauntered beside him. "So, you think Judge Fausset benefited somehow from the deal?"

"No. I don't know. He seemed genuine. Like he wanted to advise me and Miriam in the best way he could. But honestly, Max, I tend not to trust anyone even remotely linked to Simon Hilton."

Where did that leave Miriam?

That evening, Ada and Frances walked to the rec center and found few chairs available. It seemed nearly everyone at Willowdell had turned out for bingo and the chance to win the coveted prize, a five-day cruise along the Saint Lawrence Seaway.

Miriam Kroft occupied the chair beneath the ceiling fan. Short tendrils of her black bouffant flipped about her neck while a red-lined smile danced on her face.

"Max is waving us over." Frances pointed across the tables. Duncan Kroft vacated a chair next to Maxwell and moved to the seat beside Miriam.

Ada had felt somewhat relieved when Frances agreed to come out. The experience with Duncan Kroft at the pool had frightened her sister and made her hesitant to leave the bungalow.

They greeted Maxwell and settled in the chairs beside him.

Alison Vaughn bounded up the steps to the platform. She tapped the microphone and sent a screech through the speakers, jolting everyone to attention. She grinned and yelled her usual call to order, "Are you ready for some bingo?"

Cheers erupted.

"Tonight, some lucky winner—and a guest—will win a fabulous five-day, four-night cruise aboard the fabulous *Canadian Empress!* And ..." Alison paused to read her notes. "...explore the beauty and history of the fabulous Thousand Islands."

Cheers again.

"Isn't it fabulous?" Frances asked Max.

"Apparently so." He winked at Frances, and Ada caught the sparkle in his eyes.

Frances suddenly sobered. "I hope I don't win."

Ada looked askance. "Don't be silly. Why?"

"I don't want to have to choose a guest." Frances's slate gray eyes glanced from Ada to Maxwell and back to Ada.

"Well, don't choose me," Ada said. "I have no intention of going on a cruise. If I win, the prize goes to Gwen and Janet. They would love a cruise."

"You think they could get along for five days?" Maxwell chuckled.

Frances shook her head. "One of them would surely end up overboard."

"I confess, my concern would be for myself. I consider Janet and Gwen my girls, and I wonder if I could get along for five days without them."

Frances touched Ada's arm. "You'll always have me."

Ada smiled, knowing "always" would be until her sister and Maxwell Bailey admitted to themselves what seemed obvious to others.

Someone tapped her shoulder.

Samantha Milsap leaned down and whispered. "I'm sorry, Miss Whittaker, the tournament is limited to residents."

"Oh my. Yes, of course. I understand." Ada left the table and took a seat along the wall with the other spectators.

Alison called out the first combination. The tournament was underway, and Frances gave her full attention to both her card and Maxwell's, while Ada scanned the tables. *Selma Potter?* How was it Selma was allowed to participate?

Ada located Samantha, perched near the door scrolling her cell phone. She marched over. "Samantha."

The girl jumped and blurted, "I'm sorry, I don't make the rules."

"About those rules. How is it Selma Potter is participating in the tournament?"

Samantha wiped her hands on her skirt. "By proxy. Gladys Blumm authorized Mrs. Potter to play on her behalf."

A text message pinged Ada's phone. She pillaged her tote bag while she moved outside for privacy. The message from Neil read:

Please check on judge. Trying to reach for two hours. No answer. Odd. Back late tonight. Please advise ASAP.

She had not seen Judge Fausset at the tournament, and now she wondered why. She tottered a bit, trying to text and walk, but sent a message saying she would be glad to and not to worry.

She tucked away her phone and picked up her pace.

38

Ada rang the doorbell at number three, the former bungalow of Luty Mae Mears. Annie Oakley yipped, but the noise yielded no response from the dog's owner. She tried the side door of the garage. Locked. A peek in the window revealed the judge's pickup truck and his car.

Ada walked around the bungalow to the patio and knocked on the back door. Again, Annie barked, but still no sound from the judge. Sheer curtains blocked her view. She turned the knob, and with equal measures of relief and fear she found it unlocked.

"Judge Fausset? Are you home?" She inched inside. The papillon quieted when Ada soothed the creature with a soft voice and light touch.

A cell phone on the kitchen counter struck up with *Stars and Stripes Forever*. Neil calling again, undoubtedly. Next to the phone lay a small brown box.

Her breath caught. How did the judge get a box of Hegler chocolates? When she found the wrapper near the garage, she'd believed it had been tossed by whoever was behind Luty Mae's death. Now, she wondered.

Stars and Stripes Forever ended with a crescendo, and she prowled circumspectly through the bungalow. "Judge? Ada Whittaker here."

Mumbling emanated, according to the typical bungalow layout, from the bathroom. She called through the door. "Are you all right?"

He coughed. "I've fallen and I can't get up."

"Mercy. Are you bleeding?"

"Call 911. But no lights. No sirens, tell them."

She pushed the alert on her phone and advised the responder of the address and the situation and made it clear there were to be no lights or sirens. Ada spoke through the door. "They will be here soon. Can I do anything for you?"

"Yes, when they get here, turn the other way. You know, 'naked came I into the world' and all."

"Neil has been trying to reach you. I should let him know."

"Don't tell him about this. I suspect he believes my diminishing capacity caused the fire. This may confirm his suspicions."

"I understand." She did understand. Neil's concerns were not what worried the judge, but the threat to his independence these situations inevitably evoked. Ada sent a text to Neil.

> Judge at home. No worries.

At times like this, the less said the better. Minutes later the doorbell rang, and Annie resumed yelping. The front door opened. Two paramedics charged in, and Ada pointed toward the bathroom.

She picked up Annie Oakley and turned her back.

Relief swept over Neil when he read the text from Ada. "The judge is home. He's fine." He returned his phone to his pocket. "I think the unsolved mysteries at Willowdell are keeping me a bit on edge."

"Of course. You should be concerned." Jackie Senak sat across the table from him outside the pizza parlor. The smell of garlic and oregano hung in the early evening air. "Why didn't he answer your calls?"

When Jackie had called earlier, Neil agreed to meet her. Miles from Sackets Harbor, he remembered he had previously accepted the judge's invitation to join him for steaks and a game of chess.

"Ada didn't say." He leaned his elbows on the table. "Now, back to your mystery."

"Look," she touched his hand, "I appreciate you changing your plans and meeting with me. I didn't know what else to do."

"I'm glad you called. Truth is, I intended to call you." Normally confident and assertive, his sheepishness bothered him. He prided himself of being in control, but with Jackie, he wilted. It had been some time since he loved a woman, but not so long that he didn't recognize the symptoms.

His pulse raced until she pulled back her hand and picked up her cola.

"What are you thinking about?" she said. "You drifted off somewhere."

He quickly shifted his thoughts to a safer subject. "The call you overheard this morning. Do you know who was on the other end?"

"Not exactly. When Mr. Bigelow—"

"Wait. He's your law partner. Why so formal?"

Her eyes steeled. "Can we focus on the Willowdell matter?"

Neil lifted his hands, and she went on, "When *my partner* stepped out for a few minutes, I took a look at the recent calls on his cell phone and found the number."

"Did it link to Simon Hilton?"

"Only to Willowdell. Anyone in the office could have been on the other end."

Neil pushed aside his plate and tried to think who would be authorized to answer the phone at the retirement village.

"Later, I asked Mr. Bigelow—Raymond—if we could discuss the Willowdell account, but he said he had no time, he had to see a client." She lifted a slim shoulder. "Soon after, he left the office."

"Any idea which client?"

"No. But I heard him mention the name George Tuttle in his phone conversation. And something about a deputy. Holding or detaining a deputy. I ran a scan of our client list, and there is no one listed with that name, or a name similar."

Neil's heart pounded in his chest. George Tuttle was arrested for detaining Officer Bidwell. *What's their connection?*

She brooded. "I don't understand. We are partners like you said, but with this account I feel shut out."

He reached across the table and held her small, warm hand. "Maybe he's trying to protect you. Something illegal may be going on, and he doesn't want you involved."

Jackie gently pulled her hand away and shook her head. "I can't believe Mr. Bigelow would be involved in anything illegal. Integrity has always been important to him."

"He could have gotten lured into something. I've seen it before. Greed can bring down the best of men."

"No, I won't believe it. Not of him." She stared at the trees across the parking lot and sipped her drink.

The crease between her brows told him, regardless of what she said, Jackie Senak was not all that certain of Raymond Bigelow's integrity.

39

"Great," Max muttered as showers soaked the square. A sleepless night had left him irritable.

He poured himself another cup of coffee and grabbed two more brownies, asking himself the same question he had at 2:00 a.m., when he slogged to the pantry and grabbed a brownie mix. Why did *he* have to win the bingo tournament?

He'd joined the game solely to spend time with Frances. He had no expectation or desire to win. When he completed the winning row, he remained silent, but Frances, who had been keeping watch on both of their cards, jumped up screaming, "Bingo!" The competing residents groaned outwardly while he groaned inwardly.

It wasn't that he did not want to sail the Saint Lawrence Seaway or *take a late-night stroll on the upper deck under a million stars among a thousand islands* while soft piano music cooed in the background—as the brochure touted—but dare he ask Frances to join him? She might view the invitation as a commitment of sorts.

He cared a great deal for Frances and, admittedly, might be

falling in love with her. But was he willing to lay down his independence? For the first time in a very long time, he didn't have to answer to anyone. He felt a freedom to do what he pleased—within the realm of conscience.

Yet, he acknowledged, what pleased him was to be with Frances Ferrell.

When he reached for the leash that hung by the door, Stanley bounded across the living room. "Let's try to get my mind off this cruise thing, okay, boy?"

The dog hesitated before stepping into the lingering mist of the recent shower, but a tug of the leash altered his attitude. Stanley trotted beside his master's determined steps along the trail that wound through the woods along the lake.

While trying to keep Stanley on the path and out of the wet brush, Max prayed that God would show him what he should do. He paused and looked up through the over-arching branches at the clearing sky. "Any ideas you want to share with me?"

Silence.

Maxwell shrugged and moved on, deeper into the woods and deeper in thought. Perhaps he should do what Ada would have done and give the prize to Gwen and Janet.

A few steps later, he changed his mind. He should view this win as the will of God. After all, God could have filled any one of the resident's bingo cards. Yet, God gave the prize to him. He should go.

Lake Ontario rippled just beyond the edge of the woods. Mist rose off the water and blanketed the air with humidity. Max stepped out of the shadows and gazed at the gulls gliding over the lake.

He closed his eyes and lifted his face to the sky.

He could almost see it.

Misty sunrises. Orange sunsets. Soft melodies swaying in a

gentle sea breeze. His arm around Frances while they gazed at the waves from the upper deck of the *Canadian Empress*. Under a million stars. Among a thousand islands.

Clouds drifted over the sun and covered his face in shadows.

He moaned and turned toward home.

Ada stood beside her sister in the lobby, holding a small notebook.

"I don't have the authority to approve your plans for a memorial service, Mrs. Ferrell." Samantha Milsap walked away from the counter and spoke over her shoulder. "I understand your desire to honor the deceased, but you would need Mr. Hilton's consent."

"When will he be in?"

"No idea."

"We have the service briefly sketched," Ada said. "We can leave a copy for him to review."

The plan came to them over morning tea, when the conversation took on a somber note remembering Nita Beavers and Dorothy Kane. And that poor Mr. Compton. And Luty Mae, all alone, pinned and dying beneath her own golf cart. And, Ada thought, it would be an opportunity for the sheriff to scan the crowd for suspects.

"He left no information on when he will be back in the office."

"Well, where is he?" Frances placed a hand on her hip.

"His father called him to DC for a few days."

"Personal business?" Ada asked.

Samantha sighed loudly and fussed with the copier.

"Simon's focus is on the senate race. You shouldn't expect him to be here every day."

"He still has responsibilities to the residents," Frances said, her voice rising. "He can't simply dismiss us because he aspires to power."

The property manager turned to them with a flush. "Simon—Mr. Hilton—has no intention of abandoning the residents. His entire motivation in vying for a senate seat is for the purpose of enacting legislation that would improve the lives of New York's seniors."

Ada groaned. She pitied the young woman's propensity to glorify the man and parrot his talking points. "Mr. Hilton left you in charge. Obviously, he's confident that you can manage the property."

Samantha's face lit a brief moment then fizzled out.

"He trusts you to address the matters that come to your attention. I believe Mr. Hilton would be pleased to know you have taken the initiative and authorized a wonderful service for the dear residents who meant so much to him."

She scrunched a chubby cheek. "I don't know."

"What's the worst that could happen?" Frances lifted her hands.

Ada glared at her sister. "What is the *best* that could happen?" She smiled at Samantha. "Mr. Hilton's confidence in you would only be reinforced."

Samantha slowly returned to the counter then reached for Ada's notebook. "Let me see your plans."

"I need advice," Maxwell said when Gladys opened her front door the next day.

She waved him toward the sitting area. "Drink?"

"Yeah, sure. Thanks." A cat pressed against his ankles while he sat on the sofa decluttered of newspapers and unfolded laundry. Afternoon sunlight filtered through the sheer drapes. His neighbor no longer lived in the dark, and he knew he should feel thankful.

Gladys stared into the open refrigerator. "Pop, juice—"

"Water's good."

The cat leaped into a nearby chair.

"I saw you yesterday morning, moping down the sidewalk with Stanley. What had your chin dragging?" She poured water into a glass with ice, then reached into a cupboard and pulled out a plate.

"The cruise." Earlier he made the decision to go for it, to embrace the experience, to invite Frances to join him. But when he sat in church with Ada and Frances that morning, doubts assailed him.

He had to talk to someone.

"Congrats on the win. Selma brooded over her loss, but I couldn't be more tickled that you won." Gladys set his drink on the coffee table in front of him, along with a plate of sugar cookies.

He stared at the orange-frosted cookies faced with raisin eyes and a candy corn nose. Purple eyeglasses had been piped around the raisins.

"Syracuse orange." Gladys answered his uplifted brows. "In honor of Dorothy's birthday. I think she'd like them."

"I'm sure of it." Max reached for a cookie.

Gladys nudged the cat out of the chair and sat down. "Okay, Max. Tell me what's troubling you."

"Frances Ferrell."

She nodded slowly. "Saw it coming."

"But you don't know what the problem is. I don't know if I

should invite her to join me on the cruise. She might get the idea we're ... you know, an item."

She squinched her already crinkled face.

Max splayed his hands. "What?"

"You're being stupid. Spending five days on a cruise with Frances Ferrell doesn't mean you have to spend the rest of your life with her. 'Sides, the way I see it, it could be a practice run. You might find the woman irritating or annoying. Maybe she's OCD or ugly without makeup."

"Or," he mumbled, "I fall in love with her."

"The sooner you know the better, that's what I say."

"You make it sound so simple," he whined.

Gladys pointed to the orange cookies. "There's an undeniable truth on that plate, Max."

He ogled the orange cookies with raisin eyes and purple glasses. Coming to Gladys was a mistake. He should have stayed home and fought this tug-o-war on his own turf. Maxwell finally bit. "What truth might that be?"

She reached for a cookie. "You've got today to do your living. Like Dorothy, you may not be here tomorrow. You could get bumped off in the night."

40

Six days since the arrest of George Tuttle, and his lips remained tighter than the lid on a jar of pickles. Meriday received no explanation from him for the capture and detainment of Deputy Bidwell, nor any information on what had become of his partner.

The sheriff faced the next hurdle. He would return to Willowdell and interview Miriam Kroft. Someone, even though that someone happened to be Gladys Blumm, had accused the woman of murder.

He waited for a response to his knock on the front door of number twelve, the bungalow directly across the square from Frances Ferrell's. Receiving none, he strode around to the back patio and found Miriam Kroft at a table, huddled over a laptop computer.

She looked up and shut the cover. "If you're looking for Dunc, he's clearing the trails. He helps the maintenance department. It gives him something to do outdoors. He abhors being shut up in the bungalow."

"I'd like to speak to you," Meriday stepped up to the table.

"Of course. Can I get you a drink? Coffee, sweet tea, water, tomato juice."

"Coffee would be great. Thanks." Meriday sat at the patio table while Mrs. Kroft entered the bungalow advising him she wouldn't be more than a minute. His gaze fell to the short stack of papers resting beside the laptop.

He glanced at the door and spun the stack.

The top invoice read, King Tut Movers, LLC. He thumbed through the pile of sales invoices. Sofas, beds, chairs, tables. Light footsteps approached. He flipped the papers back.

The door opened. "I forgot to ask if you take cream or sugar. But I figure you for black, am I right?"

"Yes, ma'am. Thank you." He reached for the mug she offered.

"I hope we get some rain. Maybe it would wash away this humidity." She sat. Alarm flickered in her eyes before she turned the papers over. "How is it you think I can help you?"

"I need information, and I sensed from the start that you are one of the preeminent movers and shakers at Willowdell."

She tossed her head with theatrical gesture. "You noticed that, did you?"

"The residents respect you. They trust you." The sheriff had no evidence of his statement but had found pride-stroking often lowered defenses. "Folks open up to you and tell you things they may not want to share with law enforcement." He sipped the coffee.

Her red lips formed a Cheshire cat smile. "They do talk to me. Sometimes I hear more than I care to." Her birdlike eyes twinkled.

"Did Nita Beavers or Dorothy Kane or the other victims mention any issues they were having with another resident?" Meriday pulled his notepad out of his shirt pocket.

She sighed at the sight of it. "Really, Sheriff, I do wish you would cease your investigation. Accidents happen. The elderly are simply vulnerable. Why don't you let their poor, pathetic souls rest in peace?"

"Their souls can rest in peace after I have all the facts surrounding their deaths." He held her gaze, waiting for an answer to his question.

"Well ..." Miriam scratched her neck and pursed her lips. "Nita prattled about two things. Health and Stanley, her dog. Honestly, we couldn't even enjoy the monthly birthday celebrations because of the way she would *tsk-tsk* the cake and ice cream. And the way she bullied Samantha about her weight upset the girl terribly."

"Enough to drive Miss Milsap to seek revenge?"

Miriam scoffed. "Enough to drive her to tears."

"And Mrs. Mears?"

"Luty Mae liked to irritate people. She would look at someone and snicker, like she knew some scandalous secret about them. She seemed to take pleasure in draining their face of blood. They'd go all panicky, searching their minds for anything she might have on them."

"Anyone in particular?" Perhaps Mrs. Mears took her charades too far and performed too convincingly, forcing the killer to eliminate the threat of discovery.

"I don't know if she had anything particularly scandalous on Simon Hilton, but Luty Mae loved to raise his ire by racing her golf cart over the course and digging it up. The maintenance department had to repair the green several times, and the liability terrified Simon."

Meriday shifted his focus. "I understand Willowdell is a continuing care community."

"That's right. Residents are guaranteed the care and assistance they need until their final day. I feel badly for Wendall. He obviously had not been properly assessed and should have had more oversight." She lowered her voice. "Keep that between us. Residents who raise issues tend not to survive."

"Meaning?" Meriday sensed Miriam Kroft loved drama.

"Simon tends to find a way to encourage whiners to leave."

"What about Dorothy Kane? Ever chat with her?"

Her lips turned down. "Not if I could help it. No one liked her. Except Gladys Blumm." She rolled her eyes. "Those two were a pair. Always together and always fighting. Go figure. You must know about their squabble at the bingo game."

"Why do you think that is, why no one liked Dorothy?" Meriday still dug for a motive.

"Narcissistic. Everything had to be her way. And her obsession with the Syracuse Orangemen made her tiresome. I suspect she's the least missed."

He finished his coffee then said, "Let's go back to Wendell Compton."

"Completely off the grid." She shook her head. "Before he got really lost—in his mind, I mean—he would point out certain birds and talk about their idiosyncrasies and characteristics. Like migration patterns, and so on." She frowned at the sky, then looked back at him. "He'd talk about his wife. And a daughter, maybe. We had to guess with Wendell. He not only hopped subjects, he hopped time zones."

Meriday slid his notebook in his pocket and pointed toward the laptop. "Blogging?"

Her eyes fluttered. "No. Simon has me working on his next campaign. Social media stuff."

Meriday pushed aside his empty cup. "There's one more thing. I don't know if you can help me. There's a man keeping one of our cots warm down at the jail. Wondered if you've ever heard of him. George Tuttle."

Her jaw dropped slightly. She then spoke with a façade of

indifference. "Why would you think I'd know him?"

"He may have been in Simon Hilton's employ. And you working with Hilton, I thought you might have met him."

"What's he done?" She glanced at her hands.

Meriday stood and expanded his quarterback chest. "Kidnapped and bound a police officer, then left him in an abandoned warehouse."

Her neck muscles tightened. "Is the officer all right?"

"He is. But Tuttle won't be."

Her gaze wandered and did not know where to land.

———

Meriday sat in his cruiser near the exit gate at Willowdell, speaking to Bidwell on the radio. "She's lying. Miriam Kroft knows Tuttle, all right. Do a background check on her and dig up everything you can on King Tut Movers."

A tap sounded on his window. He jumped and turned to see Ada Whittaker smiling beneath a brown straw hat. "What now?" he mumbled to himself, then signed off from Bidwell and lowered his window.

"Good morning, Sheriff. I saw you were parked across the street for quite some time. Speaking with Mrs. Kroft, I assume. However, that is not what I wanted to discuss with you. I know you've been busy with this investigation and have formed your own theories, but my sister and I feel we can assist you."

He tightened his grip on the steering wheel.

"We're holding a memorial service to honor those who died so disturbingly here at Willowdell. We believe it may be an opportunity for you to surveil all your suspects at one time. I assume you have suspects?"

The scandal at Stonecroft came to mind like a recurring nightmare. The old woman had it all figured out before he could even finish the interviews. She made him look like a fool. And she was about to do it again. She'd be the one to unveil his death collector. His skin pricked, and he scratched his forearms.

"Sheriff?" Her blue eyes fastened on him.

He swallowed and felt his pride slink down his throat. "When?"

"Sunday afternoon at three."

"That's my naptime."

She straightened and scorched him with her stare.

He growled, "All right, all right. I'll be there."

"Bring your deputy. You'll need him."

She marched away from his sideview mirror. What was it she knew that he didn't?

The radio crackled. "Chief?"

He bellowed, "What?"

"Mrs. Kroft's maiden name is Tuttle. Seems George is her brother."

A flush of adrenaline tingled through his body. At last, a connection. King Tut Movers and Miriam Kroft were running a little operation out of the warehouse. But where were they getting the furniture to sell?

His gut twisted in a knot.

Was Mrs. Kroft selling the victims' personal property online, and with the help of her brother, delivering the orders?

But ... a motive for murder? He didn't see it.

A seagull dropping hit his windshield and jerked his attention back to Bidwell's chatter. "What was that?"

"I asked, do you want us to bring her in?"

"Tomorrow. We'll let her fret overnight. And let's make sure Georgy Boy sees his sister being escorted to the interrogation room. Maybe then he'll decide to talk. We need answers, and we need them by three o'clock Sunday afternoon."

41

The next day, preliminary findings of the investigation into the records of Willowdell landed on his desk. Meriday ignored the detailed copies and turned directly to the summation. He reached for his coffee mug and smacked it down when he found it empty.

Bidwell, standing by for orders, stepped to the coffee counter and began to prepare a new pot.

"Hilton authorized several large transfers from Willowdell's escrow account into his personal account," Meriday said. "The date of each transfer coincided with the death of one of the residents."

Bidwell spoke over his shoulder. "That could show motive."

Meriday grunted and leaned back, perusing and reading snippets, "A legal review declared the transfers were made in compliance with the contractual agreements signed by the residents upon entry into the retirement community ... Disclosure notices, signed by the residents, stated the required fees for entry into Willowdell were to be paid prior to occupancy ... after five years of residency become non-refundable."

Bidwell gave a low whistle.

Meriday went on, "Prior to five years, the resident receives a prorated refund based on the period of residency, except where termination of the agreement is due to the death of the resident, in which case, the prorated amount is payable to the deceased's estate."

He straightened and checked the dated signatures on the lease agreements of Dorothy Kane, Luty Mae Mears, Nita Beavers, and Wendall Compton. "All of them, over five years."

"So, no refunds." Bidwell poured water into the coffeemaker.

"The fees remain in house. In other words, the funds go directly to Hilton's personal account."

"Could be motive," Bidwell repeated. "It takes a load of money to launch a campaign for the Senate."

"According to his account balances, he already had a load of money." He spun his chair toward the coffee counter. Bidwell took his sweet time scooping fresh grounds into the filter.

"You can hardly turn on the television or radio," his deputy said, flicking on the coffeemaker, "without hearing how Hilton is the greatest thing since all-weather radials."

"Yeah. Ad nauseum." Meriday scratched his mustache. Bidwell could have something there. Could be motive. A districtwide campaign would cost a bundle.

"Hurry up with that coffee."

"It's dripping, sir."

———

Neil sat alone outside the Tin Pan Galley café reading the *Ontario Times*. The server refilled his coffee cup while he turned to the back pages to scan the legal notices before heading to his office.

Foreclosures, bankruptcies, divorce filings, estate settlements. A notice grabbed his attention. Ontario Developers is seeking a change in zoning for twenty-eight acres along the shoreline. *The shipyard.*

Hilton obtained the property through unethical means, blocking any other offer, and Duncan Kroft had sold under duress. Still, it seemed a foolish move for Kroft to sell at such a loss. Unless ... he and Hilton made a personal deal apart from what had been written in the contract.

If they had, would the firm of Bigelow and Senak have been privy to it?

The question again came to his mind, how could a man go from bankruptcy to living at Willowdell? Did Kroft get some kind of kickback, some kind of benefit they failed to disclose?

Neil had raised the possibility in a question to Jackie Senak. A question she failed to answer. Did she know? Could she, as a Willowdell attorney, be involved?

He shoved the thought away. She had risked her career in an effort to help him. He folded the paper, laid it aside, and sipped his coffee.

There was still the search of Willowdell's records. Maybe the auditors turned up something. Some kind of link to Ontario Developers, or a distinct or unusual handling of the Krofts' fees or charges. Anything that would indicate an off-the-record agreement or shadowy accounting.

He checked his watch and decided to pay the sheriff another visit.

"Chief, look at this," Bidwell called. Meriday turned away from talking with Sloan and went to see what had captured his deputy's attention.

"I found information on Wendall Compton's first wife."

Meriday leaned over his shoulder.

Margaret Duell Compton, 35, passed away June tenth ... injuries sustained in a motor vehicle accident ... real estate agent ... Surviving is her husband, Wendall Compton ...

He straightened. "Good work."

"Could Margaret be Magpie?" Bidwell faced him, his eyebrows arched. "His nickname for the person he believed to be taking him into the woods?"

"She wasn't the one holding his hand."

"Who did, do you think—take him into the woods?"

"Could have been no one. All we know is, someone pressed play on a recorder."

Bidwell turned and scrolled farther down his computer screen. "Whoa, look at her picture."

Meriday's stomach lurched. "Upload that to Compton's file and print a copy."

Neil Tibbs walked through the door of the station as Meriday turned toward his office. "Tibbs. What's up?"

"Got a minute?"

"If you're bringing me answers and not questions, I'll give you five." In his office, Meriday motioned for Neil to take a seat, then closed the door.

Tibbs lowered himself into the chair. "Any report from the auditors searching the records at Willowdell?"

"That's a question." Meriday moved to the coffee pot and filled his mug. "But I'll give you one. Yes."

Neil shook his head at the offer of coffee. "Did they find any information on Ontario Developers or any personal agreements between Duncan Kroft and Simon Hilton or Ontario Developers?"

Meriday settled in his desk chair. "Can't say they did. I had the auditors focus on finding a link between the four victims, and a possible motive. I don't recall any mention of Ontario Developers."

Tibbs brushed a strand off his forehead with a frustrated swipe.

Meriday squinted at him. Something had gotten the attorney riled. "What's this about?"

Neil shared his thoughts that perhaps a personal agreement between Hilton and Kroft had been made prior to Kroft's bankruptcy. "Something off the record that would explain the low sale price. I can't picture Duncan Kroft as foolish enough to let the shipyard go for two-thirds its value. He had to have spent decades building up his business."

"Some incentive to induce Kroft to settle, you mean?"

"It'd make more sense."

Meriday took a draw on his coffee, then said, "Look, even if there was a private agreement, it doesn't mean there's anything illegal about it. Frankly, I've got more pressing matters on my mind. Like trying to solve four possible—probable—murders."

"I know. I know." Tibbs ran his hand through his hair. "It's just, no one goes from bankruptcy to living at Willowdell. There had to be a private agreement." He scraped his chair closer. "Think about it, Leo. Where would Kroft get the entry fee? All his assets had to be dispersed among his creditors."

Meriday lowered his head and kneaded his shoulders. "Okay." He looked at Tibbs. "If an off-the-record deal, like you suggest, had been made—and it doesn't mean any crime has been committed—there's one way to learn the details. Ask someone who knows."

Tibbs told him about his trip to the office of Bigelow and Senak and about his discussions with Jackie. He leaned back in the chair. "I can't expect her to disclose anything about a private agreement. It wouldn't be fair to place her in a position of betraying client confidentiality. It could land her before the review board."

"I've met Bigelow. He represents George Tuttle, the perp who left Bidwell taped to a rafter in the warehouse. The lawyer's doing a good job keeping his client's yapper shut." Meriday snickered and tapped the file Bidwell had compiled on King Tut Movers. "But we have something that might loosen Tuttle's tongue."

Tibbs' eyes widened. "Bigelow and Senak are representing a thug?"

"Yep. The thug has got himself a high-priced attorney."

A rap sounded, and Bidwell poked his head in. "Sloan is back. He's got her."

"Is Tuttle where he can get a good look at his sister being led to the interview room?"

"Yes, sir."

Meriday's lips curved into a wry grin. "I'll be there when I get there. I want her to sweat it out awhile."

Bidwell left them.

Meriday sipped the last of his coffee, then answered Neil's questioning gaze. "Miriam Kroft. She knows more about this warehouse business than she's telling.

"She's George Tuttle's sister?"

"Yep. And she lied about knowing him. I intend to find out why. Along with why her brother risked a prison term for a sofa, and why his partner has gone underground."

Neil looked at his watch. "I've got to get to the office. Sorry I didn't bring you any answers, Leo."

"I'm sorry you brought me more questions."

"He's down by the lake." Frances pointed, and Ada turned.

Maxwell meandered along the shoreline, head low, shoulders slumped, one hand in the pocket of his red shorts and the other hand gripping Stanley's leash.

Ada started toward him.

"Maybe we shouldn't disturb him."

"Nonsense. We don't have time to waste." Ada scampered down the knoll toward the lake. Arriving, she said, "Anything you care to talk about?"

Maxwell looked at Frances coming behind her and shook his head.

"Okay, then. We have need of a preacher."

His neck flushed. "You have a pastor."

"Of course, but Frances and I are planning a memorial service Sunday, right here at Willowdell, and we want you to speak to the attendees."

"In honor of the four residents who died," Frances said. "Since they had no family, we thought it would be nice to at least acknowledge they lived."

"And to get all the suspects together," Ada said.

Maxwell's countenance perked. "Suspects?"

"With everyone in one place, I'm hoping the murderer will show himself."

"But ... who are the suspects?"

"No one and everyone." Frances gave Ada a sideways glance. "My sister practically promised the sheriff he would be making an arrest Sunday."

"Yes, well," Ada said, "we still need a preacher."

"But I didn't know the victims—not really." Maxwell lowered his eyes to the dog. "My one connection to any of them is Stanley, and I can't very well talk about him for ten minutes."

Ada understood his hesitancy. Maxwell had been thrown from the proverbial horse and hesitated to get back on. "Remember, you served the Lord at Westlake Community Church, not merely the people. 'Not unto man,' the Scripture says."

"You want me to speak at the memorial service for the Lord."

"Exactly."

He scratched his head. "What would I say?"

"Just say what's universal," Frances said. "They loved and were loved. And regardless of how or why they died, they were important to God."

Ada sent her sister an approving glance.

Maxwell looked from one to the other. "If that's what you both want."

Frances touched his arm and invited him to walk with them back to the square.

Ada lingered. "You two go ahead. I'm going to sit awhile."

While Frances and Maxwell and Stanley climbed the knoll and drifted from sight, Ada rested on the bench beneath the branches of a sprawling maple. The early afternoon sun filtered through its leaves and cast a silhouette over her denim skirt.

She placed her yellow hat beside her and ruffled her hair. Gulls cawed over the water while the sun warmed her face. A breeze blew in and lifted her hat from the bench.

"Mercy." Ada hopped up and chased the hat while it dipped and ducked and tucked itself under the tendrils of a weeping willow. She parted the fronds and stepped inside the cool shade.

"Oh—" Her foot landed on a broken limb and rolled her to the ground. "Ooh." She gripped her twisted knee and eyed the offending branch.

Is that... dried blood? Ada bent closer. Gray hairs spiked from a knob on the branch.

Her breath froze. Chills staggered down her spine.

"Mercy."

42

Meriday smirked at the sight of George Tuttle handcuffed to a metal chair in clear view of the interrogation room where Miriam Kroft awaited questioning. Sloan stood guard outside the door. Meriday asked him, "She sweating yet?"

Sloan tipped his head toward Tuttle. "He is."

George bounced a knee and repeatedly swiped at the twitch in his jaw with a shoulder. The prisoner glanced at Meriday then dropped his gaze to the floor.

"Keep him there." Meriday motioned for Bidwell to join him then opened the interview room door.

Miriam Kroft's raisin-like eyes glared at him. She had chewed the red lipstick off her lower lip, and she repeatedly opened and clasped her manicured hands. A glass of water sat on the table in front of her.

Bidwell stood by the door with his thumbs tucked in his belt.

Meriday scraped back the chair opposite. "Relax, Mrs.

Kroft. You're here to answer questions, that's all." He sat and took out his notebook.

"I am relaxed," she snapped. "Why wouldn't I be relaxed? I did nothing wrong." She slapped her arms over her stomach.

"I understand you and your brother operate an LLC. King Tut Movers."

"We own a business. Is that a crime?" Her jaw stiffened.

"This furniture you're selling, do you have proof of ownership? Something that could prove you're not selling stolen property."

"Stolen property?" Her nostrils flared. "No, I don't. But I have every right to do what I please with that furniture. Selling it is my prerogative. After all, I couldn't possibly keep it. There's so much."

"Enough to fill a warehouse?"

She steeled her shoulders. "Why are you harassing me? You have no probable cause."

Meriday groaned inwardly. Clueless people who tossed around legal jargon annoyed him. "We need to verify you're not involved in criminal activity."

Miriam Kroft placed her elbows on the table. "George and I are merely small business owners trying to make a living."

"Off the dying?"

She blinked rapidly, then diverted her gaze.

"I don't think you understand," Meriday said. "In the warehouse, my deputy saw some of the items you are attempting to sell on your website."

She lowered her chin and stared at her hands.

"That links you to the kidnapping and detaining of a policeman." Meriday straightened and expanded his chest. "The law doesn't look lightly on that. One case like this resulted in a fifty-five year term in prison."

She gasped. "Is—is that what George could get?"

Meriday tilted his head and squinched his cheek. "Selling stolen property is playing with tinker toys compared to the kidnapping of a cop. George is lucky he's in New York. In other places, the D.A. could push for the death penalty."

Mrs. Kroft shot up. "You're just trying to intimidate me."

Meriday commanded, "Sit down."

She plunked into the chair. Tears sprang to her eyes. She dropped her head into her hands and spoke through them, her voice muffled. "He said I could do what I wanted with it."

"Who?"

"Simon. He has no use for anything the residents leave behind. He just wants it all cleared out so new clients can move in."

"Hilton authorized you to appropriate tens of thousands of dollars' worth of personal property and dispose of it any way you chose?"

She bobbed her head, then lifted her face. Mascara circled her eyes. She whimpered, "When there's no family, Simon lets me have it."

Meriday made a note, then softened his tone. "Did this agreement between you and Simon Hilton compensate in some way for the price he paid for your husband's shipyard property?"

"Simon has never put it like that, but I've always suspected the possibility. When Duncan found out Simon was DBA Ontario Developers, he threatened to sue. Simon had locked out all other purchase offers for the property, securing his power to lowball the price."

"Did Mr. Kroft sue?"

She shook her head. "What could Dunc do? He had no legal recourse. And raising a fuss would get us thrown out of Willowdell."

"So, giving the deceased residents' personal property to

you is Hilton's attempt to appease Mr. Kroft's furor and ease his own conscience?"

Miriam sipped the water. "It may ease Simon's conscience, but it isn't appeasing my husband. Dunc doesn't know anything about my side business. Simon insisted on secrecy."

Meriday scratched his mustache and wondered what Duncan Kroft would do if he learned of this arrangement between his wife and the man he detested. "How do you account for the money you're raking in?"

"The accounts are in George's name."

Meriday studied her. Keeping plenty of secrets from her old man. What was she not telling *him*? "Any idea why your brother would detain my deputy?"

The veins in her neck bulged. "My brother is a fool."

"Did Hilton order him to restrain Officer Bidwell?"

"I know nothing about that. Simon may be an opportunist, but I don't believe he would ever tell George to do anything that stupid. With all the deaths at Willowdell, we were getting a stockpile of furniture, and Simon simply wanted some of it transferred to our warehouse in Watertown. Too much activity at the shipyard would invite questions from the public."

"Why avoid questions from the public? Does he have something to hide?"

"He feared the voters wouldn't understand our practice regarding the residents' personal property and would assume he profits from their death."

That sounded like Hilton. The man never seemed to make a move unless it served his lust for power. "What about George's pal? Where is he?"

"I have no idea. Where he is, or even who he is. George hires a lumper when he needs someone to help with a load." She gave a deep, tired sigh.

Meriday scraped back his chair. He gave instructions for Sloan to drive Mrs. Kroft back to Willowdell.

Bidwell stuck his head in Meriday's office door. "Chief, a call came in from Ada Whittaker."

"What now?" Meriday growled and scooped coffee into a filter.

"Says she found evidence of Nita Beavers's murder."

He spun. "What evidence?"

"Didn't say. Wants us to pick it up and get it to the lab."

His blood pressure rocketed. He rubbed a hand over his clenched jaw and turned away from his deputy. While he poured water into the coffeemaker, his hand trembled.

"Says there's hair and probably blood."

He struggled to control his tone. "When Sloan gets back, the two of you go check it out. If it links to the investigation, bring it in."

"He's there with Mrs. Kroft. Do you want him to pick it up?"

Meriday scratched his nose and his mustache, giving himself a moment to breathe. "If it turns out to be evidence, you need someone with you. There are too many conspiracy kooks ready to claim tampering."

"Yes, sir. Sorry, Chief." He left and closed the door behind him.

Meriday threw his hands up in the air. Every piece of evidence they possessed had been found by someone outside the force. Worse yet, by Ada Whittaker or one of her disciples.

Coffee dripped into the carafe and filled the small room with its calming aroma.

He moved to the window. The lake rippled golden in the late afternoon sun.

A mental review of his questioning of Miriam Kroft prodded him to look at his notes. Something had struck him.

Yes, that was it. She had said "no family." When the deceased had no family, their personal property fell into her hands.

But what about the deceased's estate?

Into whose hands did their money fall?

43

After breakfast the next morning, Frances shut the drawer of the hall table with a bit more force than Ada thought necessary. "I don't believe it. She's taken them again."

Ada looked up from the notes she had been jotting down. The memorial service would take place in a few days, and the details were still in the developmental phase. "What's wrong?"

"Samantha. She must have taken my new box of chocolates."

"She promised me she would never do that again. I believed her." Ada slid back from the table. "The box must be here somewhere."

Frances pulled a light sweater from the hall closet. "I'm going to put a stop to this."

Ada scurried to the door behind her sister and followed her up the sidewalk. "Try to calm down, Frances. There may be some other explanation."

Samantha jerked to attention at the flinging open of the lobby door.

"Where are my chocolates?" Frances's white strands had been twisted like pretzels by the wind sweeping in off the lake.

"Uh-h, there's not been any recent packages for you, Mrs. Ferrell. Uh, I will notify you—"

"You took it. You took my box of Hegler chocolates."

Samantha stiffened. A deep red swept up her neck. Veins popped near her temples.

Ada touched her sister's elbow. "Now, Frances, maybe—"

Samantha spewed, "If you're so worried about your stupid candy, you should install security cameras in your bungalow."

Ada reached across Frances with the instinct to protect her. If possible, Ada believed Samantha would have leaped over the counter.

Alison Vaughn appeared in the open doorway of Simon Hilton's office, files in her hand. She stepped to the counter. "Is there a problem?"

Samantha buttoned her lips and lifted her nose.

Alison looked to Frances. "Mrs. Ferrell?"

Frances turned and stormed out of the lobby.

Ada spoke softly. "I believe there may have been a misunderstanding. It appears my sister's recent shipment of her favorite chocolates has once more gone missing."

"They're accusing me of taking them." Samantha cast a censorious glance at Ada.

Alison smiled indulgently. "I'm sure Samantha isn't the only person at Willowdell with an unscrupulous penchant for chocolate, Miss Whittaker."

Confusion spread over Samantha's face, and Ada, too, wondered if Alison's words were meant in defense of the property manager.

"Samantha," Ada said, "do you remember when I asked you if anyone other than Frances receives shipments from Hegler?"

"Yes, and I told you no."

Ada cocked her head and raised an eyebrow. "What about Judge Fausset?"

"What about him? Mrs. Ferrell is the only resident at Willowdell who receives deliveries of Hegler chocolates."

Alison confirmed the statement, and Ada left the lobby puzzling over the matter. Where did the box of chocolates on Judge Fausset's counter come from? If they belonged to Frances, who put them there?

Gwen pulled up to the front of Frances's bungalow and parked the car. She and Janet got out. Ada hurried toward them.

When she arrived, Janet said, "We've come to help you."

Gwen unlocked the trunk and handed Janet an easel then lifted out a large, flat box.

Frances held the bungalow door open. "What's all this?"

"We're going to help Miss Ada catch a killer," Janet said.

Frances looked to Ada, and Ada lifted her eyebrows.

"We have to do something." Gwen carried the box inside and removed a whiteboard from it while Janet set up the easel. "Miss Ada told Sheriff Meriday he could make an arrest Sunday. We need to come up with some suspects. Not to mention clues and a motive." Gwen propped the whiteboard on the easel.

Janet stood aside. "Now what?"

"Pictures." Gwen pulled some photographs from her purse and taped them to the board, one at each corner.

Ada recognized the pictures of the four victims, from the Willowdell directory.

"Now, for suspects." Gwen took out a blue marker. "We'll draw stick figures to represent them. Let's start with who we least suspect and work our way to the likeliest."

"Max?" Janet peeked at Frances.

"Absolutely not." Frances crossed her arms. "He's not going on the board."

"None of us truly suspect Maxwell." Ada hurried to put out a potential brush fire. "We are merely starting with the *least* suspected."

Frances flung her arm. "Fine. Whatever."

With much bickering and discussion, the sleuths ended the hour with nine stick figures on the board, each set in a square.

Gwen stood back. "Looks like a tic-tac-toe board."

"Just think," Janet said, chuckling, "come Sunday one of them is going to have bars over their square."

Gwen glanced at Frances. "It's not funny, Janet. There are people on here we care about."

Frances shook her head. "I still say Max shouldn't be on the board."

The words of Jane Marple came to Ada's mind. *Anyone is quite capable of murder.* She kept them to herself.

Sheriff Meriday stifled the urge to rant when he received the lab report early that afternoon. Why didn't Bidwell or Sloan find that broken limb under the willow tree? They searched the area. How could they have missed it?

He settled in his chair and picked up the report. With Sunday right around the corner, he'd insisted the lab make it their top priority. The chunk of wood contained a sampling of Nita Beavers's blood and hair.

How was it that Fred didn't find any evidence of the weapon in Mrs. Beavers's scalp? The blow merely stunned the woman, and the waters were choppy. Evidence could have washed away, but it would have been helpful to know from the start.

Meriday cocked his head toward the window, hoping it offered a clearer view.

Maybe Frances Ferrell had said something. Something she'd seen that morning. He pulled out his interview notes from the day of Mrs. Beavers's death. *Drats.* He hadn't taken any notes at his interview with Frances Ferrell except that one.

A half hour later, he stood at the blue door with the white tulip swag, waiting for an answer to his knock. Deputy Bidwell, thumbs tucked in his belt, leaned against the gray Volvo parked in front of her bungalow.

Mrs. Ferrell snooped through the curtain then disappeared.

He heard muffled voices and saw women scrambling through the kitchen.

She took her sweet time but finally opened the door. "Come in, Sheriff." Mrs. Ferrell angled herself away from him and made no eye contact.

Gwen Dunbar sat on a barstool at the kitchen counter while Janet poured lemonade into a glass. They, too, averted their eyes in a classic display of guilt. Doubtless, their ringleader had them up to something he wasn't to know about.

"Hello, Sheriff," Ada said. "Did you eat lunch? We have chicken salad."

"I'm good. Thanks." He turned to her sister. "I have a few more questions, if you don't mind."

Frances led him into the living room and waved toward a chair. He sank into the leather and pulled out his little black book. She sat in the chair opposite.

Ada set a glass of lemonade on the coaster beside him, then perched on the edge of the sofa and folded her hands. "I'm sorry I can't offer you a chocolate."

He puzzled over the absence of her bird's nest do. Whatever prompted her to shed it? He acknowledged the drink, then leaned forward and spoke to Frances. "Tell me again every move you made the morning Nita Beavers went into the lake. Exactly what you saw. What you heard."

Mrs. Ferrell's slate gray eyes, set in a frame of black mascara and deep blue shadow, looked at him askance. "I can try, but two months have passed."

"Yes, ma'am, but I'd like to hear your account again. When I spoke with you the first time I didn't—"

"Take me seriously?" Frances lifted an eyebrow.

"Yes, ma'am. At the time, I believed Mrs. Beavers's death to be an accident. But recent evidence indicates foul play." In his peripheral vision, Gwen and Janet swiveled toward him on the barstools. He pulled out a pencil. "Tell me what you remember from that morning."

Frances closed her eyes and drew in a deep breath. "Okay." She looked at him. "I was on my porch watering the plants. I heard Stanley barking and Nita yelling for him to stop. It made me curious because, as I said before, I had never known Nita to have any trouble with Stanley."

"Then what happened?"

"The dog raced toward the lake, and Nita ran after him. Stanley stopped by that large maple tree nearest to the water. He stood there barking at something. Nita arrived and disappeared behind the tree. I heard what sounded like a faint splash. When Nita didn't come back into view, I grew alarmed and rushed back inside to call the lobby. I wanted someone to check on her."

"How long were you inside?" Meriday paused in his writing and watched her face.

"It took a minute to find my phone."

"A full minute?"

"No, thirty seconds or so. It seemed much longer. I felt a bit frantic."

"Is that when you called 911?"

"When I went back outside and still didn't see Nita, I had a bad feeling. So, yes, that's when I called 911."

Gwen left the barstool. "What's the new evidence?" She sat on the arm of the sofa.

"We got us a tic-tac-toe b—" Janet snapped her mouth shut at Gwen's glare.

Meriday rubbed his chin. These dames were definitely up to something.

Ada shifted on the sofa. "You did say you have new evidence."

He slipped his notebook into his pocket. "Mrs. Beavers's blood and hair were on the limb you found. Likely, someone used the dog whistle to lure the dog to the lake for the purpose of drawing Mrs. Beavers there."

Frances glanced at Ada.

The ridges on Ada's brow told him nothing. She likely held her own theories, and he hesitated to share his. Although it rankled him, her insights tended more toward the truth.

He went on, "I believe that same person hid behind the maple tree with the weapon poised. When Mrs. Beavers bent down to grab her dog's leash, the perpetrator smacked her head and pitched the victim, unconscious, into the lake, where she drowned."

Frances placed a hand on her stomach. "Poor Nita."

He turned to Ada. "The attacker shoved the weapon high up under the willow, tossed the dog whistle into the hedgerow, and disappeared into the woods."

"You may want to question Alison Vaughn about that dog whistle," Ada said. "And I wonder, is it possible a woman could have struck the blow to Nita's head?"

Did Ada Whittaker just tip her hand? Could it be that she,

herself, did not know the identity of the death collector? Then what was all this prattle and promise about making an arrest?

When he nodded, she said, "Oh, my. That doesn't narrow the field at all."

44

Maxwell rose from a short nap and placed a decaf K-cup in the Keurig. He had put it off as long as he dared. Sunday hovered on the corner, and he needed to come up with an inspiring eulogy on behalf of four people he barely knew.

With Stanley at his heels, Max took his coffee, his Bible, a notebook, and a plate of snickerdoodles and sat at the table on the back patio. He put on his readers, and with a pen in one hand and a cookie in the other, he stared at the paper.

What could he say?

Perhaps he would read the twenty-third Psalm. No. There's that part in there about walking in the shadow of death. The residents didn't need any reminder that death still lurked in the shadows at Willowdell.

He laid down the pen and tapped his fingers on the table in rhythm to the two windchimes Gladys had hung from the overhang. At least, he assumed Gladys came on his property when he wasn't home and hung the tinkling frogs and clinking colored icicles.

He stroked the dog seated by his chair. "Any ideas, Stanley?"

"Yoo-hoo, Max."

"Back here, Gladys."

Gladys Blumm lumbered onto his patio carrying two jars. "Just finished a batch of raspberry jam. Thought I'd bring some over."

"Where did you find raspberries?"

"Had Selma pick up some at the Farmer's Market."

So, she and Selma *were* looking for berries in the woods. An unexpected sense of relief swept over him. "Thanks. Have a seat. Coffee?"

"Water, if you got it." Gladys placed the jars on the table, planted herself in a chair, and picked up a snickerdoodle. "Writing your memoirs?"

"The memorial service." He reached into the Igloo Mini refrigerator he kept on the patio and pulled out a bottle of water. "Ada asked me to say a few words about the residents who died. I'm clueless. I know nothing about them."

"I heard about the service. Selma wants to attend. Not sure if I will. My back's still stinging from the darts of chinwaggers." Gladys opened the bottle and took a drink.

"Ignore them."

"What do you have so far?" She scrutinized his notes. "Nothing?"

He lifted his hands. "Frances suggested I speak in generalities, but I think my remarks should be more personal."

Gladys grimaced at the dog. "What about Stanley there? He must have taught you something about his owner. And Dorothy, well, I can think of some good points if I concentrate long enough."

"Whatever you can tell me might help."

She crinkled her face toward the sun before turning back to

him. "Wendall. He roamed, searching for something he could recognize. Like a traveler on the wrong road who believes he will see something familiar if he keeps going."

Max gave an understanding moan. "Sad."

A light washed over her face. "You know, I never told anyone, but I thought it odd when Wendall wandered out of his house in the middle of the night."

"He had some dementia."

"Yeah, but the aide always gave him medication to make him sleep. That's why they allowed him to stay alone at night. After supper she'd watch *Wheel of Fortune* with him and then help him into his pajamas, give him a pill, and tuck him into bed."

"How do you know the routine?"

"Everyone who knew Wendall knew the routine."

"Maybe the aide neglected to give Wendall his sleeping tablet. She could have been distracted."

"With all that's been going on," Gladys said, choosing a second cookie, "it's more likely someone switched his pills to keep him restless."

"Wanting him to wander?" If someone replaced Wendall's sleeping pills with something harmless and ineffective, they could have easily manipulated him and led him into the woods. "That would support my theory."

"Explain." She bit into the cookie.

"Ever since you and Selma found that tape recorder, I wondered if someone used the recorded owl's call to lure Wendall into the woods. Maybe they intended for him to get lost, hoping he would not come out alive."

Gladys clicked her tongue. "Blood is crying out from the ground at Willowdell."

Meriday perused the four files on his desk. Someone had attacked Nita Beavers and sent her into the lake to her death. And someone had seen to it the deadly brownie reached Dorothy Kane. Did that same person lead Wendall into the woods and send Luty Mae Mears on the ride to her death?

George Tuttle's conscience allowed him to capture and detain a deputy and then leave him to rot. Maybe he was ruthless enough to set the stage for four deaths. Perhaps more than four. Perhaps others had died under mysterious circumstances and were never investigated.

Meriday waved the thought aside and scoffed. He couldn't grant George Tuttle the IQ to carry out, much less plan, the deaths without discovery.

Dorothy Kane. He always came back to her. Bidwell's question as they stood over her body floating in the whirlpool nagged at him. "Why didn't she get out of the water when she felt a reaction coming on?"

Her autopsy report lay before him. *Anaphylaxis. Peanut oil. Diazepam.*

Meriday mumbled, "Diazepam. What is that? Medication for arthritis or something?" Why wasn't it brought to his attention. He placed a call.

The coroner finally picked up.

"Fred, Dorothy Kane's autopsy results. What's this Diazepam stuff?" Meriday's blood ran cold as the coroner enlightened him about its effect. Fatigue, drowsiness, muscle weakness.

Fred reiterated the woman died as a result of ingesting peanut oil, then added, "But having taken a larger dose of Diazepam than prescribed, the victim likely was incapable of getting herself out of the water. Especially if the allergic reaction left her struggling for breath."

Meriday offered a possible scenario. "Could the drug have

been crushed and added to the brownie batter, intending for what happened to happen?"

"She had taken it earlier, before she ingested the peanut oil. But I do have to say, Leo, for Mrs. Kane to knowingly take the amount of Diazepam that she took and then get into a tank of swirling hot water, she'd have been borderline suicidal—even without the peanut oil."

Meriday hung up and walked to the coffee counter. He lifted the carafe. "Why would she do that?" He filled his mug and sank again into his chair. On his desk lay the report of what had been taken into evidence at the scene of her death.

Orange swimsuit coverup. SU newsletter. Purple-framed glasses. Shower sandals. Gift wrap. Orange ribbon. "Gift wrap and ribbon?" He took a long draught of hot coffee and buzzed Bidwell.

His deputy appeared. "Chief?"

"Dorothy Kane. The stuff you bagged at the scene. You found a ribbon?"

"We found it tucked in the pocket of her swimsuit coverup, along with a piece of wrapping paper."

Meriday's heart banged against his brain. "Any card or note?"

"No, sir." Bidwell's poker face nearly folded. "They were a gift?"

Meriday chew his lips. *Someone Dorothy trusted wanted her dead.*

45

"You two go and have fun." Ada stood on the porch the next morning. Maxwell had invited Frances for a round of golf, and Ada believed their time together would do them both good.

"I'm feeling a bit squeamish," Frances said, slipping into the golf cart beside Maxwell. "I haven't been on the course since Luty Mae's accident."

Ada did not believe for a moment that Luty Mae accidentally tipped her golf cart onto her neck. No one actually placed the woman's head under the floorboard, but someone put her on that cart and sent her to her death. "You're both going to put all that out of your minds."

"We certainly will try." Maxwell smiled beneath a white ballcap. His club bag rested in the back seat.

Ada waved while they drove away then turned and noticed Simon Hilton's car in his reserved space near the square. "Oh, good. I can confirm our plans for the memorial service."

Ada entered the lobby and waited for Alison to stop fussing

with the copier. After a polite pause, she spoke to Alison's back. "Pardon me."

Alison turned with a flushed, stern face.

Ada took a tiny step back. "Is something wrong?"

"That stupid—" Alison shook her head. "Samantha. She made Simon angry. When Simon Hilton isn't happy, he makes sure everyone around him joins in his misery. His first day back from DC—his first hour back—and he goes into a rage." She took a breath. "If you don't need anything, I'm a little busy with *her* work and my own."

"I'd like to run my plans for the memorial service by Mr. Hilton."

"There won't be a memorial service."

Her neck muscles tensed. "Why in forever not?"

"That's what poked the tiger. Samantha told him she authorized a memorial service to 'honor the residents who had left us recently.' He roared, saying he didn't want any public attention brought to Willowdell, especially the kind of attention the death of four residents would bring."

Ada tilted her head. "I don't understand."

Alison's shoulders slumped and she gave a slight sigh before she turned back to the copier. "He's running for the senate. Need I say more?"

"So, he's more concerned about how he looks to the voters than he is about how the deaths have affected the residents."

Alison straightened and faced her. "Does that surprise you?"

"I wish I could say it does. Where is Samantha?"

"He ordered her to go home. He told her that he"—she sing-songed— "'didn't want to see her fat face for the rest of the day.'"

Oh, my. Ada left the lobby and started toward number thirteen. The girl must be shattered. A few minutes later, she arrived at Samantha's bungalow. Torn Simon Hilton posters filled a trash bin at the end of the driveway and spilled over onto the ground.

Samantha waddled from her garage, her arms loaded with shredded papers, her eyes red-rimmed. She paused when she saw Ada but forged ahead and shoved more of the upper and lower portions of Simon Hilton's face into the can.

Brushing away tears, she said, "Simon won't let you have that service Sunday."

"Alison told me."

"I suppose *she's* managing the lobby today." Samantha spoke through pinched lips. "This is your fault. He wasn't pleased at all that I took the initiative and authorized a wonderful service for the dear residents who meant so much to him. They meant nothing. *I* mean nothing." She turned on her heel with a snort.

Ada called, "I'm sorry this happened."

Samantha plodded back to the garage, her long skirt swaying over her scuffed canvas flats.

Ada sighed. She needed a plan B.

By the time she arrived at Frances's bungalow, she had made a decision.

Neil had been waiting a few minutes when Jackie Senak arrived and sat beside him on a park bench in the village of Parish, a town midway between Syracuse and Sackets Harbor.

"Thank you for meeting me here." She slipped the leather purse off her shoulder. "I thought it best to avoid being seen together at our offices."

Her blue eyes reminded him of a troubled sea. "What's this about?"

"After we spoke Friday night, I determined to look further into the files of those residents who recently died at Willowdell. I waited for Raymond to leave the office yesterday then I studied their accounts."

"That had to be a tough decision. You took a big risk." If Mr. Bigelow discovered Jackie's subversion, he could cause her a great deal of trouble.

"I found nothing illegal, but what I did find is disconcerting."

He focused on her lips and waited.

"When someone has lived at Willowdell less than five years and then leaves, a percentage of their entry fee is returned to them. In the case of death, the prorated fees are returned to the deceased's estate. After five years, the resident is not entitled to a refund." She bit her lip and glanced at some passersby. "The entry fees are substantial. Anywhere from eighty-nine to one hundred twenty thousand, depending on the bungalow."

Neil knew the entry fees were significant. Judge Fausset alluded to this when he moved into Willowdell. Neil asked with a sinking in his stomach, "How long were they at Willowdell, the four residents who died?"

She raised her eyebrows. "Between five and seven years."

"So, Hilton secures approximately four hundred thousand in six weeks." He leaned back. "But there's nothing illegal—"

"Not illegal, but listen." She lowered her voice. Her chin trembled slightly. "I could get in a lot of trouble."

"I don't want any negative repercussions for you." Neil placed a hand over hers for a moment. "You don't have to—"

"Yes. I do. It could be important." She straightened. "The

day after each death, Simon transferred the deceased's fees from the escrow account to his personal account and then into his campaign fund."

"Campaign fund?" He ran a hand through his hair. "You're certain?"

She nodded. "That could be motive."

———

Just before sunset, Maxwell climbed into the rusted dumpster behind the warehouse. Ada and Frances stood on the cinderblocks alongside the bin, expecting him to find a pill bottle among the trove of discarded toiletries, pantry items, and once-refrigerated leftovers.

A putrid odor rode the breeze and slapped his face.

"The stuff on top is likely Luty Mae's." Ada held down her brown straw hat with one hand and with the other pointed to a tossed tray that once held an array of creams and lotions.

"Wendall's bungalow had been cleared before Luty Mae's," Frances said, "so his things should be under hers."

"Yes, Maxwell. You shouldn't have to dig down too far."

He chastised himself. When he played golf with Frances the day before, he mentioned his visit with Gladys and her thoughts concerning Wendall's pills. When Ada found out, she insisted he take them to the warehouse so they could search the dumpster. *They* could search the dumpster. Like he would let them crawl into a giant trash can.

So here, with the sun lowering behind him, he sat on toasters and towels, searching for a small bottle of prescription medication bearing the name Wendall Compton.

"Try the other end. I think you've gone down too far." Ada peered into the heap as if trying to laser in on a target.

He tried to keep a sense of futility at bay as he continued to rummage through the unbagged trash. "Even if I find the bottle, the prints will be those of the aide. Any sensible criminal would have worn gloves."

"Criminals are rarely sensible," Ada said. "Besides, God revealed this clue to you for a reason."

Max sighed. No doubt God got blamed for a lot of things.

"That's right," Frances said. "Like when God led me to the dog whistle and Ada to the murder weapon." A light wind tossed Frances's hair, and Max again thought her striking— until her words hit him.

"Murder weapon?" He sank back on a sofa pillow, his pulse twirling. "What? Where? Whose?"

Ada explained how she had fallen under the willow tree and discovered a broken limb with traces of Nita Beavers's hair and blood.

"Sheriff Meriday says someone hit Nita on the head with it," Frances said. "Just enough to send her into the water to drown." Her voice trailed off.

Maxwell mentally replayed the tragedies. "I suspect that's his M.O. The perpetrator doesn't actually commit murder, he just sets the stage to send the victims to their deaths."

"Premeditation is clear," Ada said, "but we need the pills to prove it in the case of Wendall Compton."

Maxwell returned to tunneling and dug his hands deeper into the pile, tossing aside boxes of macaroni, plastic containers, slightly-melted spatulas. "Eh." He cringed and jerked his hand out. Something felt like the fur of a short-haired dog.

"What is it?" Frances asked.

He lifted out a taxidermized long-eared owl. "No doubt this belonged to Wendall." Maxwell handed it off to her. Again, he reached into the belly of the dumpster and pulled up a bird —white, blue, and black.

"It's a magpie." Ada took it from his hand.

"You must be in the right area," Frances said.

"But you better hurry." Ada looked toward the west.

Deepening hues of red, orange, and purple layered the sky. He had a short time to find that proverbial needle, but at least he'd landed in the right haystack.

46

Early Friday morning, Ada left number eight and set out on a power walk. She had much to think about and pray about. Later, she and Maxwell would drop in on the sheriff, hand over the bottle of pills taken from the dumpster, and recount to him Maxwell's talk with Gladys Blumm.

With a belt bag around her waist and a pink straw hat on her head she set off across the square toward the lakeside trail. At the top of the knoll, she looked toward the lake. Judge Fausset sat on a bench among the willows.

She thought of the box she had seen on his counter the evening he slipped in his bathtub and needed the paramedics. A divine appointment surely presented itself.

"Good morning, Judge."

"Ah, Miss Whittaker. Please, join me." Judge Fausset set Annie Oakley down on the grass and slid over.

Ada sat beside him. The papillon apparently remembered her and wanted to get in her lap. She picked up the dog and scratched behind its ears.

"I never thanked you for helping me out the other night. I especially appreciate you conveying to the responders not to announce their arrival. Overall, a humbling experience, to say the least."

"Were you able to get in touch with Neil?" Ada thought it best to move the discussion in a less personal direction.

"Yes. He'd gotten a call from an attorney in Syracuse and left in somewhat of a hurry."

"Oh?" Ada angled toward him.

"I didn't ask any questions." The judge turned a smile on her with a slight chuckle. "I'm grateful Neil didn't ask any either."

Ada kept her tone casual. "I noticed a box of chocolates on your counter."

He jerked back slightly. "Yes. But didn't you put them there?"

"Oh my, no."

"Then someone must have entered my home after I went in for my bath. I'm sorry. I thought you had placed the candy there, and I felt I've been amiss in not thanking you for your kindness. But now, I'm left to wonder."

"Yes, indeed. You would be." She turned to the lake. The sun peeked over the horizon and shot golden arrows into the water. Seagulls swirled overhead. Could someone be trying to cast suspicion on the judge? Very few people knew about the foil wrapper found under Luty Mae Mears's body.

Unless ... the judge was lying. But no. His brown eyes conveyed gentleness and contentment. A man at peace and not of troubled conscience.

"What is it, Miss Whittaker? You seem suddenly disturbed. I hope I didn't say something ..."

"Mercy, no. And please call me Ada. We're both too old for formalities."

"True. Call me Burton. Or Burt, if you like."

"Well, I'd best get on with my walk."

"I'm sorry. I'm enjoying your company."

Ada hesitated. She, too, enjoyed their companionship. He reminded her of Burl Ives with his rotund middle and his white goatee. "I guess I can stay a little longer. Annie seems contented in my lap." She leaned back and continued to rub the papillon's fur.

A gentle wisp of wind touched Ada's face. She closed her eyes and filled her lungs with the crisp air. Her shoulders relaxed. Until that moment, she had not realized how the stress of the last few weeks had worn on her.

Frances exited the Sackets Harbor village bus and walked the short distance to 4110 Fairfield Lane. The "girls" expected her. Ada had decided to host the memorial service in the side yard beyond her English garden, and Gwen and Janet could use her help with the planning and preparations.

After breakfast had been cleared away, and amid the lingering smells of fried bacon and fresh coffee, Gwen positioned her reading glasses and opened her notebook. "I have a list of things that need to be done to pull this off."

Frances joined her at the kitchen table.

"Wait for me." Janet ran water into the pan that had held scrambled eggs and scurried back to the table. Seated with a cup of coffee in front of her, she looked at Gwen.

"I've asked the young man who mows the lawn to help with pruning, weeding, and deadheading," Gwen said. "He said he'd put down fresh mulch and do whatever he could to brighten the area."

"The hydrangeas are gorgeous. I think it will be a beautiful location for a memorial service." Janet sipped her coffee, then asked, "What about chairs?"

"We're getting folding chairs from Miss Ada's church. I've asked Neil to see to those, since he's on the board of elders there. A table will be set up for framed photos of Luty Mae, Wendall, Dorothy, and Nita. I'm calling this the Memory Table. I've talked to the printers, and they said they could enlarge the photos I've taken from the Willowdell directory. They promised them by Saturday morning."

"Good thing we had the bathrooms updated," Janet said. "Miss Ada can be proud of them."

"Should we get a tent in case of rain?" Frances asked.

"Miss Ada said to pray for good weather." Gwen made a checkmark in the notebook.

Frances nodded. She'd seen many answers to Ada's prayers since moving to Sackets Harbor. Like when Max found the bottle of Wendall Compton's pills ...

"Wait." She stopped Gwen from going on with her must-do list to tell her and Janet of their latest search in the dumpster behind the warehouse. She related Gladys Blumm's theory regarding Wendall Compton's sleeping pills. "Max and Ada are taking the bottle to Sheriff Meriday. They're hoping he will have the lab check them."

"Gladys Blumm thinks someone switched his pills?" Janet set down her coffee cup. "Why would anyone do that?"

"So Wendall would be more alert and easier to lead into the woods," Frances said.

"Do you ever think you may be getting paranoid?" Gwen shook her head. "Now can we focus? What about food?"

"A light buffet?" Janet suggested. "A three-o'clock service time is too early for a meal, but we should offer our guests something."

"Agreed."

"What can I do?" Frances said.

"Advertising. We need helium balloons and a large poster announcing the service wired to Miss Ada's fence, near the sidewalk."

Janet snickered. "The whole village of Sackets Harbor is going to know about the deaths. Simon Hilton's going to wish he'd let the service be held at Willowdell."

"Do you think the killer will be here?" Frances sent them each an anxious glance.

"He'd better be." Gwen looked at them over her reading glasses. "Miss Ada promised Sheriff Meriday an arrest."

Ada's peace vanished when Maxwell called to her from the top of the knoll. She said her goodbyes to the judge and Annie, then scurried up the hill to where Maxwell stood beside his car.

"We need to get this information to the sheriff." He opened the passenger door and waited for her to get in.

"You brought the bottle?" she asked as he drove toward the gate.

"Yes, and I wrote down a few notes from my talk with Gladys." Maxwell wore a tightness around his mouth. Fatigue lined his eyes. "I'll be glad when this is over. I feel like I'm betraying confidences. And friends. I don't like not trusting anyone, wondering if what someone is telling me is the truth."

"I know. But as long as there are those who perpetrate evil, there will be those of us who are determined to expose it."

Riding into the village, Ada noted the scale of Simon Hilton's campaign. Yard signs. Billboards. His wide, white grin cluttered the highway. The man had won the primary, and it seemed he spared no expense vying for the incumbent's seat in the New York State Senate.

How much would a campaign of this magnitude cost? If Sackets Harbor reflected the candidate's districtwide advertising, the expense must be staggering.

Maxwell parked in the lot behind the police station.

When they entered, Deputy Bidwell approached them.

Maxwell reached in his pocket and pulled out a Ziploc bag containing the pill bottle. "We need to speak to the sheriff."

Ada sensed the deputy's struggle over the decision. His face remained expressionless, yet a thin coat of perspiration formed on his upper lip. With a nearly imperceptible nod, he led the way.

Meriday resented the intrusion, yet with less hostility than he had in the past few weeks. Like it or not, the nosey parker and the frog man had shown themselves somewhat helpful in the investigation.

Bidwell directed them to the chairs along the wall, then stood by the closed door with his thumbs tucked in his belt.

Of course, it still made his teeth grind that so much of the evidence had arrived by their hands and not those of his deputies. The dog whistle. The tape recorder. The bloodied tree limb. He rubbed his chin and wondered what they were bringing him now.

Bailey held out a small plastic bag. "We found this in the dumpster behind the warehouse. The bottle belonged to Wendall Compton."

Meriday scowled and took the bag and examined the prescription label. *Diazepam.* His neck prickled.

"It's a muscle relaxant," Ada said. "Maxwell looked it up on Google."

He set it aside. "So, the old man had trouble sleeping."

Ada scooted to the edge of her chair. "I think the pills should be sent to the lab to find out if someone switched Wendall's sleep medication for something benign to make it easier to lead him into the woods."

Meriday leaned back and placed his hands on the armrests. "Do you?"

"Gladys Blumm said Wendall's caregiver always gave him a sleeping pill at bedtime," Bailey said. "That way he would sleep until she returned the next morning."

"Yes," Ada said, "we believe the deaths were intentional. No one actually committed murder, but they set the stage for death to result."

The concept had already occurred to him. Nita Beavers drowned, but someone sent her into the water incapacitated. Luty Mae Mears didn't get in a golf cart and race off to her death unassisted. Same with Wendall. Someone intended for him to never come out of those woods alive. And the gift of toxic brownies ...

Meriday handed the bag to Bidwell with a nod, then spoke to Bailey. "Gladys Blumm, you said, knew about Wendall's sleeping pills. Seems we always come back to Mrs. Blumm."

"She also told me everyone who knew Wendall knew his routine."

Meriday tapped his fingers on the armrests and mentally reviewed his questioning of the residents. Duncan Kroft knew the old man pretty well.

Ada stood and Bailey followed her cue. "Before I forget," she said, "there's been a change in venue." She informed him of the new location of the memorial service and of Simon Hilton's position on the matter.

"What happens to your suspect pool if Hilton doesn't show up?"

"He'll be there," she said. "It's an election year."

47

Saturday morning, Ada rang the doorbell at number thirteen and waited for the property manager to answer. She held fifty flyers that Gwen had printed off and delivered to her minutes before.

The door opened a crack and one of Samantha's pale green eyes scanned her. "It's my day off."

"I have a favor to ask." Ada smiled.

Samantha's eye rolled. "You didn't do me any favors."

"Yes, I do apologize, but I believe the fault lies with Simon Hilton alone. The four residents who met death so tragically deserve to be remembered. Don't you agree?"

She slowly opened the door, revealing herself outfitted in black spandex pants and an enormous black T-shirt with a skull-and-crossbones emblem on the shoulder.

Ada entered and sniffed the air discreetly. Cat urine.

"I'd never seen Simon so angry. I couldn't even look at him yesterday after the hateful things he said to me. I'd have quit if I had any other options for employment. Sit down."

Ada scanned the gothicized room, then she sat on the edge of a black vinyl chair. "You're young. You have lots of options."

"Old people always say that. But options are for the pretty. The skinny. Not me." Samantha plunked down on the black vinyl couch. A gray cat rose from its bed under a tray table, stretched, and leaped onto Samantha's lap. She lowered her gaze and stroked the furball.

Ada leaned toward her. "I need your help, but Simon Hilton must not find out about it until you've completed your mission—should you choose to accept it."

She squinted and searched Ada's face. "You want me to do something that would make Simon angry?"

"That's not my intention, but if he were to find out, I'm afraid it would make him very angry, indeed." Samantha's face remained squinched while Ada outlined her plan. "I'd like you to deliver one flyer at each bungalow at Willowdell, advising the residents of a change in venue. The memorial service will be held at my home on Fairfield Lane."

Samantha gawped, then a smile slowly crept over her face. "That would do it. That would make Maharajah Simon bust a cork."

Ada tipped her head slightly. What could she say? Samantha could very well end up in the unemployment line, but who else could visit each bungalow and not draw attention?

Samantha removed the cat from her lap, ran her hands down her spandexed thighs, and reached for the flyers in Ada's hand. "I'm in."

Duncan Kroft thought nothing of Samantha Milsap making the rounds, holding a stack of papers and stopping at each bungalow, until she walked past his.

"Hey. Sam." He set the pruning hook on the porch step and met her on the sidewalk. "Where's mine?"

Her eyes darted over the square. "Uh, you can pick yours up in the office."

"Why? What gives?" He had no intention of going to the lobby and risk running into Simon Hilton. Besides, she had always delivered his monthly report in the past. He scowled at the notices in her arm. "What you got there?"

Samantha crushed them to her chest.

Duncan reached and grabbed the stack, scattering reports and flyers to the ground. He lowered his lanky form and picked up a notice. "Change of Venue."

He read aloud while Samantha scrambled to pick up the papers at his feet. "The memorial service to honor Nita Beavers, Dorothy Kane, Wendall Compton, and Luty Mae Mears will be held at 4110 Fairfield Lane at 3:00 p.m. Sunday. Please join us in honoring the Willowdell residents who lost their lives so tragically."

Samantha stood and ripped the paper from his hand. "You can't tell Miriam." She stared at him with fevered eyes. "Simon didn't want the service held here because of the negative publicity. He didn't want people to know about residents dying at Willowdell."

"So, Ada Whittaker is hosting it at her house." Duncan Kroft snickered. "Wonder how ole Simon will handle that."

"Not well. That's why I didn't deliver here." Sam whimpered like a kicked puppy. "I didn't want Miriam to know. She would tell Simon, and he'd try to stop it."

"Don't worry about Miriam." He gestured dismissively. "She won't hear it from me. What can I do to help?"

Her forehead crinkled. "Seriously?"

He shrugged. "Why not?"

She scratched the side of her homely face and glanced over her shoulders. With a caress of the long, goofy-colored hair sitting on her chest, Sam squeaked, "Will you make sure the staff is aware of the change of venue?"

"My pleasure." Duncan Kroft took a dozen or so flyers and set out on his mission, whistling "Yankee Doodle Dandy."

That night Maxwell turned on his side. The neon numbers on the clock next to his bed told him he had slept two hours. He lay there staring through the darkness at the five-tier shelf holding his volumes of study guides and Bible commentaries.

He had conducted dozens of funerals while pastor of Westlake Community Church, but never a memorial service for four people who had likely been murdered. He pushed himself up on an elbow and sipped water from the Styrofoam cup he kept by his bed.

"I can't take this anymore." He threw back his blanket and went to his desk and turned on the lamp. His notes for the memorial service consisted of two words. *Good afternoon.*

With a groan, he slid to his knees.

Max implored God to give him a message for those who would be attending the service. Over and over he prayed, changing the phraseology but never the petition. The hours fled with him drifting in and out of sleep.

At last, the answer came. And he didn't like it.

48

E arly Sunday afternoon, Ada stood on her porch at 4110
Fairfield Lane. Neil backed his pickup into her driveway
to unload its bed of stacked folding chairs. Jackie Senak sat in
the front seat beside him.

Ada tried to swallow the lump rising in her throat.

Neil had introduced Jackie to her earlier at church as a
friend and fellow attorney from Syracuse. He failed to mention,
however, Jackie's partnership in the law firm of Bigelow and
Senak.

Ada recognized her immediately as the woman she had
seen leaving the Krofts' bungalow the day Miriam stated she
had a meeting with a Willowdell attorney. She understood
Neil's withholding of the information. He likely wanted to
protect Jackie from undue speculation. After all, the firm may
or may not be involved in wrongdoing.

Neil parked, and he and Jackie met at the back of the truck.
"Where would you like the chairs set up?" he asked.

"In the side yard." Ada led them along the narrow sidewalk

through her English garden to a larger area bordered by trees and flowering bushes.

"This is beautiful." Jackie leaned over a wild rose. "And the hydrangeas are such a rich blue, they're almost purple."

"Yes, a very pleasant location for the service, I believe." Ada scanned the yard. The landscaper had done a wonderful job.

"I'm curious." Neil's almond brown eyes narrowed. "Why isn't the service being held at Willowdell?"

"Politics." Jackie's tone was disparaging. "Simon Hilton surely wouldn't want attention drawn to the deaths that happened on his watch. It could cost him a vote."

Ada turned to Neil. "He may arrive still upset at our holding the service. Would you mind meeting the residents at the gate? That way, if Mr. Hilton arrives—"

Neil raised a hand and smiled. "Don't worry. I'll see he behaves."

"I should stay out of sight," Jackie said. "Can I help in the kitchen?"

Ada studied her. "Of course, but why would you not want Simon Hilton to see you?"

"It's complicated."

At two o'clock, Ada stepped outside with a vase of daisies and black-eyed Susans freshly cut from her garden. She noted with some dismay that Maxwell had not yet arrived.

She made room for the flowers on the Memory Table then stood back and scanned the items she had placed there earlier. The thought to use the table as a means to unsettle the killer had come to her in the night. A good idea at the time perhaps, yet now she had second thoughts. The props could appear not merely tacky but disrespectful.

The taxidermized owl Maxwell had pulled from the dumpster sat perched near Wendall's picture, along with a cassette tape with the Beach Boys label scraped off. Of course, the sheriff held the recording of the screeching owl in evidence, but the perp wouldn't know that.

A dog whistle lay beside a snapshot of Stanley, and both were placed beside Nita Beavers's photo—again, not the original dog whistle but one Frances found exactly like it at the Outfitters Shop downtown.

A small plate of brownies and a dish of peanuts had been placed in front of Dorothy Kane. Luty Mae's photo stood over an elegantly wrapped brown box. Its gold lettering read *Hegler Chocolates*. Beside it lay an end post from a croquet set—admittedly tacky, but necessary.

She turned and spoke to Frances while her sister prepared the table for Janet's refreshments. "You should text Maxwell for his ETA."

"He'll be here." Frances smoothed the white cloth then turned and took the tray of paper plates, napkins, plastic tableware, and glasses from Jackie's hands. Gwen arrived with coffee supplies.

Ada returned to the kitchen to check on Janet.

At two thirty, she again looked out the front window. Residents arrived at the gate, and Neil directed them to the chairs. They chatted while they moved along the walkway to the side yard. Their laughter gave Ada the sense of hosting a high school graduation party rather than a service to honor the departed.

Gladys Blumm and Selma Potter arrived. Gladys walked with her head slightly too high. Selma plodded along the walk smoothing wrinkles from her blue print muumuu. Miriam and Duncan Kroft arrived next.

But still no sign of Maxwell.

Ada whispered, "Where are you?" then drew in a breath and turned to help Janet.

A tapping sounded moments later on the back door that opened into the kitchen.

Samantha Milsap stepped inside. "Sorry for coming in the back. Mrs. Kroft is here, and I don't want her to see me. I need to talk to you, Miss Whittaker."

Ada led Samantha to the study, wondering how they would hold a service with so many people trying to avoid being seen by other people.

"I don't know how Miriam found out about the service, but she told Simon. They were both in his office when he called me in. Simon ranted at me, wanting to know why I passed out the change of venue notices and promoted the very thing he had forbidden."

A tinge of fear for the young woman came to Ada but quickly dissipated. Mr. Hilton must know of the service. She wanted all suspects to be present. "What did you tell him?"

"I told him all about your plans, and that I intended to help in any way I could." Samantha's lips trembled.

Ada waited for the inevitable consequence.

"Yeah, he fired me."

Ada refrained from saying so, but she believed leaving Willowdell and Simon Hilton would be the best thing for the silly girl.

Ada stood at a parlor window searching for any sign of Maxwell when the sheriff arrived and climbed the porch steps. She opened the door to him.

"Have a minute?" he said.

Ada grabbed her black hat banded with white flowers and

followed him to the side of the house where Neil had set the chairs in perfect rows.

Leo Meriday wore a white shirt and no tie. His sleeves were rolled up to his elbows. Perspiration trickled down his trimmed sideburns. "Are you still promising an arrest?"

"I can only hope, I'm sorry to say." She noticed a slight sag of his shoulders. "But I am certain we will know more before the day is over. We will do what Jesus told his disciples, watch and pray." She answered his puzzled expression. "Body language."

He removed a folded hankie from his back pocket and wiped his brow and the sides of his face. Ada hadn't felt the day overly warm. He tipped his head toward the Memory Table. "That's what you hope to provoke with your brazen display of evidence?"

Byron Bidwell stood behind the table dressed in light gray slacks and sport coat, the bulge of a gun distorting one side. Suddenly, the deputy swatted the air. Turning and ducking, he continued to swing his hands around his face.

"Oh, my. Seems the bees are interested in your deputy. I believe I have some spray in the shed." Ada hurried toward the weatherworn building that sat on a pad of crushed stone, tucked up against the woodlot that bordered her property.

She stepped into the near-darkness. Aided by one small window at the back, her eyes adjusted. Chunks of drywall and shreds of floral wallpaper spilled over the trashcans and lay in a pile on the grayed wood floor.

She clicked her tongue and threw up her hands. Gwen had refused to pay the contractors to haul the trash away, insisting she would do it herself and save money.

"Weeks later, it's still here." She tiptoed around the pile. At the back of the shed, she searched the shelf for bee killer.

Footsteps crunched in the gravel beneath the window.

"This is a bad idea. If anybody sees us—"

Simon Hilton?

"Why are you here, anyway?" Miriam Kroft chided him. "You were opposed—"

"P.R. Why else?"

A prickling moved up the back of Ada's neck. Her chest tightened. She pulled her cell from her pocket and fumbled to open the ap to record, then slipped the phone onto the window ledge.

"What's so important? Duncan could—"

"Meriday's asking a lot of questions about the warehouse." Miriam's words came fast. "About King Tut Movers. And I'm scared of what will happen to George."

"The idiot tied up a deputy." Hilton's voice rose an octave. "How dumb can anybody be?"

"Make his attorney get the felony charge dropped. Call your father."

Hilton snapped, "Leave my father out of this."

"You have to call him. Or I will tell them everything."

Hilton laughed.

"I'm done," Miriam blurted. "I won't do it anymore."

"You have no choice. Not if you like living at Willowdell."

"George and I are taking too many risks."

"Not my problem."

"If you don't find a way to keep George out of prison, I promise I will keep you out of that senate seat." She spit out the words.

"You do, and I'll let both of you rot. My word against yours. And if anyone doubts who's telling the truth, *then* I'll call my father."

Ada's cell phone rang, startling her and undoubtedly alerting those on the other side of the thin shed wall to her presence. She fumbled to silence the ringer.

Footsteps scuffled in the gravel beneath the window.

Panic pounced on her. She couldn't let herself be trapped in the shed. She had to escape.

Ada scrambled toward the door.

Her shoe caught on a chunk of drywall. "Oh," she squealed and toppled onto the mound of debris, her hat landing nearby.

The door opened.

49

After Ada disappeared into the shed in search of bee spray, Leo Meriday moved to the shade of a Chinese Maple. Scanning the gathering mourners, his gaze paused on Simon Hilton. The would-be politician mingled with them, smiling and shaking hands until he suddenly stepped away and lifted his cell phone to his ear.

Hilton's smile vanished. He scowled and turned a slow, searching three-sixty. He then tucked his phone into his pocket and moved with a casual stroll toward the shed from which Ada had yet to emerge.

Meriday's discomfort grew with the twinge in his gut. He caught Bidwell's eye and nodded toward Hilton, then motioned his instructions.

Deputy Bidwell backed away from the table where the photos of the four victims were displayed and slipped unnoticed into the patch of woods that ran along Ada's property.

Hilton disappeared behind the shed.

A screech pierced the air. Meriday jerked and turned toward a makeshift platform where Maxwell Bailey fussed with the offending microphone. Groupings dispersed, and each attendee ferreted out a seat.

Max took the stage still chafing at the answer that had come to him in the early morning hours. *For the Holy Spirit shall teach you in the same hour what you ought to say.*

His muscles ached from wrestling with the matter.

In all his years of ministry, he had never stepped into the pulpit unprepared. He had never winged it. Standing before an audience, not knowing what he would say, was for him a nightmare.

He licked his lips and scanned the rows of residents. His mouth felt like he had arrived on camel after a trek across the desert, instead of in his Infiniti from across town. He searched for water but found none.

He faced the crowd. "Good afternoon."

Frances, seated in the front, tossed him an encouraging smile. Ada, strangely, was missing. Gladys frowned from the back row and motioned for him to get on with it.

"Today we pause to honor Nita Beavers, Dorothy Kane, Wendall Compton, and Luty Mae Mears." He forced his shoulders back and drew forth courage.

"For Nita Beavers, whose beloved Stanley was left homeless and orphaned, Death lurked behind a maple tree. Poised with the instrument of cruelty in its hand, Death struck the blow that sent the unsuspecting jogger into the frigid waters that took her life."

Duncan Kroft shifted in his chair.

"Dorothy Kane looked forward to having the whirlpool to herself late that night." Maxwell stepped away from the podium and spoke conversationally. "She looked forward to reading the Syracuse University alumni newsletter, catching up on the happenings at her son's alma mater. Dorothy sank into the warm, whirling water." Maxwell swirled his hand in illustration. "Then reached for a brownie. And took the bite of Death."

A righteous anger propelled him forward. He stepped back behind the podium.

"Wendall Compton. A man who, unknowingly, relied on his fellow villagers to watch over him. Tucked in his bed, wrapped in a sense of security. Suddenly," he paused for effect, "he is awakened. In the dark of night, Death lures him deep into the black, cold forest."

A breeze swept in off the lake and toppled the owl perched by Wendall's picture.

The hairs on the back of his neck stood up.

Murmurs rippled through the rows.

He licked his lips. "Luty Mae Mears. So tiny. So frail. So ... vulnerable. Death assisted her onto a golf cart and set her on a course of sure and tragic demise."

Neil Tibbs and Judge Fausset exchanged looks.

Maxwell hoped he hadn't said too much, disclosed too much information for an ongoing investigation. His eyes searched the gathering for Sheriff Meriday. Perhaps he should have had the sheriff check out his message before he took the stage.

Oh, wait. He didn't have a message before he took the stage.

Maxwell scowled, then boomed, "Who is Death? Who is this robber of life, this taker of breath?"

The residents made odd noises, craned their necks, crossed and uncrossed their legs, and darted glances at their neighbors.

"God knows who you are," Max bellowed, regaining their

rapt attention. He stepped to the side of the podium, leaned an elbow on it, and lowered his voice. "And wherever you go, the hound of heaven will hunt you down."

Exhaustion washed over him. Sweat had soaked the back of his shirt. He straightened. "Let us pray." Heads began to drop, but, he noted, few eyes closed.

Simon Hilton shut the shed door behind him and squinted into the darkness. He looked down. "Ah, Miss Whittaker." His lips curved in a malicious grin.

Ada swallowed. If this man perpetrated the deaths at Willowdell, he could easily rid his world of her.

He leered and baby-stepped forward.

She stared, paralyzed, unable to scream. No one would hear her above the muffled words of Maxwell's eulogy.

"Shouldn't you be at the service with your guests?"

"Yes. I should." She crawled to her feet. "If you will excuse me."

Hilton's smile vanished. "Give me your phone."

"No." Her voice tremored. "I will not." She tried to push past him.

He grabbed her and spun her, binding Ada's arms behind her back.

"Let go of me. You have no right." She struggled against him.

He patted her down. "I suppose you planned to blackmail me with this. Or take it to my opponent and have him use it to cast doubt on my integrity. Cost me the senate seat."

"I have no intention of doing anything of the kind."

His smarmy hands moved over her body until he pulled her

phone from the front of her dress. He released her with a shove.

She hit the floor.

Hilton turned aside, trying to access her phone.

Fire burned in her stomach. *Help me, Lord.* She couldn't let Simon erase his conversation with Miriam Kroft. It may be evidence. She had to stop him. Adrenaline surged through her veins. She quietly rose, then with full force flung her weight against his back.

Hilton's arms flew up. The cell phone smacked the floor. He turned with his hands fisted, his face aflame.

Ada braced herself against the wall. Her pulse pounded in her ears.

The door latch lifted.

Sheriff Meriday filled the door frame. He grabbed Simon Hilton and slammed his face to the wall, yanked his arms behind him, and locked his wrists in handcuffs. It all happened in a matter of seconds.

"Are you all right, Miss Whittaker?"

She nodded. Words could not get past the tears welling up in her throat.

50

"It's a great day in Sackets Harbor, George," Meriday said when he entered the small, gray interrogation room hours later and tossed a file on the metal table. He scraped back a chair and lowered his heavy frame.

Bidwell held his position by the door.

George Tuttle had refused to shave since his arrival nearly two weeks earlier. With the same birdlike dark eyes as his sister, he had the look of a caged animal.

Meriday placed a recorder on the table. His deputy first heard the taped conversation from his stakeout in the woods a few feet from the back of Ada Whittaker's shed. He heard the ring that unnerved Miriam Kroft and Simon Hilton. When Hilton rushed into the shed, Bidwell seized and detained Mrs. Kroft.

The sheriff pressed *play*.

Blood drained from Tuttle's scruffy cheeks when his sister's voice came from the machine. He stared at the recorder until the conversation ran its course, then swiped his hand-cuffed wrists across his forehead.

Meriday shut off the tape. "What's going on there, George? What did your sister mean, she won't do it anymore?"

Tuttle lowered his head and dragged his hands through his hair.

He turned to Bidwell in an attempt to shake Tuttle's tongue loose. "Where are Miriam Kroft and Simon Hilton now?"

"They're here, sir. In separate rooms and ready to talk."

"Maybe one of them will be willing to make a deal." Meriday shifted to rise.

George jerked his head up. "No. Wait. I will tell you what I know. If—if—"

"If we make a deal?" Meriday rubbed his chin thoughtfully. "No can do, George. Not with what you did to my deputy. But ... the judge might take cooperation into account at sentencing." He ended with a lilt.

Tuttle chewed his lips and stared at the wall.

Meriday stood.

"Yeah, okay. Okay. I'll cooperate."

"Everything, George. You got a felony charge." Meriday sat, pressed *record* on the machine, stated the time and date, and the interviewee's name. "Start talking."

"I did what Miriam told me to do." His eyes flickered. "We were dealing with the stuff, the furniture. Then one day Miriam says she needs my help."

"What kind of help?"

Sweat trickled through the top of his orange jumpsuit. "Look. We didn't kill nobody."

"You set the stage for four deaths."

"But we didn't kill nobody."

Meriday's blood boiled. He stared at the notes and gave himself a moment to calm down. Looking back at Tuttle, he said, "What *did* you do? And start with Nita Beavers."

"Who?"

"You didn't know who you were killing?"

"I didn't kill nobody. I told ya."

"Did you deliver the blow that knocked the woman into the lake?"

Tuttle lifted his bound hands. "A tap, that's all."

Meriday glanced at his notes. "Who blew the dog whistle and lured the dog and Mrs. Beavers to the lake?"

Tuttle stared at his clasped fingers.

Meriday slid his notes aside and softened his tone. "Tell me why you did it?"

"I obeyed orders and didn't ask no questions."

"What about Dorothy Kane? Who made the brownies using peanut oil, knowing Mrs. Kane would suffer a deadly reaction?"

"Don't know nothing about that."

The sheriff leaned in. "Remember our deal."

His head snapped up. "I said I'd tell ya what I know. I can't tell ya what I don't."

"Someone exchanged Wendall Compton's sleeping pills for aspirin."

Tuttle stretched out his arms over the table.

"Did Miriam lead Mr. Compton into the woods?" Mrs. Kroft's resemblance to Wendall's first wife was uncanny. She could have easily convinced him to follow her, him not knowing the difference.

"I only started the tape. I guess the old guy liked owls."

Bidwell shifted his stance and cracked his knuckles. Meriday knew the deception perpetrated on Wendall Compton in particular had rankled the rookie. He'd have to remember to ask for the backstory.

Meriday drew the file closer and focused on it. "Luty Mae

Mears. You put her on the golf cart and drove her to the green."
He looked back at Tuttle and peered at him.

"What was I supposed to do? Miriam needed my help."

"Which one of you locked down the accelerator with the croquet stake and sent Mrs. Mears to her death?"

Tuttle studied the ceiling.

Meriday pointed over his shoulder toward Bidwell. "George, you're familiar with my deputy here. You subdued him, bound him, and left him to die."

The prisoner's eyes darted to Bidwell, then to Meriday. "No. No, I planned to come back."

"But you didn't. Did Hilton tell you to tape him to a rafter?"

"No. I panicked." Tuttle glanced at Bidwell. "I needed him out of the way."

Meriday eyed him sharply. "Who's your partner? The tow mower guy?"

"I only know him as Darren."

"This Darren, he set fire to the building at the shipyard?"

Tuttle shrugged. "Maybe."

Meriday spoke through gritted teeth. "You're not cooperating, George."

"Okay. Yeah. The day of the voting, Simon needed a driver for the van. He said to lay low because of the warehouse thing and get Darren to drive, but Darren don't have a license."

"Hear that Bidwell? George is a good citizen. He wouldn't let Darren drive without a license."

"Sweet," Bidwell said.

Meriday waved Tuttle on. "The fire."

"I'm getting there." George pulled at the top of his jumpsuit and wriggled. "So I had to drive the van. I told Darren to keep you cops busy elsewhere. That's what he did."

"Where's Darren now?"

"How do I know? You picked me up when those crazy

women trapped me." Tuttle scratched his beard. "I still don't know why the van wouldn't start."

Meriday cringed. *Yeah. Even getting this moron in custody was their doing.* He scraped his chair back. "Take Tuttle to his cell."

Bidwell grabbed the prisoner's arm and yanked him to his feet.

George stumbled over the chain at his ankles. "Police brutality."

Meriday shook his head. "Don't make him angry, George."

51

Two days later, a gentle knock sounded on the front door of Ada's Victorian. She peeked out the window.

Maxwell stood on the porch, shifting his weight and smoothing his hair.

Ada opened the door. "Good morning."

"I hope you don't mind my dropping in. I haven't seen any lights on at Frances's bungalow lately, so I assumed you both were here."

Frances came to the door. "Hey, Max. Coffee?"

He stepped inside. "If you don't mind, there's something I'd like to take care of first. I'd like to talk to both of you. And Gwen and Janet, if I could."

"Sure. I'll get them." Frances lifted an eyebrow at Ada, then bounded toward the kitchen.

Ada turned back to close the door and saw the sheriff's cruiser pull into the driveway. She called toward the kitchen, "Sheriff Meriday is here."

She and Maxwell waited for him on the porch.

Frances appeared with Gwen and Janet close behind.

The sheriff exited his cruiser, fully uniformed and flanked with his weapon.

"Good morning, Sheriff." Ada had given a detailed report of her ordeal in the shed to the four people hovering around her. They had witnessed the sheriff and Deputy Bidwell escorting Miriam Kroft and Simon Hilton to separate squad cars.

He climbed the steps. "I wanted to let you know that with the evidence and the interviews with Mrs. Kroft and her brother, George Tuttle, we have enough to send it to the grand jury."

"Have a seat." Ada motioned toward a porch chair, then sat in the chair angled toward him. The others drew near and looked at him expectantly.

"Mrs. Kroft is cooperating to some degree in the hope of a reduced sentence, but I don't think she's completely forthcoming. Hilton's not talking, except to threaten to call in his father and his father's highfalutin' attorneys from DC. I expect some trouble."

"Did you find out which one of them struck Nita?" Frances asked.

"Tuttle blew the dog whistle, knowing Stanley would draw Mrs. Beavers to the lake. That's when he struck her. You know the rest."

"Oh, mercy." Ada's hand went to her throat. She glanced at the others before turning back to the sheriff. "We chased Mr. Tuttle, believing him to be guilty of detaining your deputy. We had no idea we were chasing a murderer."

"He swears his sister planned everything." The sheriff drew out his handkerchief and wiped perspiration from his face.

Janet slipped back into the house.

"And the brownies? Did Miriam make them?" Ada asked.

He dipped his head. "She wrapped them as a gift and anonymously left the package on Mrs. Kane's doorstep."

Janet returned and handed a glass of ice water to the sheriff.

"Yes, I can see it. Miriam wanted Dorothy to believe the brownies were a peace offering from Gladys." Ada looked at Maxwell. "Trusting Gladys to never use peanut oil, Dorothy would eat them without hesitation."

"Miriam placed the peanut oil in Gladys's pantry," Maxwell said. "So, Miriam really did try to frame Gladys. I feel bad. There were times I wondered."

"That's probably when she took the gold necklace." Janet looked at Frances.

Frances nodded. "Again, to implicate Gladys."

Meriday set down the empty glass and shifted his weight. "Mrs. Kane might have gone for an antihistamine, but she had taken Diazepam before she entered the whirlpool."

"What about Wendall's Diazepam?" Ada said.

"Again, Mrs. Kroft. She switched his pills for aspirin."

"I'm sorry." Gwen looked at Frances and brushed back her red curls. "I'm sorry I said you might be paranoid."

Frances winked at her. "I forgive you."

Ada turned to the sheriff. "The tape recorder. What did you determine?"

"It turns out Mrs. Kroft holds a resemblance to Wendall's first wife, Margaret, whom we believe he called Magpie. I'm speculating, but Wendall may have believed Miriam was Magpie and followed her into the woods to find the owl."

"The owl being Mr. Tuttle, deep in the woods with the recording." Maxwell slowly shook his head.

"And Luty Mae?" Frances asked.

"Again, it took both of them to accomplish. Miriam drugged her, and Tuttle placed Mrs. Mears in the golf cart. When they arrived at the green, he locked the pedal down and sent Mrs. Mears to her death."

"And the wrapper under her body ..." Ada turned to Frances. "I suspect Miriam took the chocolates from the lobby drawer."

Frances shivered.

At that moment, Deputy Bidwell's voice emanated from the sheriff's shoulder.

Meriday pressed the microphone on his lapel. "Go ahead."

"We need you at the station."

"I'll be leaving here in a few minutes."

"Now, Chief." Bidwell stammered, "Uh, please."

Meriday growled, "What's so important?"

"The feds are here."

Leo Meriday spent the next two days fitting together the pieces of the puzzle in an effort to see the whole picture. The feds did indeed arrive at the station Tuesday in the form of Chandler Hilton's taxpayer-funded—therefore, highly paid—DC attorneys. They posted bond for Simon Hilton's release and filed claims against the department, citing police harassment and the unlawful arrest of their client.

Another matter, however, weighed more heavily on his mind. When he went to his car in response to Bidwell's call, Ada Whittaker followed him.

Could she be right? Could the conversation between Hilton and Miriam Kroft behind the shed have had nothing to do with the deaths but merely with their agreement regarding the personal property of the deceased residents?

He replayed the tape several times after that and found nothing that definitively spoke to the murders. If Tuttle had not talked, Meriday would have had a hard time proving Miriam Kroft's involvement. As for Simon Hilton, neither

Tuttle nor Miriam implicated the owner of Willowdell in the death of the residents.

By Thursday morning Meriday had made the decision. He would follow Ada's suggestion. And since a phone call would likely prove futile, he put Bidwell and Sloan on a plane to DC.

52

A da answered the ringing phone on the hall table. "Hello?" She looked in the mirror over the table and ran her fingers through her short ivory strands.

"Good morning, Ada." The chipper voice of Burton Fausset sent a flutter to her stomach. "Wonderful service Sunday."

"Yes, very ..."—she had heard about Maxwell's dramatic performance and struggled for a word choice—"beneficial."

"I'm calling to invite you and your sister to my place Saturday for a barbeque. Please bring Gwen and Janet. And Maxwell, if you'd like. The notice is late, but when I walked out of ShopSmart today with a fifteen-pound brisket, I realized how much I would like to share it with my friends."

"Thank you, Burton. I'll check with the others, but I'm sure we would love to join you." She'd leave Maxwell's invite for Frances to extend.

"Wonderful. Neil and his young lady, Jackie, will be here."

His young lady? A weighted blanket dropped on her head. Neil's heart had been broken after that scandal at Stonecroft. She prayed there would not be a repeat.

With a stated time to arrive and the promise of Janet's potato salad and strawberry cheesecake parfait for dessert, they ended their conversation.

———

Saturday afternoon Ada fussed over the table on Judge Fausset's patio, making room for the various offerings his guests had brought, along with the judge's own dishes that convinced Ada the man watched a great many cooking shows.

The smell of smoking hickory filled the air and gave testimony to the sliced beef brisket spilling over the edges of the large platter in the center of the table. Gwen plucked a sample on her way to the kitchen. Ada couldn't blame her. She, too, found it difficult to wait for the meal to begin.

Jackie Senak arranged the chairs to make eight places at the table. Neil sidled up to her and touched her elbow. He leaned in with a whisper, and she smiled up at him.

A lump formed in Ada's throat. She turned away.

Maxwell and Frances paced out the distance between croquet stakes on the lawn. The cruise came to Ada's mind, and she wondered why Maxwell had never mentioned the matter. Surely, he would invite Frances.

"Isn't this wonderful?" Burton approached the table with a sparkle in his brown eyes. "It gives me so much pleasure to be surrounded by friends, sharing a meal. Everyone contributing. Everyone participating."

"And everyone enjoying themselves." Ada smiled at the judge's enthusiasm. The day they sat on the bench by the lake and talked, he'd seemed somewhat pensive. But in this environment, serving and cooking for people he cared about, he thrived.

Annie Oakley brushed against her ankle. She looked down to find the dog in search of crumbs. "How are you and Annie getting along?"

"I'm afraid I've been captured by twelve pounds of unconditional love." He beamed with the pride of a new parent.

"Time to eat," Janet called as she stepped out of the house with a pitcher of lemonade, complete with ice and lemon slices. She placed it on a smaller table set up for drinks and dessert. Gwen followed with a pitcher of sweet tea.

"Gather round." The judge called everyone together and waited for Maxwell and Frances to join the group. "Max, would you give thanks?"

Ada bowed her head and listened to Maxwell's prayer. Tears moistened her eyes while gratitude filled her heart. God had brought so much good out of the evil that had taken place at Willowdell. She peeked at the people around her while they stood holding hands.

Gwen and Janet, learning to get along. Maxwell coming out of his darkness, his resentments over the past replaced with expectancy for the future. Frances, no longer a lonely widow, but rich with friends—one, perhaps, of special interest.

And Judge Fausset. Ada looked down at his hand that held hers—firm and strong—and little Annie Oakley sitting at his feet, quiet and content.

Neil and Jackie? She could do nothing but let it play out.

With amens all around, everyone turned to the table.

The afternoon fled by with happy banter and pockets of laughter and conversation, games and grazing, until the sun made its subtle journey westward.

Nearing the end of the day, the group moved their chairs into a circle and settled down. Ada was not surprised the talk turned to the crimes of the past few weeks.

Gwen looked at Neil. "How did you and Jackie meet?" Her eyes landed a moment on the woman seated beside Neil.

"The fault lies with you, Gwen." He smiled archly. "You asked me to look into the law firm of Bigelow and Senak."

Ada tilted her head and spoke to Jackie. "How is it Simon Hilton selected your firm to represent the residents of Willowdell?" Ada suspected the story began thirty-some years ago.

Jackie's smile vanished. "With any business, nepotism reigns." Her tone seemed laced with acid. "Mr. Bigelow is a close friend of Chandler Hilton."

Neil spoke to the group, "Raymond Bigelow represented Ontario Developers—AKA Simon Hilton—in the purchase of the shipyard. Simon took advantage of Kroft's need to sell and purchased the property at a price far below its value."

Maxwell's eyes narrowed. "I can understand Duncan's resentment. But I can't understand Miriam's support."

"Like working on his campaign." Janet waved her fan at her neck, the breeze swinging her gold hoop earrings.

"We still don't know Simon Hilton's motive in the death of the residents," Frances said.

"Perhaps he didn't have one," Ada said.

Jackie's blue eyes flashed.

Neil leaned forward. "Greed. That's the usual motive."

The judge nodded. "I've seen it over and over in my tenure."

Annie Oakley yapped, and Ada turned.

Sheriff Meriday stepped around the corner of the patio. An orange ray from the setting sun struck his badge.

Judge Fausset greeted him without rising and offered him a go at the dessert table. Meriday had learned of the gathering when he called Ada earlier to tell her what his deputies had learned in DC.

"Thanks, Judge, but no," Meriday said. "I'm here on business."

Seeing the judge reminded him of another matter. He moved toward him.

Neil stood and directed Meriday to take his seat next to the judge.

"You have business with me?" Judge Fausset straightened and set the dog on the patio floor.

"I wanted to let you know, George Tuttle confessed to starting the fire in your garage." Meriday placed a fist on his hip and looked up at Tibbs, then at Ms. Senak seated beside him.

"I'm glad you told me." The judge drew Meriday's attention. "To know someone tried to burn me alive in my home, I admit, leaves me a bit shaken."

"You have Annie now." Ada patted the dog's head. "She'll let you know when someone's on your property."

"Like a security alarm, I'm afraid." The old man chuckled. "She can alert me, but she can't do much about it."

A cruiser pulled up and parked a short distance beyond the patio. Deputy Sloan stayed by the car while Bidwell approached them looking poker-faced.

Meriday stood. "Sorry, folks, but like I said, I'm here on business."

Bidwell stopped beside Jackie Senak. "Ma'am, I'm asking you to come down to the station for questioning."

The young attorney paled, then rage swept up her face and filled her eyes.

Neil stepped forward. "What's this about?"

Jackie spewed her words. "Simon. It's always about Simon."

Bidwell took her arm and escorted her to the squad car.

Meriday dipped his head at Ada, then followed his deputy.

53

Monday evening, Ada sat with Frances and Maxwell around the coffee table on the front porch of number eight. Gwen strolled the length with a watering can, and Janet sat nearby swirling the warm evening air with her fan.

Moments before, the sheriff left them. He informed them Jackie Senak—on the advice of Chandler Hilton and his attorneys—pleaded not guilty to all charges stemming from the death of the residents.

Gwen set down the watering can and settled into a chair. "How did you know, Miss Ada, that she was involved?"

"When Neil introduced Jackie, I recognized her as the attorney for Willowdell residents. But I also recognized her from what I assumed to be a family photo in Simon Hilton's office. I found it odd when she told Neil and me at the memorial service that she didn't want to be seen by Simon."

"I wondered why she stayed in the kitchen," Janet said, "even after we finished our work."

"Poor Neil." Gwen shook her head.

"Yes," Ada said. "I wish I could have warned him, but I

truly did not know if Jackie played a role in the matter. And if so, to what extent."

Frances shifted her position on the outdoor sofa she shared with Maxwell. "But why would she and Miriam Kroft plot the deaths of those particular residents? I don't see the motive."

"That's why the sheriff sent his deputies to DC—to talk to Simon's parents, in the hope of discovering a motive. According to Chandler Hilton, Jackie was seven when her mother and father divorced. Her mother eventually married Mr. Hilton. And they had a baby."

"Simon," Maxwell said.

Ada nodded. "Jackie immediately felt pushed aside and grew to resent her half-brother. Over the years, a pattern of parental favoritism—whether real or imagined—left her with a great deal of resentment and anger.

"She struggled with relationships all through high school and college. When she passed the bar, Chandler Hilton put pressure on Raymond Bigelow to make Jackie a partner in his law firm in exchange for the Willowdell account.

"According to Neil, Raymond Bigelow considered Jackie no more than a glorified secretary." Ada recalled seeing the young woman driving a Hyundai. Now it made sense. The partnership did not extend to the profits. "Jackie was assigned to meet with the residents at Willowdell who signed up for their services, while Mr. Bigelow met with those clients considered important."

"That's when she met Miriam?" Janet said.

"Yes. They soon discovered their mutual resentment. When Simon decided to run for the senate, Jackie's anger burned. She wanted him to fail, to suffer the rejection she had suffered. She enlisted Miriam, and together they plotted the deaths. They did not merely want to create negative publicity and cause him to lose the election. They wanted Simon to be held responsible for the death of his residents."

"I can't imagine living with that amount of hate." Frances shook her head.

"For Jackie's part," Ada said, "she knew which residents had lived at Willowdell over five years and if they had any living relatives who might cause trouble. She could also transfer funds from the escrow accounts into Simon's campaign fund. Her words, her actions, were all meant to cast suspicion on Simon. Giving him the means, the motive, and the opportunity."

"But there was no evidence connecting Simon Hilton to their deaths," Maxwell said.

"That's why Jackie went out of her way to create suspicion in Neil's mind."

Gwen crossed her arms. "She used Neil."

"I believe she started with that intention."

When they stood to head to their respective homes, Max remembered his unfinished business. "Uh, I have something that's been weighing on me. I wanted to take care of this last Tuesday morning."

"I'd completely forgotten you wanted to talk to the four of us," Frances said.

"Not bad news, I hope." Ada glanced at the others then back to him. "You seemed nervous standing on the porch."

Frances searched his face with her hands on her hips.

"I want to discuss the cruise I won at the bingo tournament." He scratched the back of his neck.

"Oh, yeah. Congrats." Janet tucked her fan into her purse.

"When will you be going?" Gwen asked.

"Who will you be taking?" Janet glanced at Frances.

Max dared not look at Frances. He didn't want to disappoint her, but then he didn't want to assume she would be disappointed, either. He drew in a deep breath. "I won't be taking anyone. I'm not going."

Ada frowned. "Are you sure? It sounded like a wonderful experience."

"I believe the word was *fabulous*."

Frances weighed in, "If you don't want to take someone, you should go by yourself. You'd enjoy it. You could relax. Do some reading. Meet some people. It would be good for you."

"I've made up my mind." Maxwell looked at Gwen and Janet. "I want the two of you to take the cruise."

Gwen's green eyes sparked. "Seriously?"

Janet's mouth hung open. "Us? Like, me and her?" She tipped her head toward Gwen.

"If you want it."

Janet rushed to him. Her embrace nearly robbed him of air. "Thank you. Thank you."

He looked over Janet's head to Ada. "If you think you will be able to get along without them for a few days."

Ada's face shone while she clasped her hands in front of her. "Absolutely. The girls will have a fabulous time."

After some chitchat and ideas were bandied about, Janet and Gwen headed back to Fairfield Lane. A smile remained on Ada's face while the taillights of the gray Volvo approached the Willowdell front gate and disappeared into the darkness. Ada then said good night and graciously left him and Frances alone.

Max's throat went dry. Sweat coated his palms. He forced himself to look into the slate-gray eyes of Frances Ferrell. They held a softness, a gentleness.

"You're sweet." She placed a hand on his arm. "You made

my sister very happy. Gwen and Janet are long past the age of girlhood, but Ada considers them her girls, and she couldn't be happier than to see them excited about having an adventure together."

The tension in his shoulders eased. His spirit lifted. "I confess, I debated a long time about giving the cruise to them."

Frances took a slight step back. "Why?"

"Didn't you say one of them would likely throw the other overboard?"

They laughed in a natural embrace.

Max took Frances's hand, and they strolled toward the lake. On a bench at the top of the knoll, they sat close, their shoulders touching. Surely, Frances could hear the pounding of his heart.

Cicadas sang from the treetops in the nearby woodlot while waves lapped against the shoreline in a smooth, mesmerizing rhythm.

Max placed an arm around Frances, and she nestled into his shoulder.

He heard them—soft melodies swaying on a sea breeze.

And he was there. Under a million stars. Among a thousand islands.

THE END

ABOUT THE AUTHOR

Sandra Kay Vosburgh, the author of the Sackets Harbor Mystery series, began her career hosting a weekly radio program called, "What Really Matters." She co-founded True Sisters, a ministry to women, providing the opportunity for fellowship and drawing encouragement from one another. She currently is a director of women's ministries.

Sandra began her writing ministry by sharing her testimony of salvation through Jesus Christ in *Decision Magazine*. She went on to publish articles about her trips to third world countries and taking hope to those long held under the rule of communism. She currently writes devotionals for Standard Publishing.

Growing up on a dairy farm in western New York gave

Sandra not only the ability to milk cows, bale hay, and drive a tractor but an appreciation of nature's beauty. Her stories, set in the stunning Thousand Islands area, reflect this love of the woodlands, lakes, and mountains. She allows only her favorite characters to get lost in them.

Sandra is a speaker, Bible teacher, and pastor's wife. She and her husband have five children and fourteen grandchildren. They currently make their home in the warmer state of South Carolina.

You can connect with Sandra at www.sandrakayvosburgh.com or find her on Facebook.

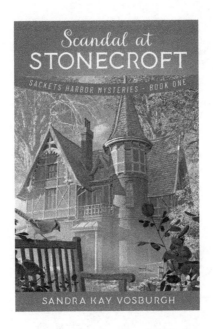

Scandal at Stonecroft

by Sandra Kay Vosburgh

Sackets Harbor Mysteries - Book One

Twenty years after the disappearance of the treasurer of Stonecroft Resort, an article appears in the Ontario Times, "Whatever Happened to Harold Ramsey?" reigniting Sackets Harbor with whispers, rumors, and gossip.

The townsfolk believe Ramsey embezzled funds and left town with Kate Darby. Blair Ramsey believes her husband is dead. Miss Ada Whittaker believes Felix Zohlar knows more than he's telling, and

Felix Zohlar believes wealth and influence, like blood applied to Hebrew doorposts, will cause the hand of justice to pass over.

scrivenings.link/scandalatstonecroft

Blue Plate Special

by Susan Page Davis

Book One of the True Blue Mysteries Series

Campbell McBride drives to her father's house in Murray, Kentucky, dreading telling him she's lost her job as an English professor. Her father, private investigator Bill McBride, isn't there or at his office in town. His brash young employee, Nick Emerson, says Bill hasn't come in this morning, but he did call the night before with news that he had a new case.

When her dad doesn't show up by late afternoon, Campbell and Nick decide to follow up on a phone number he'd jotted on a memo sheet.

They learn who last spoke to her father, but they also find a dead body. The next day, Campbell files a missing persons report. When Bill's car is found, locked and empty in a secluded spot, she and Nick must get past their differences and work together to find him.

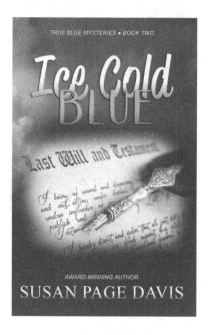

Ice Cold Blue

by Susan Page Davis

Book Two of the True Blue Mysteries Series

Campbell McBride is now working for her father Bill as a private investigator in Murray, Kentucky. Xina Harrison wants them to find out what is going on with her aunt, Katherine Tyler.

Katherine is a rich, reclusive author, and she has resisted letting Xina visit her for several years. Xina arrived unannounced, and Katherine was upset and didn't want to let her in. When Xina did gain entry, she learned Katherine fired her longtime housekeeper. She noticed that a few family heirlooms previously on display have disappeared. Xina is afraid someone is stealing from her aunt or influencing her to give them her money and valuables. True Blue accepts the case, and the investigators follow a twisting path to the truth.

Scrivenings
PRESS
Quench your thirst for story.
www.ScriveningsPress.com

Stay up-to-date on your favorite books and authors with our free e-newsletters.

ScriveningsPress.com